The One Thing Worth Doing

The One Thing Worth Doing

John Pope

To my parents

Part One

Chapter One

The party was starting to wind down. As waiters cleared away the remains of dessert, a few guests had already made their exits. But Martin Cardwell, flushed with wine and happiness, didn't want the night to end. The guest of honor, he stood surrounded by the engineers he'd been working with these last ten days.

"What are you going to do if the bubble really bursts?" asked Joël, leader of his host company's team. Since Martin's arrival in Paris the two had joked nervously about tech stocks, which in early 2001 were doing even worse than in 2000.

"Ask me tomorrow. Tonight is no time for French pessimism!" Martin said, accepting a refill of his glass by a passing server. He'd just cemented Dendroid Micro's first European partnership, after all.

"You do have momentum... so how bad can the market really be?" said Joël with an ambiguous smile. "It can't keep going down, not when the... how do you call them... *animal spirits* of so many have already bet so much. And if worse comes to worst, it's only a job."

"No! Well, kinda," Martin conceded. He'd co-founded Dendroid, so it was far more to him than a "job." Yet their product was strictly commercial, far from the world-changing stuff he had always hoped and expected to build. It had been years since he'd worked on anything he actually believed in, but of course this wasn't the time or place to get into that.

"We felt so sorry for you, staying late every night," someone said.

"It's the choice you make," he responded easily. His audience looked dubious.

"See, that is how one *shrinks the world*," Joël said, to general laughter.

Martin winced. The Parisians had been super nice, but understandably couldn't resist poking fun at his marketing department's latest inane slogan. Could they maybe have a point? Silicon Valley evangelism sounded so pious and obnoxious over here. He'd have to revisit that… sometime.

"You will disrupt us all," added Joël, "without even leaving your cubicle!"

Recovering, Martin played along, rubbing his hands together evilly. "Don't worry, creative destruction is only for our enemies."

He went on like that, spurred by the booze and the novelty of being the center of attention. Afterwards, walking back to his hotel, he couldn't explain it to himself. He hated the cliché Valley engineer persona; why adopt it when his listeners, apart from Joël, didn't know him and wouldn't get his provincial little joke? They might have even been mildly insulted. Here they prized stability, after all. Their company was huge; his, a small startup about to receive its first funding. That placed him much higher on the status totem pole in California; here it was the opposite.

Sticking to the Boulevard Saint-Germain, the one street he sort of knew, he made his way past couples and groups of bar-hoppers crowding the sidewalks in the warm weather. He thought of Gail, who'd text-dumped him the day he left California. She had done him the favor of being honest, and he'd seen it coming anyway. Still, their exchange bothered him, even as its details, like tiny toads, hopped beyond his mental reach. He sat on a bus stop bench and thumbed through the messages.

What are we doing to each other? Good question.
You have been phoning it in for months. Close.
In fact, you always phoned it in. That was it. Ouch.

Martin often took forever to notice when someone he cared about no longer cared about him. If enough gestures and rituals of friendship remained, he might hold onto his fey goodwill for years, shrugging off unfriendly or undermining actions as mere bad optics. So it showed a kind of progress that Gail's acid words had burned straight into him. Yet he couldn't blame her. He was married to Dendroid; nobody would put up with that for long. And that's how it would be while his life was set up this way…

"Set up this way" — as if somebody else had done it! His own choices, small and large, spread out over years, had built this zombie lifestyle where everything but the job got phoned in. When people asked how he was doing, he'd often say: "Living the dream." What was that dream, even? To stand apart from the daily hypnotic reality and be able to say: this is who I am, where I'm going and why… well, he'd never managed it. And couldn't remember really trying. He certainly hadn't planned out the person he'd become — had anyone? It had all just happened.

Walking again, he thought back to grade school, when he and his best friend Terry would play for hours on end with nothing but some plastic dinosaurs and a pile of dirt. One day in the park, they'd strayed off the path and almost stepped on an enormous beehive. Backing away, they stared at it, petrified, for some minutes. As Martin calmed down, he began to feel instead an overwhelming, silent awe, an intuition that each bee and the hive as a whole acted in harmony with an age-old pattern, as if part of some mysterious grand design whose origin and goal remained unknown. For months afterward, he'd thought about his own actions, those of friends and family, about what design they might be part of. It seemed there must be another reality, behind the one you could see. At that age, he'd had very elevated ideas of adulthood, assuming it would involve heroic self-exploration, a quest for real answers. Starting with why he was who he was, not someone else: a question more important than the sun!

Back then he could afford to ponder things, explore, follow his mind wherever it went. Who had time for that anymore? He used to at least have ideals. Or wanted to have them. Or wanted to want to have them. Just a few years ago the internet had been on the verge of creating unprecedented, dazzling possibilities, tools to break humanity's ignorance and fragmentation for good. He'd played his own small part in it, but today, barely into the new millennium, it seemed all those innovative companies had sold out or been co-opted — Dendroid included. Was he now any different from all the other nerds stampeding to the Bay Area from the four corners of the Earth, seeking nothing more original than a big payday?

Sonic debris wafted up from the street: urban hum, sirens, the bright arpeggio of a car horn. Somewhere, a washing machine churned its mindless rhythm: wa-wa-WOO-wa. Martin's head felt twice its normal size, filled with pain jelly. He flicked his eyes open. The noonday glare exposed the cracked walls and dented chairs, the cheap dresser: lonesome, humble objects, anonymous by design, with their aura of no aura at all, made to be used, then forgotten. He forced himself vertical, somehow ending up in front of the bathroom mirror. His body must have done it while his mind trailed a half-second after, as the consciousness researchers claim. Instead of the cubist portrait or mutant he felt like, it was only a coarser version of himself staring back; hollowed cheeks, a mid-forehead crease: a precursor, maybe, of Face 2.0. But these thoughts and last night's even gloomier ones were somewhat ridiculous. His coworkers, Swanson in particular, would've mocked him mightily, had they known. Here he was, lucky enough to be doing what he liked, what he excelled at, established in the one world he knew…

It was actually way past time to get in touch with Swanson. Martin had only left him one brief voicemail since arriving in Paris, and had barely checked email. While he was at it, he could regale everybody with the details of his triumph. Yeah! The hotel provided no way to connect, of course, so after a plate of viscous peanut noodles across the street, Martin stopped at the local internet café. Buying a ticket good for thirty minutes, he fumbled his way in the darkness, past rows of disembodied heads that floated in front of screens, passive canvases for the images playing across their features. He found his designated PC, then started through the unread emails, oldest and most delete-able first. He stopped short at one from Swanson.

Subject: Dendroid funding

Didn't want to traumatize you when we still weren't sure, but I guess I better say it before someone else does. Jones-Wolff reneged on their offer, right before the final signature. Trying to figure out what happened. Anyway, now we gotta crawl back to the other VCs to beg for a deal. Our cash runs out at the end of this week. Will let you know more once I do myself.

Martin pushed his chair back, staring into the shadows. What the hell? The funding had been nailed down — otherwise he'd never have come to France. This could not be happening! But indifferent keyboards around him clack-clacked in reply: it could happen, had happened, and only a handful of people in another country would give a damn. He scrutinized the email for signs he'd misunderstood. Fingers trembling, he scrolled through the other messages. No followup. Why would Jones-Wolff, one of the biggest venture capitalists around, pull out? Their consultants had kicked all possible tires. One had indiscreetly told him Dendroid's competitors were "not even wrong." But maybe technology wasn't the problem. Maybe Jones-Wolff themselves had blown up. He laboriously typed a response, cursing the French keyboard layout. With his job in the balance, he forgot last night's heretical anti-Valley thoughts. He'd cancel the rest of his itinerary, book the next available flight, crush any software problem…

Minutes after sending his message, though, he was astonished to get a reply from Swanson in California, where it was past 3am.

Subject: URGENT — WAIT!!!!!

Had no chance to tell you earlier — Dendroid is kaput. Nothing anybody can do now. However, I have a clever plan… Hang out for a couple days. Will explain when I get there.

- Swan

Chapter Two

S wanson Geach threaded his way through the piled-up moving boxes and clumps of people talking in the hallways. Despite his agitation, he couldn't help noticing the conversations lower to a whisper when he passed. As if everything were his fault. As if he hadn't just lost more, in so many ways, than all of them put together. The company was only part of it.

Banking left, he reached the sanctuary of his office and slammed the door behind him. He sat at his desk and massaged his aching eyeballs. Like Dendroid Micro's other executives, he'd been there since 5am winding the place down, in his final act as VP of Marketing: auction off the physical assets that afternoon, settle the remaining intellectual property issues, compose a farewell press release. Somehow he'd managed to act above it all, not lashed out at the idiots probably responsible for the company's shocking implosion. At least that part of the torture was over.

The noise from the movers died down, and for a moment the office went eerily quiet. The fountain in the fake lagoon outside his window soundlessly sparkled. Swanson's tanned, handsome face lapsed into a scowl. He hated silence. Keep on the go, he thought, bounding to his feet though there was nothing consequential left to do. He checked his laptop and immediately regretted it: word of Dendroid's abrupt demise was already surging through Silicon Valley, reaching the whole world he cared about. Competitors and enemies were all over the online forums, savoring his misery. He read on, stomach gone sour, unable to stop, mentally noting the worst gloaters for future reference. Then the message machine caught his eye: eleven new voicemails. Maybe one held a miracle.

"Howdy, Swanson!" Josh, his headhunter. "Long time no talk! Sorry to hear about…" Naturally Josh couldn't afford to wait until the corpse was cold. Couldn't he see, though, that going straight back to work after such a heartbreaker was impossible? Let alone at somebody else's company. Swanson hit the delete button. "Hi, I got your resumé from…" Argh, another. Delete. "Hello Mr. Gea-" Delete. Delete. Del*ete*. "Hey, Swan…" started the last one. Shit. It was Martin, from a couple days ago, with an update on his Paris trip: he'd landed the new partnership. Ah, the irony. Obviously he hadn't been reading his email. Now he'd get all the bad news at once.

Swanson shrugged. He and Martin had co-founded Dendroid, but the truth was that he himself had far more skin in the game. Engineers like Martin inhabited a Silicon Valley with a completely different hierarchy from that of the players — the executives people visually identified with a company, the ones who decided *what* to build, not how, who were in the news, who might one day have political influence. That was his track, and with Dendroid he'd sensed a whole new level of status within reach. He'd had one decent-sized success, but this was now his third failed startup in a row. The naysayers would have a field day. Starting with his father, who so often hinted to him that he should pursue art, his real talent, not waste his life on frivolous tech nonsense. Given his dad's condition, Dendroid would probably be Swanson's last chance to prove that his failures were the flukes, not his triumph.

He groaned and looked around. The only things left to pack were his presentations and strategy reports. Quality material that would come in handy when he did all this again…

Again?

We did everything right. Now I'm supposed to politely start over, take a few more years to claw my way to where I should be now?

As he mulled backhanding the documents, the symbol of two wasted years, into the trash, somebody knocked. Before he could bark out a negatory, Ralph, the VP of sales, opened the door and poked his head in. Despite the situation, he looked pink and cheerful.

"Yo, sport! You done?"

"Uh huh." Swanson felt glad to escape his thoughts for some small talk with a trusted ally. Ralph's balding dome swiveled back and forth, scanning the room.

"If it weren't for the boxes, I wouldn't have guessed. Looks the way it always does in here: barren."

Swanson cracked a half smile. He knew everybody thought his spotless office, lacking any visible papers or personal effects, was the product of some clean-desk management ideology. But even in childhood he'd kept his methods and intermediate results to himself. Few things showed cluelessness and lack of style like gratuitously tipping your hand.

"You?"

"Yeppers, all done. It's just that I'm..." Ralph choked up theatrically, "I'm gonna miss that damn ergonomic chair. We were made for each other. Those beautiful legs, that perfect seat..." He burst into fake tears.

"Stand tall, big guy. There'll be other chairs."

"Still can't believe we blew up," said Ralph, forgetting his bonhomie. He stepped into the office and pulled the door shut. "I was sure this was going to be The One. How could all those money people hump our legs for months, then drop us just like that?"

"Something turned us radioactive."

"You pissed? It was your baby, after all."

"Hell yes," Swanson spat out the words. "And if somebody monkey-wrenched us..."

Major setbacks always felt like a personal affront, a violation of the natural order, but none more than this. Who'd ever seen a venture capitalist — a VC of Jones-Wolff's caliber, yet — spend months on due diligence, demand an exclusivity clause, verbally commit, then pull out without a word? Worse, JW's partner in charge of the deal had been his closest friend in college, Duncan Shipley. In general, and especially in the Valley, loyalty was for saps. But this was different. Duncan had literally saved his life once. It did not compute that he'd let this disaster happen without so much as a warning. Or had he *made* it happen? No. Impossible. Yet since then he'd avoided all contact.

"Did JW even give us an excuse?"

"Surely you jest," Swanson said, popping his last antacid. Nobody knew he and Duncan were friends, not even Ralph. That way, he'd reasoned, it couldn't be claimed that Dendroid's funding had come through personal connections, rather than the company's merits. The real virtue of keeping it quiet had turned out to be very different: everyone in the company, if they knew, would now be blaming him for his JW buddy pulling the plug.

"I just don't get," he continued, "why all those outfits made offers before we chose JW, then wanted nothing to do with us. So what if we passed them over once upon a time a few weeks ago? Our projected numbers were fantastic!"

Ralph pantomimed a striptease: "Customer list, thadda-bump! Future earnings, woohoo!" He finished with an approximation of a belly dance.

For the first time in weeks, Swanson laughed out loud. But his thoughts came right back to chew at him. Their last hope had been snuffed out the night before, by a notorious vulture capitalist named Woodring. His money *was* green, but knowing they were on the brink, he'd offered terms so draconian that the Dendroid team had just looked at each other and walked out. Instead of a hot startup with a competitive product, A-list customers, and ten million in the bank, they were toast.

Swanson sat up. "Let's get outta here. How about a cold beverage?"

Ralph brightened like a thirsty cartoon character who's been offered a sarsaparilla, and gave several hearty doggy nods.

Swanson snapped his briefcase shut. "I'm parked out back."

The hallways were still full of employees, exchanging contact information. Even the old-timers seemed traumatized by the sudden collapse. A summer intern approached Ralph, who gave him a business card and began commiserating. Swanson paced, pretended to look at his phone. Hell with these guys, he thought. This place was just a paycheck to them. They'll find another. Ignoring the intern, he abruptly clapped his hand on Ralph's shoulder. "C'mon, man, it's over." Ralph glanced back at the intern, shrugging faux-helplessly as Swanson dragged him away. Their steps echoed as they crossed the deserted shipping and receiving area, Swanson tall and athletic, Ralph shorter, with a bouncing, adolescent gait. "One last exit out the anus of ol' Dendroid," lamented Ralph as they pushed out through the double doors into the windless, oppressive heat.

Swanson's banana-yellow Lotus crouched in front of a row of eucalyptus trees, which at high noon gave almost no shade. Each man opened his respective door, climbed gingerly into his seat, inhaled the dense aroma of overheated leather. Ralph's cell buzzed. His eyebrows shot up when he saw the caller ID. Before the car's top was halfway retracted, he was bellowing into his phone. Swanson countered by peeling out, then revving his engine at the edge of the driveway, but Ralph, a hard man to annoy, just talked louder.

Swanson had been too busy lately to notice, but as they zoomed through their now-former business park, the place was littered with vacant buildings. Company logos were either left to the elements or with 'for lease' signs pasted over them: the latest plunge from Valley peak to Valley valley, all in a matter of months... These boom-bust cycles — the peristalsis of money — were only getting more severe.

"Come again?" Ralph yelled into his phone. "Unbelievable! And such beautiful timing. I knew they were swine, but this…" He nattered on until Swanson pulled into the parking lot. "Gotta go. Mmmbye."

As they walked through the heat waves shimmering off the asphalt, Swanson, without turning, said: "Well?"

"Let's get some alcohol in you first. You'll need it." Good old Ralph: when holding gossip, milk it for all it's worth.

True to its neon sign, the Hotsy-Totsy Club opened at six every morning — a faded holdover from the days when Sunnyvale was mostly apricot orchards. The cool darkness inside, saturated by decades of cigarette smoke and stale beer, had one shot of color: an orange shag carpet, grizzled and greasy as a giant, unwashed fright wig. Across from the bar, past the tiny dance floor, a leprous dartboard hung, flanked by photos of the Rat Pack with fake dedications to the owner. The clientele was two-tiered: alkies and suits. A fly on the wall, had it been a blackmailer or a day-trader, would have made a fortune from all the personal indiscretions committed there: intraoffice affairs, corporate secrets blabbed, business plans left behind. But the hard-core Hotsy regulars, having other matters on their minds, couldn't be bothered. It was the one bar in the city where nobody looked up to see who just walked in.

Ralph exchanged a five for two brews, then tapped the bottom of his bottle on the top of Swanson's, cackling as it foamed over. Swanson looked at him wearily.

"Dude, you are so tiresome. Out with it already."

"That was my boss from a few companies ago. A little birdie — actually, he's a big fucking birdie — told him Jones-Wolff is announcing their next investment soon. Guess who."

"Hit me."

"HellaDyne."

Swanson's voice raised in spite of himself. "They shafted us to invest in our direct competitor?" He evened his tone. "No way."

"Yes way. Twelve million bucks."

Swanson tried to stay calm, to make sense of what he was hearing. The betrayal it implied could not be real. JW was a very top-down shop — maybe the order had come from Duncan's boss.

"I don't get it. The Hella people are absolute clowns!" boomed Ralph, with that robust faith every salesguy needs to have in his cause. "We have — well, had — better technology, better management, better customers… It won't take Jones-Wolff a month to realize they've screwed the pooch."

"By then we'll all be elsewhere," said Swanson, who'd mastered his face but wanted no more of the subject. Talk was pointless; he needed hard data. "Speaking of which, my spy network must be slipping — seems every headhunter in the Valley already heard the same news you did."

"Swarming, aren't they? But it's just to keep their rolodexes up to date. I've already done a bunch of callbacks — there are no jobs out there. Anyway, I'd bet a million bucks nobody knows the Jones-Wolff part yet. They're on the case because somebody in Quality Assurance posted a heinous rant about us on fucked-firm.com last night."

"One of our own? Great."

"Don't worry: the targets were the VCs, not you," said Ralph. He finished his beer, then slapped another fiver on the bar. "So, what's next for His Majesty?"

"My personal code of manliness and taste for vengeance say I should get right back in the saddle. But it sounds like there is no saddle. Besides, this is my third dud in a row. Time for a break."

"Hey, I've *only* worked at dot-bombs. You at least hit it big once."

"Well, medium big…"

Though Swanson's salary was common knowledge, he always played down the money he'd made before Dendroid. He could take as much time off as he wanted, not that he would open up about it to a blabbermouth like Ralph.

"I admit," he went on, spinning around on his barstool, "I'm hooked on the competition. Compared to some of the bastards I play hockey with, I'm still small-fry. I wanna run the show myself, maybe try corporate turnarounds."

"Didn't you do real estate for a while?" asked Ralph, who managed to enunciate clearly while tossing peanuts one by one into his mouth.

"Yeah, working for my mom, to help pay for school. I wouldn't want it as a job, but as an investment, sure — a hands-off one."

"It's way more solid than this startup shite. If I had the dough, I'd buy some properties, rent 'em out, hit the beach, and never be heard from again."

"Hah! You'd last about a week," said Swanson. He stared blankly at the sports results streaming by on the television. "Maybe I should hang in Paris awhile. I haven't been back since ninety-five."

"Why'd you leave?"

"I couldn't let the whole internet thing go berserk without me. I knew I'd never have the chance for a ride like that again."

"Got that right," said Ralph, gloomy once more. "Explain it to me: the year 2000 was supposed to break every piece of software in existence. The industry zooms past it without a single problem, then the market decides to tank. A year later and it still hasn't bounced back."

"The stupid money is long gone. Remember pets.com? Or that company, you know, the one selling a widget for your monitor that schpritzed out a scent, depending on which website you were visiting?"

"Loved it. Can't remember their name, either, but I do remember the twelve million in funding."

"That kinda nonsense gave everybody a bad name."

"Now we're in the toilet with 'em, doing the backstroke."

"Lotta great companies in there, too. Think how much intellectual property just *vanished* this year."

Ralph finished his beer in one long glug. "Meanwhile HellaDyne lives on. So much for Darwin. Well, I better head back. The auction's in the parking lot in a half an hour, and I wanna bid on my chair."

At the office Swanson said a few goodbyes, loaded his boxes in the car, put the top back up, and made for the freeway. On impulse, he took the long way, through Palo Alto, up Sand Hill Road, to cruise past the Jones-Wolff offices. The news of JW's investment in HellaDyne had hit him like an arrow between the eyes. He'd played it cool in front of Ralph, and though talk wouldn't change anything, goddamn it, this demanded an explanation, big time. Reneging was bad enough; to then invest in HellaDyne was the act of an enemy. That was not possible from Duncan, given all they'd been through — yet he'd owned the whole deal. There had to be some explanation. Duncan's Ferrari wasn't in the lot. No use trying his house; he'd moved recently without saying where, and the JW staff would of course never give out such information. Swanson speed-dialed him. Straight to voicemail, like the last dozen times.

Pulling onto 280, Swanson turned the air-conditioning up a notch and eased back in his seat, determined to think about other matters. After weeks of running on fumes, dealing with a situation beyond his control, he needed to get ahead of the curve again. He took a deep breath and slowly exhaled, suddenly glad he hadn't shredded those presentations on his desk. His long-term place was here. When the time came, he'd know what to do, who to call. And it would be his show. CEO positions in the Valley didn't require decades of apprenticeship — on the contrary. The proof was in the business section of the paper every day, where another little snot-nose, still in his crusty pajamas, would launch a half-baked product from his bedroom and get showered with money.

But he needed to reorient, to have one of those periodic confabs with himself, mercilessly appraising his career choices, social contacts, CD collection, wardrobe, love-making techniques, investments, savoir-faire… Maybe he took it a little far, yet what could be more important? Already at twelve he'd been age-aware, made the most of what you were supposed to make the most of at twelve. All the more so today, with forty coming up fast. The men's lifestyle magazines often profiled some poor fool who'd ignored or botched a major turning point in his life, right when the stakes were highest. Stylish, dominant 'before' photos morphed into pathetic, befuddled 'after' photos. Do what you like, the day would come when you'd realize you'd crossed a line somewhere, that your options and energy had waned, leaving you to march on while time, the great enemy, galloped away with piece after piece of what you'd taken to be yourself. The job was to push that reckoning as far into the future as possible, prune life to its essentials, fortify the necessary, jettison the rest.

His exit approached. In two minutes, he'd be home. Home, where there'd be nothing to do or any reason to even get up tomorrow. Where the horror of long, empty days would be stretched out like a never-ending Sunday afternoon. At the last second his foot, obeying a law of its own, hit the gas. The Lotus surged past the turnoff, and he surged with it — free, after all. Why not keep right on driving as long as it felt right? Blast the music, head up the coast with only the clothes on his back: Portland, Seattle, then Vancouver, Hudson Bay… But at Daly City, when all he wanted to do was keep moving, traffic bogged down, then stopped. After twenty minutes he abandoned the Ultima Thule idea and looped back, southbound again. Winding at first, the Pacific Coast Highway straightened out near the ocean, pointing down the coast, into the sun.

Blue Rondo à la Turk came on the radio: a tune he hadn't heard since Paris, where the bistro next to his office only ever played that one Brubeck disc. The insistent piano motif still brought to mind the same synesthetic reverie of animated Mondrian-esque Lego blocks vaulting over the Seine in rhythm with the music, bounding up, then plunging down the stairways of Montmartre. The saxophone entered, evoking smoky bars, fancy cafés near the Place de l'Opéra, elegant women swinging their shopping bags along the Rue Saint-Honoré. An integral vision: that time and place, that short piano riff… Mind-debris, really, a melody hinting at how life might be lived, leaving you free to fill it in however you liked. It could be your sole memory of a city or a relationship or a whole period of your life, yet still influence your future decisions more than any rational plan.

Ah, Paris… Wangling that transfer from San Jose had been sweet, his first major career coup. Not just anybody would have raised his antennae for opportunities in other countries, or had the nerve to interview for the position after only a year at the company, or bluffed a knowledge of French, then backfilled at night classes before the move. Or, once there, squeezed so much juice from that particular orange.

And Martin was there right now. How long had they mumbled about buying a rental property somewhere cool? With the tech industry in tatters and both of them now between jobs… Why not do it in Paris, for that matter… Sit on the grass of the Quai Saint-Bernard with a glass of Bordeaux, visit small museums on rainy afternoons… Maybe Céline was still there, still single… At worst, he could visit once or twice a year, use it as a refuge from all the bullshit once he did go back to work. His mind raced. Airfare would even be a tax deduction. Find an apartment, do the deal — that'd be easy — then hire some student to be caretaker when neither of them was around. Ralph might often be full of it, but he'd hit on something back at the Hotsy. Real estate was the one investment you could trust, long-term. Swanson's friends always thought he was joking when he said that — until last April when the Dow dropped 600-plus points in one day. They'd laugh even harder at this Paris idea — a strong indicator it might be exactly the right choice.

He drove home, so tired now that his pupils oscillated from side to side — snake eyes. Best to have a quick meal, then lights out. Wait until tomorrow to press his contacts for information about Duncan, to investigate the Paris idea…

Once he did lie down, the thoughts wouldn't stop: the sneer on Woodring's face as they walked out of his office last night, the Dendroid team's shocked dejection this morning. But also those possibilities in France, which had his blood singing… He gave in. After a long shower he put on a freshly laundered shirt, splashed on some cologne — his helpers when tired — and confronted his ideas with reality while they were fresh: Paris apartment prices, history of the dollar-to-franc exchange rate, tax laws. By three in the morning, he'd attacked his plan from every angle. No doubt anymore: it was a masterstroke. The numbers didn't merely work; they screamed to be acted on.

He got up from his desk, ready for sleep, when a little gong sounded: incoming email from Martin. Where'd he been the last few days, anyhow? So… he finally read that obsolete email that Dendroid was in trouble… but now he wanted to come *back*. No! Swanson sat down again. He had to act right this second, while Martin was still over there, before naysaying reasons set in. Banging out a reply, he could feel the arc of circumstances, this time, bending to his will.

Chapter Three

From a bench in the center of the square, Martin watched as a slow-motion tide of shadow washed over the Place des Vosges. Picnickers stowed their baskets. An old man tossed his last breadcrumbs to the pigeons, then shuffled off. Lovers stood up shakily, plucked grass from their hair. Above the treetops, the brick and stone façades lining the square soaked up the rusty light, their tall windows bouncing sunbeams in all directions.

He laced his hands behind his head. How did the first humans react when the sun sank into darkness and the moon rose? Easy for us to be calm about it... For that matter, why do we still say the sun sets, hundreds of years after discovering that we're the ones moving? Soon we'll use more than a fraction of our brains, assisted by computer prostheses or genetic enhancement: sustain attention for long periods, hold dozens of items in short-term memory, express ourselves with precision, if only when thinking to ourselves: the-waning-of-the-sun's-incident-angle-due-to-rotation-of-the-earth-when-viewed-from-a-given-point. Drop our vague, truncated summaries, the old, false maps, and approach the actual territory. By then, though, humanity might already be in its latter days, clinging to life on a planet coming apart at the seams. Technology, instead of helping us understand consciousness or probe the nature of the universe, might only serve immediate survival needs, relaying imminent dangers: deadly pollution spikes expected throughout the southern hemisphere this week, severe heat flashes across Siberia, an earthquake-induced tsunami predicted to temporarily submerge the land mass once known as California...

Back in the present moment, a gendarme was motioning him toward the nearest exit. Martin crossed the street and took a table in the agreed-on Café Hugo. Soon he'd finally hear Swanson's plan. Probably some debauchery or other to mourn the passing of Dendroid. Just what had happened, anyway? Did anyone even know? It was painful to think of Dendroid in the past tense. Good times, possible riches, all that work… just gone. On another level, not that he would tell Swanson, it was a relief. The company's thrust, e-commerce analysis, was not remotely fun programming-wise, and the social implications for ordinary people — the customers of their customers — were not entirely clear.

His waiter arrived and Martin pointed at the menu for a glass of wine. So lame. But he wasn't ready for the humiliation of trying to say *un bon vin blanc*. Maybe printed French would be easier. He picked up an abandoned newspaper from the next table. Some words were easy: *dynamique, socialiste*. Then there were toe-stubbers — *ras-le-bol, aussitôt* — and acronyms: SMIC, PIB, UMP… The familiar-looking *main* or *essence* meant something very different in context.

Tossing the paper aside, he signaled for another glass. Lamplit apartments now dotted the square. Some had their curtains open, revealing crystal chandeliers, gilt wallpaper, ceilings twice the normal height — ample spaces where oligarchs or heads of state could cavort in luxury, deploy a network of forces and possibilities completely strange to him. Far above, a pair of birds made slow circles in the metallic-blue twilit sky, their bat-like appearance giving the façades a melancholy, Transylvanian grandeur.

Well into his third glass of wine, he felt a tap on his left shoulder. Turning left, he caught himself and swiveled right. There stood Swanson: grinning, solid, carefree — like the Swanson of old.

"Lookin' good, man," he said, play-punching Martin on the arm. "Sorry I'm late. Crashed when I got to the hotel and slept right through my alarm." Then, casually: "Too bad about Gail."

Martin started. "How the hell did you —"

"I know all, see all and hear all."

He waved the topic away with a gesture. "You're pretty chillaxed yourself, compared to last time I saw you."

"Yeah, I was getting to be a basket case there."

No shit, thought Martin, who'd witnessed it first hand. Their morning commute, for example, had once been the best part of the day: stopping by Jolt n' Bolt for a caffeine infusion and some banter with their sexy baristas, bombing down 101 in the SwansonMobile with KPOO's drive-time blues hour cranked, trading work gossip… But the fun had evaporated in inverse proportion to the company's growth, as the stress twisted them both into pretzels. The day before Martin's Paris trip had been the worst. Swanson, on some other planet, steered with one finger, changed lanes for no apparent reason, ignored the drivers who honked or flipped him off.

Martin couldn't take any more. "Swan, would you cut it the hell out?"

"What?" He said innocently, raising both hands off the wheel — upping the ante.

"You may be a good driver, but see those other people? They aren't. So slow down. Then go get some help. You're a mess."

"Help? *Me?* You sound like my grandmother. I am *fine.* The last thing I need is a shrink," he yelled, whipping around to wave at a hottie in a strawberry-red Beetle.

"Great, whatever — but don't take me with you. Let me off at the next exit and I'll find a goddamn bus. I mean it."

They'd finished the commute in silence. That evening Martin caught a late ride home from another co-worker, and so hadn't seen Swanson since. Now his friend sat there at his ease, his arm draped over the adjoining seat, sunglasses tipped up on his head. As if the last few months hadn't happened.

"So much the better about Gail, though," Swanson was saying, "You're a free man in Paris."

"You gonna tell me about your mysterious plan?"

"You don't need to go back to work right away, do you?"

"How come you always answer my questions with questions?"

"Do I?" Swanson grinned.

"I haven't started hunting for another job yet, if that's what you mean."

"No, I mean how are you situated, in general."

"Financially? I have a little bit saved up."

"Have you ever considered doing something totally different?"

"Aside from a few months off? Sure, I think about it now and then. Teach English somewhere exotic, maybe try the Peace Corps for a year..."

"The Peace Corps," Swanson echoed, drooping his eyes and slumping his shoulders for a little extra sarcastic topspin.

"What's wrong with that?" *Why am I being defensive?* "I've considered it for a while now." *No I haven't. Why lie?*

"Aren't you a little old for that, Martin?"

"I didn't realize peace was just for twenty year-olds. You have anything more age-appropriate in mind?"

"Glad you asked. Remember that idea of buying a rental apartment? Well, it hit me that now is the perfect time."

"Wait, you're thinking of this? A Valley creature like you?"

"The Valley is screwed, and who knows when it'll bounce back. If Dendroid couldn't get funded in this environment, nothing can. Meantime, I'm not going to stand around like a dummy."

"So, an apartment. O-kay. And the location?"

Swanson spread his arms with a comically beatific expression.

"Eh? Here?"

"It's one of the top tourist destinations in the world, and for a European capital, it's cheap right now."

"What could I bring to the party? I don't even speak the language."

"Deep calculation shows it will be twice as easy to maintain and cost half as much if there are two of us. Plus, we always talked about going in on something together, and I wanted to give you the chance. Do you speak any French?"

"*Bonjour, rendez-vous, merde, voulez-vous coucher avec moi.* I think that's it."

"I was fluent when I worked here; it won't take long to ramp back up to speed. I can manage the business transactions while you're learning. After a few weeks of lessons, you'll be able to cover the basic stuff."

"Uh, Swanson? I haven't said 'yes' yet."

"You will, you will. This plan is too beautiful!" He unfolded a napkin and began drawing charts. "The dollar is crushing the franc right now. It always goes in cycles, so we can sell later if we want, when the dollar goes back down, and make a bundle just off the change in the rate, even if real estate prices here stay flat. But they won't; they'll go up for sure, like in most major European cities. Even more after they introduce the euro next January. The way to make a real killing would be to get mortgages on two or three places —"

"Three apartments? *What?*"

"For now let's say we just buy one. We can always expand later."

"Okay, suppose we make money. What about taxes? The I.R.S. is bad enough without adding the French version."

"Yeah, they've had a few hundred extra years to perfect their methods of bureaucratic torture. We can collect rental fees in the U.S, though, and get taxed there. We'll pay property taxes in France, but that's simple. Wouldn't it feel good to know your money's not all stuck in the States, let alone in the goddamn stock market?"

"Sure, but…"

"Don't you owe it to yourself to take a few months before going back to do the shit you already know how to do, over and over for the rest of your life?"

"Yes. Maybe. I mean, I don't know."

"Short run, neither of us has job prospects. Now is the perfect moment for adventure! Why not, just once, take a path without knowing where it leads?" Swanson actually sounded sincere.

"How much work are we talking about, and who does what? Who cleans the places and handles guests?"

"We can find a student to do that; it's not like it takes any experience. As for staying in the place ourselves, let's say we each get two free weeks a year? Anything beyond that, whoever stays pays the other one half the rent. If either of us has to sell for some reason, the other can buy him out or we sell the place and split the profits."

"Sounds reasonable, I guess. Have you written any of this down?"

"It's between us, so where's the problem? Have we ever disagreed about anything important?"

"Nah, aside from politics," admitted Martin, feeling himself getting pulled in. "But how would we actually do this? We'd need months to buy an apartment and get it ready."

"Shouldn't take that long. We can rent a cheap place meanwhile."

"Supposing I join you in this insane boondoggle. What happens to my life in Sunnyvale?"

"Life? Excuse me? What life? There's no job and no woman, either. What's left?"

"Oh, just my parents, my friends, my stuff, my *existence*."

"You don't have to live here, just pony up half the cash and help me bootstrap the beast. Then go back to California once the business is running on its own. Or build huts in the Gobi desert. Or stay here awhile, if you want."

"Just like that."

"Yeah, just like that."

"I'll consider it."

"Fair enough. Look, I'm starving. There's a restaurant on the Place de la République that does great *moules frites.*"

"Mule frights? Suuuurrrre."

On the credenza beside their table, a colossal mound of shellfish encrusted in ice towered over them, reminding Martin of that legendary Himalayan peak, brushed by a bird's wing once every thousand years: only when the feathery contact wears down the entire mountain can the wheel of karma stop turning and the world come to an end...

Swanson was on his cell, speaking French in low, dulcet tones, probably reconnecting with some woman from his Parisian past. If he suffered from jet lag, he didn't let it show. Not that he would have: one of his rules was to never let himself be seen when below par. He'd been that way ever since Martin first met him, a long, long time ago.

They hadn't always been close. In the lower grades, they never ended up as classmates or in the same circles. With high school came cars, girls, intoxicants, the quest for personal style. Old groupings fractured, creating new ones. Swanson's posse in particular fascinated and repelled Martin, the way they roamed beyond the reach of authority, their feet not quite touching the ground, seemingly well-behaved but ultimately doing as they pleased, certain that whatever went wrong would be quietly fixed, that once the fun and games were over, big things were waiting for them. Not that Swanson was a snob. If you approached him in the presence of his friends, he welcomed you without any hint of politeness, natural as could be. It was theoretically possible that he'd hidden the snobbishness, thus performing a double-snob. But no, if Martin felt outside a group he could've easily joined, it was his own doing. Cliques meant labels — jock, stoner, geek — and a bunch of unwritten rules, if you wanted to maintain membership privileges. He always drifted away before it got to that point, back to the group of those like him who had no group, guided by an instinct he'd never understood but always obeyed.

If not for a chance incident at their high school's graduation party, Swanson might have become just another forgotten childhood acquaintance. Martin was hanging out with some friends who'd pulled the old vodka-in-a-baggie-inside-a-bottle-of-orange-juice trick. At the height of the festivities, he overheard a familiar, precociously resonant radio-announcer's voice. There stood Swanson, facing a semicircle of his buds, making summary judgments of one after another of them while they listened, slack-jawed: this one was in love with himself, spending every recess at the boy's room mirror; that one a chronic masturbator, petrified of real girls; that other a petty thief, who bragged about ripping off all his neighbors…

Martin backed away unnoticed. This… from Swanson? To hoard all that dirt, then serve it up in front of everybody concerned? Even years afterward, Swanson refused to give Martin any reason for the incident. A mysterious creature, there all along, had risen from the deep, belched out fire, then vanished beneath the surface… Yet you couldn't help admiring the nerve of it, when in the same situation you would have invented some pretext to water things down: offend no one, make nice even with the jerks you'd rather avoid, while magnanimously telling yourself you wanted to go easy on *them*.

When they both ended up at Stanford, Martin stayed in touch, discovering that Swanson was far more interesting than he let on. At first, they mostly argued. Not in a hostile way, but more in an amused, how-can-anyone-think-this-way way, each giving the other a target-rich environment as well as a worthy opponent, a testing ground for ideas that would never come up among like-minded friends. Discussions that might start over a bong or a bottle at Swanson's frat house, where hip-hop from the stadium-grade stereo shook the floorboards, would continue into the night in Martin's bamboo-curtained co-op room, beneath the posters of Che and Gramsci, who gazed into the future, toward justice and the common good. Often as not, they'd abandon their debate over the patriarchy or the merits of *Atlas Shrugged*, and go pick up girls. Swanson would lead, plowing into a group of unknown women like a polar icebreaker, impervious to bitchiness or frosty receptions, confident that one or more of them were dying to be rescued from an evening of boredom. He'd open with anything. Once, he'd won a bet by simply exclaiming "cauliflower!". While he got their attention, Martin would enter from the other side, apologize for his amigo, then find a woman of the more low-key persuasion. A good cop-bad cop routine that worked the whole time Martin was at Stanford…

Swanson finished his call, jotted something down, and continued exactly where he'd left off.

"Unfortunately, Jones-Wolff's offer was strictly verbal, so there was no legal breach of contract."

"What happens when this gets out, though? Doesn't reputation matter, even to those scumbags?"

"They're the go-to people," Swanson shrugged, "they have the capital, they get to do what they want."

"Such as fuck us with impunity."

"Perhaps you'll find this shocking, Martin, but some people out there really aren't very nice. However," he raised his index finger, "you're in Paris without a care in the world. There must be a reason."

Martin dropped his keys at the front desk, expecting to take a very long walk. His flight home, paid for by Dendroid in what already seemed another life, was tomorrow. But he still had no solid answer for Swanson. For days he'd wandered the streets, circled monuments, ruminated in sidewalk cafés, hoping Paris itself would tell him. By tomorrow, in any case, the choice would be made. On the Place Saint-Michel, he stopped at the fountain, supposedly the one place on Earth where if you were patient enough, whatever person you were waiting for would eventually pass by. A break-dancer with bright blue hair set down a boom box, cranked the volume, and began his routine. *Boom, klak, a-boom-boom klak.* A crowd gathered. It seemed that everyone but him had a purpose, knew where they'd be tomorrow. Martin moved on, toward the river.

He descended a wide stone staircase to walk along the Seine. Down here the city's rhythm was slower, more intimate. Gulls cried. Water ploshed against the bank. On the far side of the river, fishermen baited their lines, set up their poles, unpacked lunch. Tour boats glided past.

Apartment scheme or no, jumping straight into another job was out, even if tech somehow un-crashed itself. Big companies were full of entrenched egos and bureaucracy. Startups promised autonomy, potential impact on the industry, stock options — but the recipe was always the same: take job; tenderize brain for fifteen hours a day, fry until burnt and crispy; watch company rise or implode; emerge from cave into sunlight; soak well in beer, bronze in front of TV; simmer for three or four months, stir occasionally; bring job offers to a boil; return to cave…

Before this trip he'd sometimes brooded over the tactics of his career, but not its overall direction. Consensus opinion in a pressurized, self-referential place like the Valley was that there was no alternative. What were you gonna do, join the clueless outside world? Even so, friends of his had bailed, started families, gotten advanced degrees. Others had entered that floating world, the 'between jobs' zone — hanging out in coffee shops, chatting online, pimping their blogs.

His motivation used to be the programming itself, which had grabbed him while at school and not let go. Having decided to major in philosophy, he'd happened to watch someone in his dorm write code for a video game. Martin stayed for hours, absorbed by the guy's impeccable mastery, the way he chose his own problems, how and when to solve them — the whole time walking a tight-rope, since one missed semi-colon, he said, might mean days lost in hunting down the mistake. Computer classes in high school had been dry; this was *cool*. Soon Martin began working part-time for the dorm guy's video game outfit. Coding spread across his days like kudzu, choked off everything else in and outside class, turned his junior year into one long caffeinated hacking party. Aristotle and Kant dropped away, unable to compete with the instant gratification of making the computer do his bidding. His first thoughts on waking and the last before sleep were the bug he needed to fix, the next tweak, the elegant design he'd cooked up to amaze his peers — the only people he knew, incredible as it seemed today, with email addresses.

Now they were all grandpas in nerd years, and the game had drastically changed. Compressed product cycles — where even the rate of acceleration increased — meant less room for creativity. Software had become more standardized, using preexisting code libraries, documented in mind-numbing tomes that had to be choked down every few months just to stay current. Less mojo and more Lego. It had been years since he'd designed anything from scratch. Yet he'd stayed at it. Maybe he hadn't known what else to do with himself? He did enjoy the technical challenges, the cash, his work friends. But no, what really kept him at the trough was that only there could he conceive a project, build it, set it in motion and get the rush of containing — all by his own will — the centrifugal forces that constantly threatened to send the entire contraption flying apart. He'd organized his existence around building stuff, triumphing over emergencies and deadlines — without, until this Paris trip, considering another way to get that kind of adrenaline fix. Or whether life might offer something better.

Not that any of that meant he should drop everything to join this apartment scheme. He always fell in too easily with other people's ideas, especially Swanson's. To say no was probably wiser. He walked along the river bank, muttering to himself: "Great idea, sorry that it doesn't make sense for me right now…" He sighed. Tomorrow, then, back to Sunnyvale. To his prefab one-and-a-quarter-bedroom, in a cul-de-sac lined with identical boxen. Where there were no sidewalks — no *sidewalks* — forcing you to drive for even the piddliest errand. Where urban planning catered to industry's need to lodge the bodies that supported the heads that contained the grey matter that cranked out the code, designed the hardware, sold the product. No wonder the entire peninsula, viewed from a plane, resembled a circuit-board.

His occasional fantasies of leaving usually involved a sleepy little town in Marin County. He'd run an off-road café with hardwood floors, gingham tablecloths, a cat in the window. There would be a house outside town and a girlfriend, a bright young thing with a goofy sense of humor. On off-days they'd be lazy, make love all morning, drink coffee on the terrace in their kimonos, maybe read or take a hike afterwards, head into town at night to hear some jazz… But now that felt like a shift into neutral. What he'd blurted the other day about the Peace Corps had been no accident: a radical departure was what he needed — and here it was, handed to him. For a couple months, if that's all he wanted. While his parents were well and he had no wife, kids, or other commitments. Instead of stumbling into a major change, as he always had, he could create one. All the weight of the question moved to one side of the scale: yes. *Hell* yes. Even if Swanson's scheme fizzled. He turned around, waved to the anglers on the opposite bank, then bounded up the stairs, whistling.

Chapter Four

Swanson was trying to uncork a bottle of wine with a pair of scissors.

"Damn it, Sébastien! You're French — weren't you brought up to carry an opener with you at all times?"

"Do you expect me to take care of *everything* for you? Isn't it enough that I put this roof over your head? And Americans are supposed to be so competent!"

"Yadda yadda."

Swanson impatiently pushed the cork into the bottle, then filled the plastic cups set out on the formica table. Lit by an uncovered bulb, it was the only furniture in the kitchen, apart from their chairs.

"Gentlemen, a toast," he cried. "To Sébastien, who arranged these temporary headquarters, launch pad for our coming world domination!"

Martin seconded it. "To Sébastien! To world domination! Yarrrr!"

"I brought a house-warming present," said Sébastien, placing a large cheese on the table with exaggerated ceremony.

"Wheeeeewww," gasped Martin. "Smells like an old sock."

"You don't know what heaven is," replied Sébastien, who leaned over it and made little scooping motions with his hands to better take in the aroma. "Ahhh…!"

"French machismo for you," Swanson shrugged, "The runnier and stinkier, the better."

Sébastien struck an offended pose, dropping his excellent English for a moment. "You weeell nev-aaair und-air-stand zees country! Only when this cheese gets up and walks across the table will it be ready to eat."

Martin found it hard to avoid laughing along with this guy, whose grin implied you and he were in on something together, without it ever becoming clear what that something was. Beneath the meticulously tended three-day beard, which seemed to have been rolled on pre-grown, like Astroturf, was a face neither handsome nor ugly. It was the mischievous, effervescent glance that, according to Swanson, worked wonders on the objects of his fleeting affections, be they women or men.

Martin poured some more Bordeaux. "So, Sébastien — you're at a cable company?"

"Yes, a few months after Swanson here went back to the States — the traitor — our department got downsized. I then spent the best year of my life so far, doing nothing whatsoever. When the money ran out I started working for LOSSY and have been there ever since. What I do amounts to receiving people's requests to terminate TV service, then pretending I didn't receive them."

They looked at him blankly.

"*Je vous explique*. Let's say you want to end your contract with LOSSY. You send us a letter using an *avis de réception…*"

"Registered mail," Swanson interposed.

"…to tell us you want out. My performance is evaluated, though, on how much extra revenue I generate. So I do whatever I can to prolong the process, in order to extract," he smiled that smile, "as much money as I can from you. One illegible word in your letter, and I send it back. That means another three weeks, on average. Once I receive an impeccably completed form, I delay as long as possible before I process the request. Half the time I ignore it anyway, then make up some excuse if you write again."

"What if your boss finds out?" Martin asked.

"Are you kidding? My boss insisted I do all that! Whether it's legal is his problem. Some customers get so worn down, they stop trying to terminate — I earn a bonus for every five of those. Others explode. Then I get angry myself — I mean, what gives them the right to yell at me? I didn't create the process! Eventually, you begin to enjoy saying 'no' all day. It makes you strong. I got so good at it that they put me in charge of Customer Satisfaction." He paused for effect. "Bwahahahaha!"

Martin and Swanson burst out laughing.

"It helped me with seduction, too," he continued, "I wasn't afraid to hear 'no' anymore."

"When were you ever?" asked Swanson.

"Of course I wasn't stupid enough to let it show, but sure, rejection bothered me. A little. Now I truly don't care. No matter how much I desire someone, I imagine him or her as one of my customers, and even the most drastic non doesn't touch me." He sliced himself some cheese and tore off part of a baguette. "So, what is your crazy scheme, again?"

"An apartment rental business…"

"That's very nice," Sébastien cut in, "But enough about you — let's talk about me some more."

Swanson tossed up his hands. "Welcome, ladies and gentlemen, to Sébastien World."

"Oh, all right — go ahead."

He listened to their plan, nodding here and there, then said: "It's a very good idea, but there are certain unwritten rules you need to know. Fortunately, I used to go out with a realtor, who taught me all kinds of things — the G-rated parts of which I will generously share with you."

While Swanson took notes, Sébastien gave the lowdown. Assume the real estate agents will try to cheat you, especially since you are Americans. Don't bother with listings that don't show the size in square meters. But watch out: that size might differ from the *loi-carrez*, the actual habitable space. A top-floor apartment with a sloped ceiling, where it's impossible to stand upright in certain areas, would have a smaller *loi-carrez*. Make sure the building has an elevator — tourists won't walk up four flights of stairs. Forget central air-conditioning, hardly anyone has it.

"Why not?" Martin asked.

Sébastien stuck out his thumb. "It's hard to retrofit these old buildings." Then the index. "People are used to doing without it." Second finger. "Many are cheapskates." Ring finger. "Most methods are against the law."

"Against the *law*?"

"Especially in the expensive areas. I mean, the boxes outside New York apartment windows? Those are *ugly*. And it's illegal to be gratuitously ugly in Paris."

"People just suffer in the heat, then?"

"It's a lifestyle choice. At least we're not contributing to global warming. Oh, another thing: the bathrooms and showers here are…"

"Microscopic."

"While you Americans…"

"…just keep getting bigger."

"You said it, not me. That will mean some remodeling. Also, find out whatever you can about the *syndic*, the company that manages the property. All apartment buildings have one. They charge you big fees and often do absolutely nothing. I want to be a syndic when I grow up. Which *arrondissements* are you looking in, by the way?"

"The third or the fourth, I guess. The Marais is popular with tourists and I lived there before, so I know it better than the others," said Swanson.

"Good. It's expensive, but still cheaper than the sixth or seventh."

"Is it better to have a shared bank account?" asked Martin.

"Why would you want to do that?"

"Since we are *partenaires*…"

Sébastien thrust out his hand. "Wait — unless you two are sleeping together, don't say *partenaires*. You are *associés*. As for a shared account, I see no advantage. What you do have to worry about is getting a loan, unless you came over with suitcases full of cash, like good Americans."

"I can see that the main downside of this venture," said Swanson, "will be you annoying French people."

Martin poured another round. "Are you really so bad?"

"We are an acquired taste," said Sébastien, "like you guys, the Germans, the Russians, and everybody else. We do tend to be hypercritical. You Americans think we hate you or that we're snobs — but we judge each other even more. If the average Parisian goes to a party, he'll stick with the people he knows and not talk to anybody else. His great fear is looking ridiculous, unlike you Americans, who don't fear it enough."

"You're not that way."

"I said the *average* Parisian." He looked at his watch. "Well, enough cultural lessons for today. I'm supposed to get together with this guy at ten."

"Er, it's already ten-fifteen."

"We just met today," he said from the door. "I thought I'd better get him used to waiting for me." Then he disappeared, leaving only the afterglow of his Cheshire-cat grin.

For Martin the days went by quickly, a blur of apartment visits. Between appointments, he and Swanson were having the kind of open-ended conversations they hadn't had in a long time. Evenings, Swanson mostly caught up with his old Parisian friends. Of course he had a perfect right to — it wasn't his fault Martin knew nobody here. After feeling a little put out at first, Martin came to appreciate the solitude, which let him try to digest the unfamiliar impressions that bombarded him every waking minute.

As they furnished their temporary digs, he discovered another side of his friend, who'd invest long hours choosing placemats, silverware, coffee equipment. But the private Swanson had always differed somewhat from the public, type-A Swanson. Martin himself might spend days on hot-rodding a laptop or shopping for a bass guitar, but kitchenware… Maybe he had something to learn. Like many of his engineer friends, he'd always surrounded himself with unstylish, mismatched objects, acquired more or less at random. As if it were something to take pride in. He'd probably never appreciate style or beauty the way some did, but it really was juvenile, in Paris of all places, to not try to know his own tastes, or pretend he'd rather not have any.

The ground rules at headquarters needed no stating. The two had never been roommates, but during the bootstrapping of Dendroid, they'd worked out of a single open room for the first six months — one toilet, a hotplate, and a mini-fridge for thirty people — where you quickly learned everyone's third-rail dislikes. For Martin, no audible techno or hip-hop, no fried food; for Swanson, no abandoned messes or chit-chat before the morning's first coffee. The common area split into zones. Martin gravitated to the sofa, where the wifi signal was strongest, while Swanson usually hung out at the kitchen table with an espresso and a Clairefontaine notebook, tabulating data and ranking apartments they had seen. On his own, Swanson was also investigating what was up with Duncan. More from worry than anger by now, especially when he found out Duncan had been canned by Jones-Wolff. Nothing about him made sense anymore. Their mutual friends in the Valley said he seemed to have vanished without a trace.

"Mais, ma puce…", the reedy blonde purred into her minuscule, baby-blue cell phone, *"tu sais que c'est impossible. Je t'ai déjà dit milles fois. Arr-êt-es… Écoute, il y a du monde. Je te rappelle. À plus…"*.

She rose to greet them in a low, tobacco-mellowed voice. *Bonjour, est-ce que je peux vous aider?* Hearing their accents, she seamlessly switched to English: Oh, you are Americans? You speak French so well… No, no, you are far too generous, blah, blah. Swanson. Martin. Monique. In the future we will have to arrange for nicer weather for you, etcetera. All the better for looking at apartments… Were you interested in a particular property? Yes, the *deux pièces* on Boulevard de Sébastopol. Oh, *c'est un quartier très animé* — one can see that you know Paris well, and so on.

Swanson asked about the apartment listing they'd seen in the window. As he launched into Sébastien's list of talking points, Monique's mobile eyes openly looked them over. Her mouth began to set; finally she leaned forward and asked sharply: "*Vous êtes des marchands de biens, c'est ça?*" Ha, ha, *mais non*, not professional real estate people at all — just normal buyers, interested in the apartment. She gave a sigh that said: What to do? A client is a client. Foreigners, even Americans, sometimes came prepared. She nodded. If you want, we can look at it right now. Yes, that would be ideal.

After locking the office, she led them across the broad, noisy rue Saint-Antoine, then onto a parallel side street. As they passed a corner café, Martin noticed a dark-eyed waitress, setting the outside tables. She looked up abruptly, triggering a sudden, crazy hope. But her gaze went past him, to a waiter on the opposite corner who was making the thumb-and-pinkie gesture for a phone call, pointing at his wrist for "later." She smiled. Martin stopped a moment, pretending to tie his shoe to take in, even vicariously, this slice of Parisian life you might see in a movie or a Doisneau photo — the kind of thing he'd been wishing would happen to him.

He rejoined Monique and Swanson, staying a little behind to let their conversation float back to him, the slippery French sounds meaning no more than the cooing of pigeons. These stolen moments were the best. Not obliged to speak or understand, he could play the cultural anthropologist: observe the architecture, passersby, store windows… At home, none of it would have registered: the overcast sky spreading its pearly, matte light over the buildings — so old on this street that they leaned into or away from the street like a drunken chorus line — or the Japanese tourists up ahead, who fixed their hungry attention on unexpected things, now peering as one into an Italian bookshop named, in bright yellow letters, *Tour de Babel.*

A few minutes later, Monique smartly punched in the door code of an imposing multistory edifice. Its lobby was modern, surfaces polished, mailboxes gleaming. In the courtyard, behind the proud façade, Martin was amused to find that the unified structure was actually a hodgepodge of buildings stuck together over many years, huddling like actors backstage with their makeup off.

As she opened the apartment door, Monique explained that the owner had lived there since World War II; when he'd fallen ill, his son offered the place for sale as-is. "Which makes it an exceptional bargain. You just need to use your imaginations a bit." The entry hall extended past a sordid kitchenette to the living room, a large space made smaller by clutter and fustiness. Shelves and piles of bric-a-brac orbited around a lumpen sofa facing an ancient rabbit-eared television. An overflowing ashtray, an opened bottle of orange juice on the floor… a human being had lived right here, been interrupted as everyone must eventually be. And here they were, strolling through his space. Martin, oddly guilt-struck, momentarily unsure what to do with himself, went to the window. He looked down in surprise: the neighborhood on this side of the building was another world from that by which they'd entered: bars, fast-food places, an old-school neon-signed X-rated bookstore… nearby, two linebackerish hookers in garish miniskirts loitered in a cobblestone alleyway that looked hundreds of years old.

He rejoined Swanson, who was already making a careful inspection, alert to signs of mold, bad plumbing, structural decay. Neither spoke, unlike the first days of their search, when Swanson, or Martin through him, asked question after question, for practice. They had cast their nets wide, zigzagging all over the "heart of the Marais"— which, if you believed the real estate agents, extended for miles in every direction.

"We need to decide what we're looking for," Swanson had said at the beginning — three weeks ago now. "A complete re-do takes time and work but lets us set up the place the way we want. Some only need minor TLC; they cost a lot but are ready to go. Figure a six percent interest rate on an eighty percent loan, amortized over fifteen years. The payments plus insurance come to eleven percent of the principal..."

"My vote is for a cheaper one," Martin cut in. "Forking out so much cash makes me nervous."

"Dunno. A place that needs minimal work means we could start renting right away. My mom did fixer-uppers for a living — they always take longer than you think."

"I can't afford to put half my savings into this," said Martin, glad to have something to assert. "Unless it's priced to sell, I say we pass."

"Okay boss, just don't come complaining to me later," Swanson had said.

Afterwards, on the sidewalk, Monique gave a brief history of the area and its surroundings: the former importance of Les Halles, the way people had torn down old buildings in the Marais, replacing them with whatever they wanted, until Malraux saved the entire district. Of course much had changed since then, as it does in cities. In the mid-nineteenth century, today's ultra-chic Île St. Louis had been the bottom of the barrel, the only district that the royalty of the mind like Baudelaire and Gautier could afford...

When she left, Swanson turned to Martin.

"Are we agreed this one's a winner?"

"Yeah. The nabe's not perfect, but..."

"Well, nobody comes to Paris to sit in their room."

All the way back to headquarters, Swanson thought out loud. "It isn't the Marais. Still, it's a fantastic deal — there's space for a whole family, easy. If the seller's in a hurry, maybe we can lowball him. Ten percent off the price and a mortgage would give us great leverage. If we charge twelve-hundred a week, that leaves our profit at…" At times he became so engrossed in calculations, he almost walked into traffic. Martin grunted a response now and then. He enjoyed details; his professional life revolved around them. Just not grubby investment numbers. He preferred observing their neighborhood. Compared to downtown's glittering stores and apartments, it seemed to belong to another city, with its grimy kebab joint on the corner, the wholesaler of wigs, the stationery store whose display — an electric typewriter and its cardboard advertisement, featuring a pipe-smoking gent and a lady with a foot-high bouffant hairdo — was covered in a fine, blueish dust.

As they reached their building, a tall man ducked into the night club next door. Probably the manager, at such an early hour. The place's relentless boom-chi-boom-chi started around ten on weekend nights, a musical Chinese water torture that lasted until morning.

Martin elbowed Swanson: "Ever find out the deal with this place?"

"No. Let's ask right now."

In their lobby, Swanson hit the front desk buzzer. The concierge, a pleasant, sleepy-eyed Portuguese woman named Paula, appeared a minute or so later.

"Yes," she sighed, after hearing him out, "everyone is angry about the noise."

"Good! Perhaps we can start a petition."

"However," she continued, with a tight smile, "they urged me not to complain."

"What?"

"You need to understand," she lowered her voice, "many tenants here have no papers. They come from all over: Nigeria, Poland…

Portugal, too. Every week new ones arrive: musicians on tour, businessmen here for a deal... They come, knowing they'll never go back. The last thing they want is a visit from the police." She shrugged. "I am a citizen since my husband is French, but I understand how they feel."

Can't blame them, considering what they'd be forced to go back to, thought Martin, though it was usually pointless to say such things to Swanson. They got off on the fourth floor, where the hall was filled with its usual mix of cooking smells: fried rice, roasted meat, boiled cabbage. The people behind the odors were rarely seen, but the thin walls revealed more than enough — which couples fought, which fucked, and which, generally the loudest, did both.

"I talked to Sébastien about the next steps," Swanson said. "First, we hire a notaire — a real estate lawyer. After comes the *promesse de vente*, where we make the down payment. Once we sign that, we're out thirty thousand euros if we renege. Then we get a loan, since we're not paying cash. The final signature is a month or two later."

"Wow. I thought we'd be renting the place out by then." Martin thought for a while. "Well, if it's gonna take that long, I'm gonna pop back to California after the *promesse* and see what's growing in my fridge."

Chapter Five

Almost to water level now. At SFO a landing plane always seemed to be diving into the bay, and from a passenger window you couldn't see terra firma until the wheels touched down. Everything was naturally computer controlled, which for most people meant error-free. As a programmer, Martin knew better. Airplanes were pretty damn robust, of course, but what did he know, really? Most technology permeating everyday life was powered by commercial code that inevitably shipped with bugs. Deadlines and human frailty often meant fixing just the showstoppers, leaving the rest for the next software release. Even if machines eventually programmed themselves or each other, their flawless code might be maladapted to a messy human world speckled with edge cases and contingencies. The lowly users, as now, would have to trust without being able to verify.

At baggage claim, suitcases were already on the conveyor. Passengers swarmed anxiously, pounced on their belongings, then marched away, yelling into their phones with accents that sounded nasal, strange: luvya, hunny; buh-bye. He was home, in circumstances unlike any he could have imagined when leaving for Paris: the breakup with Gail, Dendroid's implosion, co-ownership of an apartment rental biz…

The oddness only evaporated in the airport shuttle, as he watched the familiar cities go by. Ahead on the left was Panoptical, its new headquarters towering purple and enormous above the dusty freeway shrubbery. A worldwide enterprise for years now, they'd reached the point in their lifecycle where it felt imperative to erect a Phallic

Corporate Monument, that Silicon Valley archetype whose meaning to everyone outside the given company's upper management is always: time to short the stock. Still, props were due. Panoptical had been his first real job, his true alma mater. The video game outfit he'd left school to join didn't count, since they never produced, let alone sold, anything. It was more a pretext for Martin and three other guys to consume absurd quantities of donuts, impress each other with clever but useless ideas, and brag they were "building a company." Months later, having drifted from one dorm room or coffee shop to another, bleary-eyed and smelling like a zoo, they'd dissolved the cabal. That taste of freedom, though, made it out of the question to take some normal job or slink back to school.

But he needed serious remedial study. Moving in with his folks to regroup, he'd stumble downstairs to their drafty basement at the crack of noon, to hunch over his ancient, tiny-screened Mac. Around it he piled teetering stacks of second-hand textbooks in the shape of a horseshoe, as if encircling a shrine or temple. Using discipline he didn't know he possessed, he'd slog through exercises in data structures or network performance until late at night. Then came the reward: connecting to Usenet via his parent's dialup connection. The programming-related newsgroups, being free-form online billboards, were open to all, but dominated by a handful of gurus who seemed to live at their keyboards, advising or passing judgment in a gnomic tone of genius: cranky, impatient, yet open-handed with their hard-won knowledge, even when responding to numbskulls or competitors. Wisdom existed to be shared, went the ethos. To reduce the amount of stupid code out there, no matter whose, was A Good Thing. In a world stupefied by noise, what could be nobler than to add more signal? Finally, an adult activity worth believing in. Plus, one got to wear both a virtuous white hat and an anti-establishment black hat. Until the early morning, Martin would read every message in every group that mattered, separating the noobs from those who spoke wisdom in this guild he meant to join. Many of the sharpest hailed from Panoptical.com. There, and nowhere else, was where he'd work.

Reducing his Stonehenge of books to those recommended online, he took apart each example, exercise, and wisdom nugget, connected them to what he'd already learned, then moved on to the next. All else — women, friends, phone calls, favorite TV shows, his gig playing bass with Vomit Launch — went by the wayside.

Once he felt ready, he ginned up a resumé, providing the other donut-eaters as references, and sent it to Panoptical. His contact there, a genial, corpulent redhead with the improbable bluesman name of Deacon House, recited the same mantra for months on end: don't worry, we've gone through all the proper channels, be in touch soon. Unable to wait anymore, Martin called HR one day, claiming to be a tech journalist; in less than two minutes he was on the line with the head of the operating systems group. To phone him directly had to be verboten, but there was no longer much to lose.

"I don't know who gave you my number," barked the manager, "but you've sure got some balls."

Martin flinched, ready to hang up.

"Can you come over for an interview today? I need more people with attitude."

Martin's flimsy resumé fooled no one, but in those days they welcomed a little chutzpah. A few hours later, he was in. The HR guy Deacon, either not remembering or pretending not to remember Martin and his many phone calls, gave him a tour of his new home, with its rumpus room decor: gadgets everywhere, a paper maché flying saucer hanging from the lobby ceiling, pinball machines in the chill room.

In many ways it felt like school: someone always in the building, be it Saturday at 4am or New Year's Eve… the same fear of falling behind, of dropping a stupid remark, of being — or, worse, *said* to be — one of those who couldn't cut it. Most programmers turned out to be phenomenally sensitive to hierarchy, whatever they claimed to the contrary, and worse gossips than a coffee klatsch of old biddies. Sooner or later, every conversation circled back to salaries, titles, and sexy projects, especially when the undeserving got them. The Ayatollahs at the top had weighty responsibilities, which gave them license to snarl at their co-workers or bosses when in the mood, or show up late for meetings and put their feet up on the conference table, letting everyone else stare at the soles of their sneakers for an hour.

They weren't all that way. Hojo, for example, whose nickname came from winning an undergrad bet to eat a stack of pancakes in every Howard Johnson's between Bakersfield and San Diego. The fastest, most error-free coder in the company, he was also known as an approachable wizard — a rare commodity among senior engineers who often simply shouted "no!" at those who knocked. Newbies and executives alike would camp outside his office door, hoping for advice or blessing on a project, and Hojo usually made time, even if it meant he finished his own work at 3am, while his questioners had been asleep for hours. To blow off steam, he'd pull a prank or two: fill his girlfriend's cubicle to the brim with styrofoam peanuts, or kidnap the VP of Sales on April Fool's day and stage a mock trial, convicting him of corporate treason for violating truth and logic. Such were the joys...

Martin started awake as the shuttle hit the speed bump of his cul-de-sac, a term he could now translate literally as 'ass of bag'. On the counter were stacks of mail his brother had been collecting for him. The first piece of non-junk was a $900 phone bill — most of it roaming charges in Paris for calls to Swanson. Damn parasites. If they caught you off-guard, they made more off you in one billing cycle than they did the entire rest of your life. Flopping onto the sofa, he took hold of the small plastic rectangle and switched on the other rectangle across the room — something he hadn't done or missed since he'd left. A couple of talking heads snarled at each other.

Past midnight he woke up, famished. The fridge being empty, of course, he shuffled to the garage, feeling a slight thrill as his trusty Saab started up. California did have that in its favor: a private chariot, with no worries about catching the last Métro. As he turned down aisle four at the local Food Mart, he almost ran into a guy clutching a couple party-sized bags of Cheez Bombz. It took a second to recognize Stan, a fellow grunt at Panoptical. Major awkwardness. They'd worked on several big projects together and hung out a lot, even outside work. Then one day Stan stopped talking to him, rebuffing all overtures. They hadn't spoken since. He was pudgy then, even more so now — and not looking pleased, not at all.

"Hey, Stan! How's it going?" Martin offered to shake.

"Okay," mumbled Stan, ignoring the outstretched hand. He tossed his swag in the cart with a nervous rodential squint, as if ready to burrow into the breakfast cereals.

"What you been up to?"

"Nothing."

"Hey," said Martin, surprised at his own determination to get an answer, even a lie: "What happened back at Panoptical? All the sudden you started acting as if I'd run over your grandmother."

"Uh — it doesn't matter, does it?"

"Maybe not, but I still want to know."

"Why don't you ask Barry?" He turned his cart around and scuttled off.

Well, that was a name from a bygone era. At the time of Stan's freeze-out, Barry headed their division, with Martin his supposed lieutenant. Everything had been super-political. Another group kept postponing their deliverables to Martin's project, not even bothering to hide their attempt to make him fail. It got so bad Martin broke the 'never complain, never explain' rule with Barry, alluding to 'enemies' trying to sabotage the project. It had seemed wiser not to name names. But Barry must've thought — or chosen to think — he meant Stan, and had told Stan. The timing and Stan's own words left no doubt. Why? Maybe it was that damn party Barry had hosted. A last-minute crisis prevented Martin from going, though he'd been looking forward to it. Hard to believe Barry could have been so offended, but from then on he'd only spoken to Martin when necessary.

Martin ambled through the frozen food section, mechanically tossing items into his cart, his image of that period breaking into pieces and reassembling into unexpected patterns. So many odd interactions now made sense. Once home, he lay in bed, staring into the dark. Code was so much easier to unravel than human beings. When else had he missed the signs? Well, there was the real estate agent who'd sold him this house, then insisted on getting together after the sale. Martin had always wondered why, especially when the guy left after a couple beers, clearly annoyed. He'd made thousands on the sale, but now it was obvious: he'd expected a tip or a gift. Martin had sleepwalked through the entire conversation — the agent's motivation hadn't even appeared on his radar. Jet lagged at 3am, plenty of similar incidents came to mind; he was still ruminating on them, feeling chagrined but a little less stupid, when the sun came up.

Late one evening, a group of ex-Dendroid engineers gathered around a basement pool table in west Mountain View. They'd been the core of the engineering department, and Martin was eager to hear what they were up to now. It was the first time they'd all been together since the company's demise, which inevitably was where the conversation started.

"Can't believe nothing's surfaced about our getting screwed at the last minute," Tooch was saying. "Not even rumors."

"Big companies are croaking every week now," replied Matt. "Who's gonna remember lil' ol' us?"

Sam took a long pull on his beer. "Maybe it was for the best."

"How's that?"

"Mind you, I don't have proof that it would've happened, but a couple nights before we went under, I saw something on the white board in the executive conference room. Something… heinous."

The room went silent.

"A diagram," he went on, "of an interface for third-parties to connect to our customer data."

Everyone started talking at once.

"That would've totally violated every privacy commitment we ever made to our customers," boomed Ben, who stood a head taller than anyone else. "Worse, it would've boogered up my beautiful architecture."

Greg stroked his chin. "Management would have presented it as a *fait accompli*. The only way to stay in business."

"Worse, they'd have been right," said Matt.

Martin listened, as shocked as everyone else. He hadn't heard about any such plan, which seemed to confirm his worst fears about the direction of Dendroid and tech in general. Being engineers — fanatical about privacy, opposed to invasive marketing — they batted around every aspect of the nasty moral dilemma they would have faced. Somewhere in the middle, though, Martin began to detach. It just didn't seem like his fight anymore.

Tooch, noticing he'd tuned out, elbowed him. "So, dude… Paris! What's up with that?"

Everybody started grilling him. The apartment venture seemed strange to them. Was it an overreaction to the Dendroid fiasco? An excuse to goof off? A mademoiselle? The implicit assumption being that taking a hiatus from Silicon Valley, even in its current pathetic state, was what was odd. He let them guess, having no pat answer. How could he explain that in some ways he was going back to Paris to figure out why he wanted to be there?

The day before his return flight, Martin got in the Saab to pick up some stuff for Swanson — the last to-do on his list. Mostly this trip had gone as planned: he'd hung with friends and family, visited favorite bookstores, even had dinner with his headhunter, for formality's sake. But the run-in with Stan and the revelation that Dendroid had considered selling out their user's privacy had pretty much spoiled the homecoming. What had these last years been about? Instead of making a difference, he'd made a little money. Now he was in limbo: unclear if he wanted to return to California in two months, and even less sure about the Paris thing…

Whoops! The white clouds of oleander masked Swanson's house so well that Martin almost drove past it. He parked in the driveway and took out his list of what Swanson wanted and which room it was in. Opening the door, he stood there, shocked. His first thought was: earthquake. Instead of Swanson's usual meticulous order, the sofa was turned upside down; CDs, photographs, books lay scattered on the floor. He stood still. Whoever did it might still be there. He held his breath, but with his heart thumping wildly could hear nothing else. Through the half-open door wafted the oleander's heavy perfume. Backing away, neck hair standing on end, he stumbled to the car. Using both hands, he finally got the key in the ignition, then pulled out of the driveway so fast he almost hit a passing jogger. After a couple minutes, evasively changing streets even though nobody was in the rear-view mirror, he stopped to phone the police. He doubled back and stationed himself across the street to wait. Soon a couple of black-and-whites slid next to the house, sirens off. Two cops went inside, while a third waited for Martin to cross. His big pink face puckered as he squinted into the noonday sun.

"You the one who called?"

Martin nodded, then recited his story.

"Friend of the owner? Know where he is?"

"Paris."

The cop wrote down Swanson's info, then pivoted toward Martin. "You know, somebody called us just before you did, saying she was almost run down right in front of this house. Her description matched your car." The cop stared at him for a few long seconds. "Mind if I take a look at the vehicle?"

Martin paled. "*My* car?"

"Are you telling me no?"

"No! I mean, go ahead."

As the cop began rummaging through the glove compartment, Martin idly wondered if people had ever put gloves in there. Then he remembered last year's road trip to Mexico. Shit — someone had brought weed. They hadn't left anything behind in the car, had they, any paraphernalia? He couldn't remember. Why the hell was this guy checking him out anyway, when he was the one who'd called? The cop took his time, leaving Martin to imagine getting thrown in the same jail cell as the thugs who'd just ripped off Swanson. Who'd naturally exact some kind of horrific retribution…

But there was nothing in the car and nothing else to say to the cops. The next day, Martin left California again, without regrets.

Chapter Six

Covered only by her long, flowing hair, the nymph ran her fingers through the satyr's curls. But her gaze went past him, with the nostalgia and regret of a midnight swimmer who's seen wonders at the bottom of the lake, then been forced to return to the banal life of the surface. The satyr perched on a rock, trailing a forgotten lyre behind him, a lusty expression on his goatish face. Their drama, frozen in stone above the building entrance, went unnoticed by the pedestrians below. Only Martin paid any attention, for once not caring if he was taken for a tourist. Like so much of what he saw in Paris, though, he could get no further than the surface. It was doubly frustrating because Swanson knew all the mythological references, the artistic styles, and such, but for some reason never liked to talk about those things. What required no specialized knowledge to see was that the sculpture, unlike the weathered double doors beneath it, looked brand new. Things had changed since his childhood trip to Paris, when the monuments and long rows of apartments resembled rotten teeth, blackened by the dirt of centuries. These days, as Monique had explained, the city took its *patrimoine culturel* more seriously — as a source of civic pride and tourist revenue — and was cleaning landmarks all over town, often for the first time. Orators, stone gargoyles, generals on horseback, their patina of age and distance exfoliated, now stood there in nude surprise, like freshly plucked chickens.

A portly, well-dressed man, a sheaf of papers under his arm, keyed in the entry code and beetled ahead while the doors were still opening inward. Swanson and Martin followed him in, to the offices of their notaire M. Gauffre. As they'd done their first time there, for the *promesse de vente*, both stopped short a moment to take in the enormous cobblestone courtyard. Martin clapped his hands to hear the echo.

"I still say you could fit a hockey rink in here."

Swanson smiled. The space distribution of urban Europe had surprised him too, when he'd first lived there. All those unexploited square meters, in one of the most expensive neighborhoods on the continent — try finding that in New York or San Francisco. Any façade, especially in the single-digit *arrondissements*, might conceal some unexpected marvel: a curved double staircase leading to a palatial entrance, a lush garden… When a street door opened around here, even the locals gawked.

"This may get rocky," said Swanson. "Gauffre told me the seller was bitching and moaning 'cause we moved up the signature date."

"What choice did we have?" said Martin. "You've gotta go deal with the robbery, and no way can I do the transaction."

"True. Anyway, he'll shut up once he's got our money."

The office was already humming. A ballet of notaires and secretaries darted in and out of offices, balanced stacks of documents, zipped along hallways. Swanson and Martin were quickly ushered to a large conference room. At the far end of the polished wood table, shuffling the morning's dossiers, sat M. Gauffre: silver of hair, blue of suit, radiating comfort and satisfaction. The bookshelves behind him were filled by bound archives dating back to the 1800's, the gold-embossed years shining like the helmets of soldiers in formation, prepared to march in case of dispute or disorderly conduct. The seller, M. Mignot, wore the same green polyester shirt as at the *promesse de vente*, a shirt from another milieu than the sober elegance of his notaire's silk suit and canary yellow power tie. Clothes that demonstrated life's randomness more than words ever could: two people whose paths would otherwise never have crossed, except perhaps to stand next to each other in the Métro, who after this meeting were unlikely to see each other again.

Everyone stood to shake hands, then settled into leather chairs that hissed luxuriously. M. Gauffre distributed copies of the sale document, then read it aloud, point by point. He often made asides, which were so often sprinkled with *tout à fait* or *effectivement* that Martin began to keep count. What else to do, lost in a sea of unfamiliar words, reduced to turning the pages or laughing when the others did? His thoughts wandered back to bio-computing implants. One use might be tracking your own verbal tics, with a visualization option to generate charts or graphs. For incremental self-improvement, Benjamin Franklin-style, there'd be a way to check the monotony of your conversation or create an alert when you used up your quota of "like," "you know," or "kinda." If others uploaded their data, you could compare and contrast with those in your age group or profession, chart the vocabulary of different socioeconomic levels, political leanings…

M. Gauffre raised his voice slightly. "Now for the financial portion of the contract."

Martin and Swanson exchanged a glance. The mortgage should have been a no-brainer; in the United States banks would've begged to give them a loan. Here, the first six institutions they'd approached refused to even talk to unemployed foreigners, no matter how fat their account balances. "If you have as much money as you say," asked one bank officer, "why do you want a mortgage?" Swanson, incredulous, explained that a loan would allow him to invest his capital elsewhere, at a much higher rate of return. The man recoiled as if he'd just been offered a vial of snake-oil or a pair of x-ray specs to see through women's dresses. Finally they'd found Sabine, an ambitious young banquière who wanted to build her clientele and was willing to take a chance on them. The only catch was having to pony up far more of a down payment — for Martin, most of his savings — than was common in the States.

Now there was a long silence. M. Mignot had just said: "*Hélas*, my father, who owned the apartment, passed away last week."

M. Gauffre put on a serious expression: "*Je suis tout à fait navré d'entendre cela.* Please accept my condolences."

"I haven't managed to remove his belongings from the apartment," the seller continued, "so I would appreciate another month to do that, especially since we had to move up today's meeting."

Swanson straightened and coolly replied: "Unfortunately we cannot oblige you, as our first rental clients arrive in two weeks. We will need seven days to move our furniture, which still leaves a full week in which to arrange your affairs. Of course we'll be happy to dispose of whatever you leave behind."

Without understanding anything, Martin saw the seller stare a long moment at Swanson, then whisper some remarks to his notaire, who relayed them in hushed tones to his *confrère* M. Gauffre. The latter, after some back and forth, shrugged, making a 'what can I do?' face. M. Mignot narrowed his eyes and spit out the words: "*Très bien. Soit.* I accept your generous proposition."

When they broke for coffee, Swanson explained the interchange.

"You are one cold fish." Martin laughed uneasily. "Would it hurt to give the poor bastard a few weeks to move his stuff out? He accommodated us, remember? Why pretend we already have clients?"

"Because it's business, Martin. If you let your emotions take over, you're at the other guy's mercy. You have to think: would he give me any slack if we switched sides on the deal? I can tell you, having watched my mom do this for a living then going through it myself, that not one in a hundred would. They're nice and polite, but their actions prove they're looking out for themselves, like everybody else. If we'd let that guy take his time — and he might not even have been telling the truth about his father — I guarantee we'd still be waiting for him to clear out three months from now. I shouldn't have even offered to let him leave stuff behind."

Martin had nothing in his experience to counter that.

"Plus," Swanson continued, "that's just how I get in a deal — any deal. I can't help it. By the way, I made some progress while you were gone. First, the concierge put me in touch with a decorator."

"Who speaks English?"

"Well enough. She does lots of remodels, so she has carpenters, painters, electricians — the works. That is huge. I didn't know where we'd find all those people — then somebody with a whole team fell in our lap. We may have to pay extra for the one-stop shopping, but it'll be worth it."

"We're leaving it up to her how the places will look?"

"No. I mean, give her a little creative leeway to make her happy, but we should tell her what we want."

"Er, okay," said Martin, "what do we want?"

"A few nice prints, an antique or two. Not the 1930's art-deco shit they sell on the rue St. Paul: nobody wants to stay on the set of a Garbo movie. Make sure she finds one nice, high-class centerpiece — an armoire, a desk, whatever — the other stuff can be less expensive."

"Such the little homemaker."

"Hey, I watched my mom do this stuff for years. The decorator's name is Donatella, by the way. She'll be in touch next week. Also, I persuaded my cousin to do a quick-and-dirty website for us. Once they finish the renovations, we can take some pictures and start advertising. I'll be back way before then, but just in case, I made up a to-do list."

"Damn, Swannee, what am I, a child?"

"No. Well, yes — for now. You said so yourself. I mean, even if you spoke fluent French, you'd still have to get used to the way things work here. The protocols are different."

"How's that?"

"You know the way the weekly métro ticket goes from Monday to Monday, and not seven days from the day you buy it, like most other cities? It's like that with everything. There is always some piece of knowledge you can't do without. It's obvious once you know the trick, but until you do… well, you'll see."

M. Gauffe's secretary herded them back to the conference room. Eleven *tout à faits* and fourteen *effectivements* later, Swanson and Martin were officially in business.

Chapter Seven

Now this is a crappy, backwards way to learn, thought Martin as he lay sprawled across the couch doing his grammar homework. Indirect objects, complements, reflexive verbs… Fine, but demanding all that at the beginning was like studying engine repair before learning how to drive. How had he acquired English? All he remembered was tracing a big letter A over and over so that it fit within the blue lines of his notebook. The rules came much later: after imitating others, after building a network of phrases. According to his undergrad linguistics class, words were arbitrary signs, whose meaning came from differences with other words. Yet to differentiate them, you needed to know a few in the first place. It must have been a slog, constructing his own childish edifice from a chaos of sounds — especially, later on, with the words that mattered most. How long had it taken, in those years before search engines, to undo the confusion Janice Bergenmuller, from his third-grade class, caused when she pulled him into the shrubbery in her backyard one humid summer day and slid down her panties to proudly show him her 'cock'?

He'd expected French to be like a new programming language: pick up some vocabulary, the basic syntax, add higher-level phrases, make variations on them, eliminate the habitual mistakes, clarify the grey areas, imitate those who were fluent, generate new combinations. Human language was far messier, with more exceptions than rules. Worse, French added gendered nouns, the subjunctive, arbitrary prepositions, *faux amis*… Speaking directly to people now, instead of through Swanson, feelings of incompetence stung him daily. Just that morning, a store employee had offered him a sample of free dish soap. His "*Merci, ça suffit*" was supposed to mean "Thanks, I already have plenty." After her eyebrows shot up and she raised her hands in mock self-defense, he looked it up at home: "Enough already! Buzz off!" Fortunately, the French reputation for snootiness was either undeserved or buried under enough politeness that he didn't notice. Even the waiters gave him slack, echoing his "Uhhhn kersant eht ooon Avion" back to him, with a straight face as: "*un croissant et une Évian.*"

Improving had become an obsession. He wouldn't reach fluency, not in two or three months here. But he could drill the little he did know until it was fluid, automatic. Isolate his weaknesses, like any skilled musician or athlete, then hammer on them until they became strengths. Avoid his usual temptation: to invent elaborate practice plans instead of mastering the basics. He picked up his book again. *Il faut que je comprends.* No, no, *que je comprenne…*

Hours later, after grammar class at the Alliance Française — the sole item on his schedule until Swanson returned or Donatella got in touch — Martin strolled down the boulevard Raspail, looking forward to another unstructured afternoon, spread out before him like a plate of ripe fruit. Then he remembered the front door lock at headquarters. It needed minutes of persuasion to open sometimes, and was on the point of failing for good. Asking the building management to repair it, Paula the concierge had said, was "a pretty dream," adding that if he wanted to try it himself, the materials could be found at the big department store across from the Hôtel de Ville. It shouldn't take long; by now he knew the fastest paths through the maze of Châtelet station, how to get from métro line four to line one while avoiding the stairwells that smelled like an open sewer, which platform had the out-of-tune violinist and which the unknown genius accordionist whose Bach fugues echoed through the long passageways.

In the department store a bloodless remake of a Janis Joplin song droned on. Music this lame could only be the work of a whole chain of fools: the singer, who recited the face-ripping words 'take another little piece of my heart' as if they'd come off a cereal box, the executives, distributors, and other functionaries who never listened to their own 'product,' audiences who accepted whatever was fed to them. A four-minute encapsulation of the decline of the American music industry: still squeezing the withered teat of the Sixties, even as the file-sharers pushed them towards the tar pit...

Down one level, in the *sous-sol*, was the vast, chaotic hardware department. Employees rushed past, ignoring Martin's mumbled questions, until finally one took pity and pointed him to the doors and windows section. But when he opened the boxes at home, he found the knobs came with no hardware to attach them. Back in the *sous-sol*, the clerk pointed out that one also needs two small screws. And why, Martin stammered out, didn't you tell me that before? Because — in English this time — each door plate is different. Home again, it transpired that the two screws required some special francofuck kind of screwdriver. Again, to the clerk: any other tools he might happen to need? No. But in attaching the handles, he discovered he'd bought two left-handed ones, not thinking, since they had all been mixed together in the same bin, that they might come in non-identical pairs.

By the time he finished, it was dark out.

The next day Donatella called, and suggested they meet in a café/bookstore on the rue Vieille du Temple. Given her outsize telephone voice, Martin was surprised to find a short red-haired woman of a certain age, who kept her dark glasses on indoors and wore a bright green peacoat with a pink checkered scarf: the kind of outfit that few but the Italians could pull off. She handed him a buttery-soft leather portfolio with the word *Sprezzatura* embossed in gold letters. Martin perused the photos of her work, feeling unqualified to judge it. Well, he'd do his best. All this had been dumped in his lap by Swanson, who could hardly come back later and complain.

With their coffees still to finish, he tried to make small talk. Crisp and direct in business matters, the most Donatella would say about herself was that she'd come from the Abruzzi thirty years ago for a short vacation, never to return. There'd been a husband, children too, but Martin hesitated to press for details. It was his brand of discretion, which some mistook for disinterest. His former long-term girlfriend Laurie, an avid consumer of pop psychology, had viewed it as a symptom of deep-seated personality problems, in the end calling it 'the deal breaker.'

Donatella stopped short: "Is anything wrong?"

He'd twisted his face into a grimace, angry over a situation that no longer existed. "No, it's nothing." He relaxed, almost laughing at the truth of it. "Nothing at all."

At the apartment, groping for the light switch, Martin sensed something was wrong. He hadn't been there since before the sale; now it was filled with a vile odor, which got overpowering in the main room. Old clothes and junk were strewn everywhere. In the center of the floor was a huge pile of very used kitty litter.

"*Mais, c'est le bordel ici !*" Donatella exclaimed.

"Excuse me?" Did she just say there was a bordello here?

"It is a catastrophe, a… mess."

Martin frowned. "Sorry. The previous owner wasn't very happy with us. I didn't realize he was *this* unhappy."

Holding her nose, she examined the walls and fixtures and state of each room, then motioned him outside to the hallway.

"If you want to rent this apartment to tourists, you will have to redo it completely. The floors, the walls, the electricity, it will all have to be replaced."

He nodded uneasily. Swanson's initial two-months-and-get-out calculation was looking further and further from reality.

"It won't be cheap," she warned, "There's nothing here we can use."

"Well, the fact that you have your own team," Martin improvised, for the sake of something to say, "is worth a little extra."

A surprised look passed briefly over her face. "Yes, they're excellent."

"See what a nice guy that seller turned out to be?" said Swanson.

If you hadn't antagonized him, thought Martin. "Yeah, yeah."

"Did you emphasize to Donatella how little money we have for this project and how important it is to do things economically?"

Martin pursed his lips. No way Swanson cared about the price. He just didn't want to get out-bargained. "Not exactly. I kinda let it slip that since she had her own team, we were prepared to pay a little more."

"You *what?*"

"That's what you told me," he feebly tried to recover.

"Martin, I said that to you. In confidence. Never give away information like that when you're negotiating! You are such an *engineer*. You have to complain that the price is too high, that you'll need references from satisfied clients before you can even consider such a large expenditure, blah, blah. The pressure has to be on her until the deal is done."

"Why so adversarial? She doesn't seem the type to take advantage."

"How do you know?"

"Well…"

"You don't. It's like the seller: you can't know what people are capable of until you're in a deal with them. Do what you can to them before they do it to you. Otherwise, you're just handing your money to a total stranger."

A few days later, Donatella's estimate arrived, impressive in its detail and unfamiliar vocabulary. The bottom line was several thousand euros over what Martin had expected. He showed it to Sébastien, who said: "I have no idea what most of this stuff should cost. Check the prices of the materials if you're worried she's ripping you off. I see she gave you the option of an electric toilet. Do not go for it — even if you think it sounds different or cool. It will break every week, just at the wrong time, and you will hate yourself and your life. Not, of course, that anything like that ever happened to me."

"Where would we be without you, Sébastien?"

"In the desert, my friend, helpless as two fluffy bunnies. However, it amuses me to descend from my mountain-top and resolve your tiny problems. Another thing: she will probably pay her people *au noir* — in cash. That way she avoids taxes and pockets the difference. Let her. It comes from the government's pocket, not yours."

Martin forwarded the estimate to Swanson, casually mentioning the virtues of paying *au noir*. A week later, having received no response and eager to get on with things, he gave Donatella the go-ahead.

Drrooongggg.

His eyes fixed on the computer screen, Martin ignored the doorbell. No one ever used it. Probably somebody had gotten the wrong apartment. It was also a non-optimal moment for an interruption. He'd spent the last couple days consulting for a friend back in California, and was at last closing in on the main bug. He could now force the program to fail in the same way it did at the customer site — most of the battle. Apart from the extra dough, it felt great to be back in his element instead of stumbling around in the dark, as he often did in Paris. Just a few more test runs and… Drroooonnnnnngggggg.

Groaning a little, he checked his watch: eleven in the morning. A package delivery, maybe. Before standing up, he searched for a task to give the computer. Years of optimizing code had trained him to optimize his own time, and like a puritan, nostrils twitching at a hint of sin, he was always on the lookout for ways to do one task after spinning off another that would continue on its own. Looking a step ahead, he realized that he needed to download a large file to reproduce the client's bug. He typed in the command to kick it off, then pushed his chair back. Now — ah, endorphins! — all those megabytes would be hot and ready when he returned to his desk. He sprang to his feet, pulled on a t-shirt, scooped up yesterday's socks from the floor, tossed them in the direction of the hamper, nudged a stack of papers about to fall off the desk, then sauntered to the door, using his knee to straighten up the coffee table as he passed. At the threshold stood an unknown woman; medium height, off-blonde hair, wearing sweat pants and a hoodie. After dramatically scanning the hallway in both directions, she leaned forward to whisper, in a strong, non-Parisian accent: "I need to come in. It's urgent." Without waiting for a response, she entered, closing the door behind her. "I'm sorry to bother you, but I don't know what else to do," she spoke rapidly. "I live down the hall. This morning my husband threatened to kill me. I suppose you can hear it when he yells and throws things."

Up and down the hall, one heard cries of love and hate every day. Any of them could've come from her place. He'd never spoken to his neighbors, didn't even know their names.

"I am Madame Dupont," she went on, as if guessing his thoughts. "I've lived here with my husband for years. Since I got pregnant, he has started beating me every night. I need to get away from him, but I have no money and no family here. It's hard, it's hard." She wiped away a tear.

"Have you called the police?"

"My husband said he'd kill me if did!" She sat on the sofa, shaking her head, silently rocking back and forth. Martin looked at her discreetly. Her pregnancy, if real, barely showed. He ran a hand through his hair. To help this person would cause him no big inconvenience.

Had he ever come to anyone's aid? Never, apart from a few charitable donations, given when asked.

"What can I do for you?" he finally said.

She brightened a little. "If you could loan me two-hundred euros, I'll be able to take the train to Marseilles. I have friends there."

"Why don't you ask them for the money?"

"It would take too long! My husband might do anything in the meantime! Tonight, even!" She cradled her stomach in her hands, looking down. "Oh, this is hard, it's hard."

He stood there, unsure of what to say or do.

Still gazing at the floor, she said: "I will send you the money as soon as I get to Marseilles." She took a crumpled piece of paper from her purse, then earnestly wrote down his name and apartment number.

"Please. I have no one else to turn to."

On the pretext of looking for cash, he went to his room to gain time to think. It wasn't a matter of money; he wouldn't miss it. Maybe he'd help someone out of a horrible situation. He remembered what Paula had said about people in the building, afraid to call the police even when in need. He returned to the living room. She hadn't moved.

"I'm sorry, I don't have any money here," he found himself saying, though he had enough cash on him.

She responded at once: "There is a machine just down the street."

He rubbed his jaw. He could pretend his account had just a hundred in it and give her that… Such stingy generosity made him ashamed. Either give her what she asked for, or nothing. What the hell. But now he'd have to go through with the charade of the ATM. They rode the elevator in silence. The only words that came to mind were either inappropriate — so, how long have you two been married? — or suspicious: when is the baby due? Paula, who might have corroborated this story, was not at the front desk. On the street, the woman gave an incongruous wave to the pharmacist, who stood on the sidewalk, smoking. He waved back uncertainly. The ATM spat out crisp new bills. Martin handed them to her, his stomach grinding, even as he told himself that it was the right thing to do, or, at worst, something that wouldn't hurt him. She thanked Martin profusely, then flagged a taxi, asking for the Gare de Lyon. As he walked back toward the apartment, shaking a little, her story began to fall apart. The pharmacist, still smoking his cigarette, told Martin he didn't know her. Of course. Was her carefree wave that of a woman whose husband had just threatened to kill her? There was no Dupont on the mailboxes or building directory. He went back up to the apartment, ashamed, angry only now at the woman but even angrier at himself. So many questions I might have asked, he thought, discrepancies I ought to have noticed. Why didn't I apply any common sense? Because she caught me off guard. Because I feel guilty for doing well. Because I give way to people who have a lot of momentum…

From down the hall came the sounds of hammering and a kind of belly-dance music played through a cheap radio. Martin knocked, then entered through the half-open door. A few pipes dangled where the kitchenette had been. The noise came from the bathroom, its entrance covered with a plastic sheet to prevent dust from escaping. Inside, vague, otherworldly shapes stumped around. The main room was empty apart from a coffee table and the previous owner's green, threadbare sofa. Donatella paced in circles around it, talking on the phone in Italian. She waved to Martin, then motioned for him to look around. Even the walls were gone. Their exposed framework exuded a sharp, chalky odor, overpowering any remains of the kitty litter smell. The formerly claustrophobic rooms were now in limbo, waiting for their new role, stripped of all personality. Where's the other man, they said, who stayed here so long? And who are you? Why should we be yours just because you paid someone money?

He reentered the living room, where Donatella was just hanging up. She turned to Martin.

"How do you like it?"

"You did all this in a couple days? Incredible!"

"Tearing things down is always the easy part." She patted the stack of catalogues on the table and cleared a space for him to sit at her makeshift command post. First came the big items: bed, dresser, desk, chairs. On her laptop were pictures of furniture she'd seen in antique stores *à la campagne*, the countryside, which apparently meant 'anywhere outside Paris.' He gamely shifted to French. With professional patience, she gave items and prices, advised against faux pas like putting an art nouveau lamp on a Louis XVI table. To his annoyance and relief, she soon slipped back into English. After an hour of toasters and lampshades and brushed-nickel fixtures, Swanson's discourse on creative leeway came to the rescue.

"Donatella," Martin said, "I can see you understand what we're looking for. I trust your choices for the rest."

She laughed. "I was wondering how long you would last."

Curious to see the bathroom deconstruction, he moved aside the plastic tarp covering the door. The three men chipping away at the tile stopped and stared up at him. In their dour expressions, he saw himself through their eyes: Da Man. The-one-who-writes-your-check, that is, with a you're-my-bitch attitude they would assume lurked underneath. Back in the Valley Martin always programmed, even when in a management role — to show he hadn't completely joined the Dark Side, but also to avoid having too much power over others, which was almost as unpleasant as them having power over him. Here there was no middle ground. Worse, his role required French, in which every conversation was still an improv performance.

"Bonjour," he said. *A little too loud.* They hesitated a moment, then intoned: "Bonjour, monsieur." *Uh, oh. I'm bugging them.*

I would like — *what's the conditional? Je voudrais…* to introduce myself *me presenter…* Argh, too formal.

He flailed on. These recent Parisians were foreigners too, without a native speaker's leeway in understanding his bad accent or butchered grammar. They weren't so ill-humored, though, and even started calling him 'chef.' Laughing now, they tried out their English on him, mostly one-liners from old action movies: "*Allez, chef!* Make. My. Day!"

When the bonhomie petered out, Martin went off to do what seemed the French boss-like thing: celebrate this meeting with baked goods for all. As he returned from the boulangerie, though, he saw the fragrant bag of goodies as more a guilty attempt to ingratiate himself. What is this boss complex of mine, he wondered. Is a pecking order or the authority to hire and fire intrinsically wrong? People repair cars for others, rescue their pets, operate on their livers, and those others reciprocate with their skills. Different contexts, different roles. Somebody has to be the chef here — why is it so wrong if it's me?

"As I said when you guys bought the place, it's not the greatest neighborhood," Sébastien remarked as he munched on what was ironically billed as a *chien chaud*. "It's full of — what do they call those people in New York, the ones who don't live there?"

"Bridge and tunnel people?"

"That. The area is called Les Halles because the big market halls used to be right there. This street," he gestured behind him to the pedestrian-only rue St. Denis, "used to be, and partly still is, a red-light district, if you walk that way a block or two."

Great, thought Martin. Why had they focused so much on the rental unit, and so little on its neighborhood? But he wanted to keep things light today, not go into his second thoughts about the apartment boondoggle, which, given the remodeling delays, would be lasting way longer than the famous two months. He also wasn't going to bring up that woman who'd come to his door asking for money, let alone confess that he sometimes felt lonely and miserable and ready to slink back to his safe existence in California, where he at least knew what he was doing.

"We'll advertise the boulevard de Sébastopol address, then," he said, "and have people enter from that side."

"There is a certain charm to Les Halles, if you look up at the façades, not down at the stores. Anyway, if your tenants see something they disapprove of, just tell them," Sébastien shrugged his shoulders ineffably, "it's a colorful place."

"Hopefully they'll spend their days on tourist stuff and be too tired to notice." Martin held up his glass. "Is this what you French call a milkshake, by the way?"

"Sorry, I should have warned you. For some reason, we make delicious ice cream but terrible milkshakes; good coffee, but weak, foamy cappuccinos. Those are our two worst culinary sins. Whereas you in the States…"

"I know, I know. But you guys import our worst stuff: burgers, hot dogs — excuse me, *chiens chauds*…".

"Hold on, I know your secrets better than that. We do not — and will never — have corn dogs, turducken…"

"Bah, nobody actually eats that stuff," Martin deadpanned.

"Deep-fried Twinkies…"

"Admit it, you still love us. Which reminds me: how did you learn to speak English so well?"

"Oh, the usual way."

Martin thought for a second. "What was her name?"

"Elizabeth."

The waitress came by to check on them. Sébastien turned towards her, smiling, and said something in a low voice. She laughed and pretended to sternly shake her finger at him.

"Now I see your other full-time job," Martin observed after she left. Like Swanson, it seemed Sébastien enjoyed having an audience for his boldness.

"Job? It's art! A way of life! If something happens, great, if not, hey, you're just practicing. Of course you don't behave like those assholes who say rude garbage or harass women on the street. Just be friendly. I think our waitress likes you — go ahead, you try."

Martin shook his head, horror-struck. "No way! You've heard my French."

"Doesn't matter! Just babble — use that American accent."

"I hate the American accent."

"Who cares about *you*? *They* think it's *exotique*. You could also buy a ridiculous little dog, if you want a conversation starter. Pound for pound, nothing gives better results than *un p'tit chien ridicule*. Except for a baby, if you can borrow one."

"I'll look into it," said Martin. "Now, what else do I need to know about this area?"

"I can show you most of it in half an hour. Starting with this eyesore," said Sébastien, gesturing toward the Forum Les Halles complex. "It was built in the seventies. Now they're going to tear it down and start over." Run-down and artificial it was, no denying — the past's version of the future. After finishing lunch they circled it, starting at St. Eustache cathedral and finishing at a taxidermist on the Rue des Halles, whose display sported a clothesline of dead rats, hanging upside down in a neat row. "You see? Something for every guest!" said Sébastien.

Martin sighed. If you overlooked its seedy aspects, though, the area wasn't so bad. Restaurants, night life, a short walk from some of the biggest tourist sites in Europe...

"Anyway, you're stuck with it now," Sébastien grinned, reading his thoughts. He checked his watch. "I have to go. Better get your French together. Next time I won't let you off so easily."

Chapter Eight

Well, looky thar, thought Swanson. Just about the last person he'd expected to see in this part of Sunnyvale: his old buddy Duncan. In the parking lot of a low-end coffee shop, getting out of… well, it couldn't be his car. Duncan drove a red 550 Barchetta, the latest entry in a long-running, half-serious competition between the two of them: whenever one bought a new ride, the other got one even bigger or fancier. Swanson cut across a couple lanes, flipped a U, and parked next to Duncan's vehicle, a babyshit-brown Honda Civic. It literally looked lived in. What the…?

Duncan — it was him all right — sat in a booth by the window. Swanson slid into the seat across the table.

"Yo, Dunk — the Ferrari in the shop? It must hurt having to cruise Sand Hill Road in that piece of shit."

Duncan looked up from his menu. "Hey," he mumbled, as groggy as if he'd just gotten out of bed.

Swanson tried to keep his voice low. "What the hell, man? I've been calling you for months. I heard you left JW."

He took a hard look at his friend: the five-day stubble, the blotchy skin, the eyes, shifty where they'd once been transparent. A face in eclipse.

"What happened?" Swanson pressed on.

"You mean to Dendroid? Man, I was in deep shit with people I don't even want to think about."

"Those people paid me a visit," replied Swanson, certain of it as he heard his own words.

Duncan sat up, eyes wide. "You?"

"Turned my place upside down. Maybe you better tell me what's going on."

"Look…" Duncan's voice trailed off. He stared out the window. "I've been a stone fuckin' crackhead for a year and a half." He turned to face Swanson's shocked expression. "I know, I know — a total dead-end. Lots of other shit went with the lifestyle. I burned through everything I had, went into debt, then started gambling, trying to claw back to zero. I lost my ass, had to get an emergency loan. You can guess the rest."

The waitress brought Swanson's coffee. He sipped, struggling to find words, to recall anyone he knew who'd so much as tried crack.

"How the…? I mean, you were practically the straightest person at Stanford…"

"I hated working at JW," Duncan said, his jaw set. "A bunch of self-important assholes, who funneled millions of other people's dollars to companies that half the time made no sense. The paycheck was incredible, but the pressure the last couple years got just hellacious. So I'd do blow sometimes, to keep going when I was under the gun, then drink to come down. I tried crack at this party. Pretty soon my only friends were people who got high all the time. Shit takes you over, hollows you out. Before I knew it, all that money wasn't enough to even keep me afloat."

Swanson would never have imagined any of this for Duncan, the most generous, together person in their frat, who at six-four literally towered over everybody, calm and indestructible. Once he made a decision, nothing got in his way. His few bouts of wildness were the raucous all-night poker games he liked to run, though they were well within house standards. Their friendship dated from one of those scrotum-tightening freshman year hazing rituals. Swanson had ended up in a drunken stupor so deep that Duncan drove him to the hospital. All he remembered was the doctor who pumped his stomach telling him he was lucky to be alive. Duncan didn't leave until the next day, when it was clear Swanson had made it without serious damage. Naturally, Duncan was razzed for it the entire year: who but a total wusscake worries about another drunken pledge?

Until now, there had never been a way to pay him back. And much as Swanson wanted to strangle him, Duncan mattered more than any failed startup. His solidity and resolve made him one of the few people Swanson had ever admired. Who on top of that had saved his bacon. But in this harsh new light it became clear that Duncan couldn't apply that resolve to his own behavior. Not that that let him off the hook.

"Why kill Dendroid, though?" Swanson pursued. "You guys — well, you, to be exact — told us we had a lock on the funding."

"You have to swear to keep this to yourself."

Swanson nodded.

"As I'm looking for a way out of debt, I get an anonymous call. Maybe it was somebody connected to HellaDyne or one of their financiers. Anyway, he is aware of my, uh, situation, and offers me a big wad to kill the deal with you guys and fund them."

"Why didn't you fucking tell me?"

"To shield you from any aspect of that mess," Duncan said, gazing out the window again, as if the wrong turn he'd taken were out there somewhere. "What happened with your house is exactly what I wanted to avoid. I had no choice but to take that guy's offer. The people I owed explained in detail what they'd do to me and my family if they didn't get their cash right away. It sounds like some bad movie, but those people don't bluff. I panicked."

"You know I owe you. But there is a limit."

"You have every right to totally disown me." He faced Swanson again, miserable. "I shouldn't have dodged you. I hoped I'd get past it all, then explain what went down. I never imagined those bastards would go after friends who had nothing to do with it."

"I'd been phoning you non-stop. They must have come to the wrong conclusion."

"Yeah. I had to give them their money piecemeal, 'cause that's how I got paid. I guess somewhere in the middle they got impatient and hit you. By the time I paid them off, they'd taken everything. Which is why I'm eating here and driving *that*. I cannot tell you how sorry I am about all this, and that Dendroid went under. I was sure somebody else would fund you guys. You were miles ahead of those other turkeys."

"Just FYI, there's a lawsuit on the way. Remember my old boss Kyle, the CEO? He just told me he's going after JW and you personally."

"I'll stonewall the mofos," Duncan replied. "There's no trace of what happened. Whoever got me that money isn't gonna broadcast the fact."

Swanson paid for his coffee and left. He was late to visit his dad in the hospital, and in no mood to hang around and lecture Duncan on the insanity of his awful new path. It was so not the life Duncan was meant for — but a person could know better and still become a slave, unreachable by friends or anyone else.

Setting an iced tea on a low table in his backyard, Swanson flopped into a deck chair. Past the rhombus of manicured lawn, above the climber rose that scaled the high wood fence, a few puffy clouds hung in the sky. Lotus land, California-style.

Gotta tell him sometime, he thought. Cardwell's a grown-up, he'll roll with it. Swanson took a long sip before making the call. He'd stick to business matters; no need to mention his father's illness for now. The prognosis wasn't good, but plenty of people with less fortitude and joie de vivre than his dad had beaten cancer. When Martin picked up, Swanson spoke without any introduction or greeting, the way they always did.

"How's Paris?"

"Let's just say every day brings a lesson."

"Was I not right about the codes?"

Martin laughed. "You were right about the codes. I'm discovering new ones all the time. I feel like a complete goober here. Then there's the language." Martin recounted a few comic mishaps, including a surreal dialogue he'd had in a café, back when he thought the word for 'toilet' was *abattoir*.

"So… What's the deal with the robbery?"

Swanson sighed. "Well, the house is back in order, but the insurance claim is still pending."

"Meaning I should expect you in what, three weeks?"

"Um, not exactly."

"Hm?"

"Look," said Swanson, "I have bad news and strange news. Which do you want first?"

"Let's start with strange. But before I forget, Donatella wants the next installment."

"Has she finished the demolition yet?"

"The bathroom's still in process."

"Wait until she's completely done," Swanson insisted. "Then wait another week or two. We have to set the tone. Otherwise, she might leave us hanging until she's in the mood to finish the job. Tell her, I dunno, that our U.S. bank has delayed all international money transfers."

Martin sighed. "Okay, whatever. Gimme the strange."

"I found out what happened."

"You mean who robbed you?"

"Why Jones-Wolff flushed us."

"*Tell.*"

"I can't. Not all of it. Let's just say that someone involved with the decision had a big monkey on his back. His solution involved kinda sorta completely screwing us."

"What solution…?"

"I don't know all the details, and I don't want to."

"Wha…whaddya mean? Let's nail his ass!"

"I can't. I've known him for years and owe him you can't imagine how big time. I cannot rat him out, no matter what happens."

"He takes the company we all busted our humps to build, flushes it down the toilet, and you want to let him walk?"

"I'm not happy about it either, believe me. But even if we tried to nail him, I know this guy: he covered his tracks very carefully."

"When did you find out?"

"Couple days ago. He was — maybe still is — in way over his head with some very nasty people. They're the ones who broke into my house. He claims everything's resolved now."

"How wonderful for him. Send him my best." Martin paused. "If that wasn't the bad news, what is?"

"Kyle informed me that he and the idiots at the-company-formerly-known-as-Dendroid plan to sue Jones-Wolff."

"Are you kidding? Great!"

"No, bad. Very bad. They insist that I, as a principal involved in the negotiations, stay in California to help prepare the suit."

"Oh, fuck."

"Fuck is right."

"Fuck those fucking fucks! That'll take months. You gonna do it?"

"I have no choice; I was at the center of the deal. If the suit doesn't get laughed out of court right away, there'll be a discovery phase; I'll need to hang around for that as well."

Swanson held the cool glass to his forehead. He'd never imagined Kyle would go after the VCs. To antagonize the money dispensers in such an insular community as Silicon Valley was suicide, the equivalent of walking around with a skunk under your arm. Sue one and the rest will shun you, too: freeze you out of partnerships, contracts, social circles… not for a month or three, but until Earth itself was a scorched, vacant nubbin. What had gone down was unfair — more than Kyle knew — but trivial compared to the exploits of, say, the original captains of industry. The Dendroid folks weren't exactly starving, helpless Bedouins, either. Many already had already moved on to new jobs, the way one was supposed to. In a year, they'd barely remember what happened. Martin was not taking the long view just yet.

"That's beautiful. First you cover up for some asswipe who single-handedly vaporized our company, then, now that we've passed the point of no return over here, you leave yours truly holding the bag."

"I know, I know. Look, the suit won't get past the preliminaries. They're gonna try to claim Jones-Wolff defrauded us on purpose — extended a fake offer to keep us out of circulation, ruined our chances with the other VCs in order to maximize their investment in Helladyne, which they'd planned from the beginning."

"Sounds pretty plausible to me."

"But not what happened. I was in it up to the eyeballs — there is no way they'll be able to make that case. Meantime, it looks like you'll have to hold down the fort for a while, ol' buddy."

"Hold this!"

Swanson could practically hear the bird being flipped.

"How," continued Martin, "can I carry a business here by myself? I speak French like a three-year old."

"You'll do fine. Just fake it 'til you make it."

"Fake this!"

Part Two

Chapter Nine

At noon sharp, with the Place de la Bastille full of people going about their business, air-raid sirens began to wail. Martin started, glancing involuntarily at the sky, then returned to his *omelette mixte*, laughing a little at himself. No one but him had paid any attention. To react, let alone look around, was for tourists; yet here he was, after a year in Paris by now! His initial siren encounter had come in French class last October, weeks after 9/11, when everyone's nerves were still frayed. Some students hid under their desks, even when the teacher explained it was only the French early warning system, tested on the first Wednesday of every month since the war.

Since *the* war, people usually said. As if there'd been only one — or two, with the so-called 'great' war. As if mankind had not been at war, one place or another, without a pause, since the beginning. Nobody seemed to see that if the world were a house, one room on fire meant the *house* was on fire. Now the U.S. was pounding the rubble of Afghanistan into finer rubble, with Iraq in the crosshairs. He felt proud that the French were standing against it. Fortunately they didn't blame him for the actions of his government. Not to his face, anyway. I voted against those people, Martin would say. Yet even politicians he sort of liked and had voted for were endorsing the madness.

"The world is broken, dude. Forget about it," Swanson had advised that morning. "Worry about your own patch and let the rest take care of itself."

"Just what the warmongers and the power-mad rats want to hear."

"You can't change any of it. You just feel guilty, 'cause you're here in the land of milk and honey."

"We still gotta track the government's lies, follow the money and the arms." It must be better than nothing, Martin figured, though it didn't feel like it. "Anyway you should be the guilty one," he added, "having not been here for a year." Swanson had only arrived that morning, but that was no reason to hold off giving him shit.

"But look how well you've done without me!"

"Yah, yah," Martin had replied, unsure of what attitude to adopt. He should be more pissed than he felt, having joined this Paris business with such hopes and getting a lot of stress instead. Especially when Donatella's team discovered that a weight-bearing beam underneath the kitchen had rotted, and it became clear that his stay would be extended indefinitely. Things only got back on track after Sébastien wrote a — hilarious — threat-filled letter to the building's management company. But that was all old news; what good would come from harping on it now?

"I knew you'd come through," Swanson said.

"Bah, save it," Martin had answered, blushing at the fact that he was blushing.

"I'm kinda surprised you're still here, though."

"At headquarters? It's okay, now that the nightclub got shut down after all."

"I mean in Paris."

"Oh, it's growing on me. Consulting from here works okay; plus, every time I look, the Valley is in worse shape."

"It hasn't hit bottom yet, either."

And with that, Swanson had gone off to sleep. It had been good to get a little face time with him, Martin thought as he paid his bill and headed up the rue Saint Antoine. They'd talked a lot during the early stages of the renovations, with Swanson asking for status or passing on gossip from the Dendroid lawsuit. Then his dad had died, and Martin had hardly heard from him since. As usual, though, he'd put his finger right on what was eating Martin, who could've returned to California months ago yet kept on not doing it, despite the expectations of family, friends, and headhunters.

Martin pursed his lips. He had no plans to go back anytime soon, and had even forced matters by renting out his Mountain View place for a year. Despite his remarks to Swanson, the job market had little to do with it. Rather, it was that he'd only answered the most basic challenges of Paris: all his vague hopes on first signing on to Swanson's thing still applied. For now he'd escaped the salary-man loop, an opportunity that might never repeat itself. To leave without accomplishing something new and different would be an epic fail.

His now-decent French had allowed him to read Tocqueville's dissections of the North American character: petty! insipid! anti-poetic! If all that didn't apply to him already, it certainly would if he got sucked back into the all-consuming Valley bullshit. Also, people there had very set ideas of who he was and what he could do. Here he was unlimited by anyone's perceptions but his own. Would there ever be a better time to address the big questions, the kind he didn't even know how to formulate yet?

He turned left onto the rue Saint Paul to look for a couple knick-knacks to replace Donatella's gaudy vases of cattails, which the renters all hated. He could've, maybe should've, dropped this errand on Swanson — let his *associé*, who'd spent the better part of a year kibitzing from his armchair in California, do something for once. But a diddly task like this was a nice break from coding, and Swanson was no doubt still asleep. There were heftier missions to give him, anyway.

His phone buzzed: Moon, the cleaning lady and Jill-of-all-trades for the rental place.

"Monsieur Martin! Help! There is *un problème dans l'appartement! Il faut que* you come right now! It is the *ballon d'eau chaude! Ça ne marche plus!* It does not work!"

The hot water balloon? The hot water bottle? Whatever. Moon, a dependable housewife recommended by Paula, didn't freak over nothing. Martin turned around and speed-walked to the apartment, on the Boulevard de Sébastopol. Answering the door was a tall, round-shouldered man wearing a checkered cardigan sweater and a look of strained good cheer.

"Richard Peterson," he announced, shaking Martin's hand. "Sorry to have bothered you." He nodded a couple times, agreeing with himself. "We don't want to be any trouble, but after the long flight, our daughters are all dying for a shower. I'm sure you can understand…"

In the main room, four pre-teen girls were splayed out, fiddling with their phones or fanning themselves as they watched television. None even looked up when he entered. Moon broke free from her conversation with the wife. "Ah, Monsieur Martin! The problem is the *ballon* — here, I show you." She marched into the bathroom and dramatically pointed to the hot-water heater mounted on the wall above the bathtub.

"*C'est en panne!* No hot water come out!" Before he could ask, she added: "I call my plumber, but no answer."

After fiddling for a few minutes, he gave up and phoned Donatella; no luck. Not likely that Swanson would know a plumber, either. The only option was one of those 24-hour handyman services, whose advertisements pollute the mailboxes of Paris. *Dépannage d'Urgence! Intervention Rapide!* He pulled a fistful from a drawer in the kitchen and gave them to Moon: this was no time to fumble around on the phone for the sake of practicing his French. When she finally got a reply, her eyes opened wide, staring into space, while her free hand pantomimed, as if her interlocutor could see her gestures and be enlightened or persuaded. The voice on the other end cried, loud enough for Martin to hear: "*J'arrive !*" — "On my way!"

Martin knew from *j'arrive*. It meant anywhere from thirty seconds to three hours. He let Moon take off, then turned to Mrs. Peterson, who plainly wanted a word.

"It is really a disappointment to have something so basic not working. We've already lost half our first day on this."

"Yes, I'm very sorry."

"We're very sorry, too," she replied sharply.

Martin forced a smile. "I understand."

"That's very nice, but what do you intend to do?" Her husband stood there with his fixed, fearful smile, while the daughters pretended not to hear. Clients had pressured Martin before. A few months earlier, the television inexplicably stopped working, leaving the guests, two professionals in their sixties, beside themselves. "We're news *junkies*, you know," said the wife, her neck muscles straining, "He can't go more than a few hours without it. This means a ruined vacation for us, absolutely ruined." No refund for them — on principle. Anybody who visits Paris to watch TV... Besides, a week doing something else might permanently change their lives for the better. Another couple complained about hookers in the alleyway across the street, next to the shuttered X-rated bookstore. Their ten-year old might have seemed more traumatized if he hadn't spent the entire conversation blowing up mutants on his video console. Another nyet. The Petersons, however, had a legitimate beef. Before he refunded any money, the right thing would be to call his associate, as they'd agreed to do in such cases. But Swanson hated to spend money on repairs, let alone refunds. He would second-guess Martin's decision, whatever it was, as he'd done since they'd bought the damn apartment. He was never the one facing the angry client. He'd make a zero-sum game out of the smallest dispute, even when a small concession would buy the kind of client goodwill that leads to repeat customers and friendly recommendations. His business sense was incredible, just not for the kind of business that lasts longer than a deal. Hell with it, Martin decided; offer five percent off the rental fee and let the haggling begin. Mrs. Peterson accepted immediately, though, and walked off with a satisfied look. Nobody had taken advantage of *her*.

Rather than try to distract these people, Martin suggested they go enjoy Paris, promising not to leave before the problem was fixed. He flopped onto the sofa once they'd trooped out and, thinking of those two news junkies, turned on the television. The news, as usual, was both nauseating and boring, an endless loop of the same fifteen minutes of information: the West Bank situation, freedom fries, saber-rattling from the usual faux-macho 'realists' — all of them serial draft dodgers. Same old same old, with enough variety to give the illusion that, underneath, it was not the monotonous game of power that had blighted so-called civilization since the beginning.

Eventually the plumber, a wiry, harried-looking man named Blago, arrived. In a mixed salad of French, English, and some third language, he explained that since the water of Paris was extremely hard, the ancient water heater had in effect become a giant calcium deposit. Not only did it have to be replaced, it would take a whole team to remove it. Two hours later, Blago handed Martin the bill.

"Yikes! Fifteen hundred euros!?"

Blago made a sympathetic face. "Unfortunate. That is urgent price."

The antique stores on the rue Saint Paul looked bleached in the afternoon sun. One window sported an enormous print of a happy, robust young woman holding a glass of wine; Martin squinted to read the caption: "*Vins de France: Santé, Gaité, Espérance.*" He went in. Still needing a knick-knack or two, he was also in no hurry to return home to hear Swanson complain about the price of the water-heater. It wasn't like there'd been another way out. Swanson could bitch all he wanted; now that he was here, he'd see how much time even small tasks needed, what things really cost. And revise his cheapskate ideas, like using students as apartment managers, which had been a total disaster. Martin felt lucky to have found the very reliable Moon, though even she had her limits. Living outside Paris, she couldn't help guests with late-night emergencies, or handle a situation like today's on her own. She could have arranged for the plumber, but never paid out so much cash on the spot. If he hadn't been there as the owner, the Petersons would probably have moved to a hotel, demanded their money back, and written ugly comments on every travel website they could find.

He picked up an old paperback with the title: *L'homme, cet inconnu.* Out fell a postcard with a black and white photograph of an unnamed city. He read the back:

> *Tunis, le 10.2.39*
> *Ma chère Anca,*
> *J'ai perdu tout l'espoir de vous voir, car vous ne voulez pas*
> *venir à Tunis, même plus vous n'avez pas voulu me prévenir*
> *pour que j'aille à vous trouver à Paris! Quant à la guerre,*
> *espérons que Dieu nous garde de cette cataclysme!*
> *Votre sincère ami,*
> *Sacha*

Did Anca ever visit him in Tunis? Did Sacha come to Paris? Where had they met, how had this postcard, perhaps unread since 1939, ended up here? And what about Anca? Maybe she'd been a spy, a *collaboratrice...* Or perhaps Jewish, denounced by a neighbor then murdered in Auschwitz, her belongings appropriated by the traitor and washing up here, with the shipwreck of the years, on the rue St. Paul... He replaced the postcard and set the book down. Most big events, the ones that get to count as history, must be murky underneath, too. Yet history's big picture might essentially be right, even if built on approximations and half truths, the way that the postcard seemed solid despite consisting of quantum particles that are here, there, or both. Future historians would presumably be studying not just the pixels of the famous, but mountains of plebeian blog posts and selfies. His own leavings, assuming they didn't vanish into the Great Bitbucket, currently fit on a mid-size hard drive. Perhaps far in the future some post-apocalyptic scavenger would find it while pawing through an endless graveyard of computer detritus and study it by the light of burning tires. Or a lab-coated researcher, in a clean-room miles below Earth's blasted surface, who'd adjust her glasses to better examine his humble emails, technical articles, family photos, recordings of the band...

Martin continued through the shop toward the back, where two ladies of a certain age fanned themselves and chatted: one garrulous and well-dressed, the other behind her desk, listening patiently.

"Since the divorce," the first was saying, "I've had no income at all. I may even need to sell my apartment and move in with my daughter."

"That would be a shame; it's such a lovely place!"

"You met my ex once, didn't you? The old bastard is faking some sort of financial disaster and wants to cut off my alimony."

"Are you sure he's faking it? So many are doing badly these days. Even the wealthy can get an unpleasant surprise..."

"Oh, he invented it all right. This is a man who owns a dozen houses. He only gave me that apartment to keep me quiet." She sighed. "Maybe I ought to go back to America — everyone is so nice there."

Martin looked up. She caught his eye so quickly that it almost seemed she'd been talking for his benefit.

"Sometimes, anyway," he said.

On hearing his accent, she switched to English.

"Oh, an American! I knew it! Nadia always knows. I was in your marvelous country recently."

Martin, amused by people who referred to themselves in the third person, played along and asked where.

"New York — for a documentary on world hunger I'd produced," she sighed. "The premiere was going to be a block from the World Trade Center — on September 12."

"Oh."

"Yes, oh. I put up half the money myself, and have been trying to recover ever since. Now I may need to sell my apartment."

This was way too much information. Was she a compulsive revealer, or trying to flatter him with these confidences? He played along, for grins.

"Why don't you rent your apartment on the internet?"

"What do you mean?"

Martin briefly described his business.

"That sounds wonderful!"

"It depends on your apartment, of course, where it's located, how it's furnished…"

"Would you like to see it? It's two blocks from here! I can show it to you right now," she said excitedly.

"Okay, why not?" This was going further than intended, but apart from Sébastien he hadn't received a single invitation of any kind from an actual Parisian. Easy enough to leave if she became weird or her place was a pigsty. As they left the shop, the owner gave him a knowing, ambiguous smile that Martin only remembered long afterwards.

They walked down the rue Saint-Paul. Nadia, talking non-stop, abruptly crossed the street just before the rue Charles V, forcing a car rounding the corner to skid to a halt. Not turning around, she delicately fluttered her hand in the air, the international oh-don't-mind-me sign of a lady of quality. In the space of one block she'd exchanged greetings with the postman, a shopkeeper, and an old lady fussing over a pair of chihuahuas. She was a neighborhood fixture, though by now even Martin could tell she wasn't French.

"Have you lived here long?" he asked, trying to place her accent.

"Three years now. The apartment belonged to my ex-husband, but it became mine after our divorce."

"And in Paris?"

"Oh, for years, on and off. Here we are — first door on the left."

He followed her into a small entry area that opened out into a long narrow loft space. The carpet, walls, and furniture were all hospital white, except for a vermillion sofa. Stacks of cardboard boxes huddled against the wall.

"I'm sorry the place is so cluttered. I printed a thousand brochures for the film, and had to ship them all back here. Have a look."

He thumbed through the weighty, glossy pages, larded with pictures of Nadia, taken over the years alongside various celebrities — a fashion designer here, a bad-boy artist there, a Crown Prince, a politician. At lawn parties, dinners, charity functions…

"Fancy company," he said. All this had what to do with documentaries, again?

"It wasn't always easy meeting some of those people, but I can be quite persistent," she said, with a little smile.

The photos showed no signs of fakery. Au contraire, the subjects all seemed at ease, lounging around with one of their own. Yet who knew if those spheres of wealth and fame overlapped with other, more mercenary ones, whose sticky web of charm or deceit might snare victims unable to disentangle themselves, except at great cost…

"Those contacts are important," she went on. "I didn't want to say it back there in the shop, but my main problem now is that the Parisians, of all people, don't seem to understand how much it costs to produce a film. In New York, nobody used to ask money questions. Unfortunately all my contacts are in difficulties at the moment. Do you know anyone who might like to invest?"

"It's really not my area."

"Well, tell me more about your idea of the internet," she pivoted briskly. "Are these rooms big enough?"

"Oh, sure. Of course, you'll want to add some tourist-friendly touches…"

"If I did, I could rent it out?"

"Why not?" Martin replied, caught up in the idea, "I'll introduce you to our decorator, if you like. We could put your apartment on our website. We'd ask a fee for handling the advertising and reservations. My guess is you could charge twelve-hundred euros a week."

"That would solve everything!" she said, eyes wide.

"It's just an idea. I'd have to discuss it with my co-owner first."

"I don't know how to thank you!"

As he left, she handed him another brochure. "Here's another for one of your wealthy friends," she said as she closed the door, "I know you Americans always have a few."

Chapter Ten

Things might have turned out differently, Swanson mused long afterward, if he hadn't visited the Centre Georges Pompidou that day. If the red-eye from San Francisco had arrived late as usual, instead of on time; if he'd spent a few minutes more or less yakking with Martin at the apartment, or found some other Paris attraction in order to stay awake... Whether he'd have tried to change fate if he'd had the power, well, that would be a Martin kind of question, or the plot of a bad movie. It was what it was. Museums had been his father's way to beat jet lag: feast your eyes and stay vertical. The old man — who'd been a special guest at the Pompidou's inaugural ceremony twenty-five years before — would've raised an eyebrow at the ways of fate. And chuckled at the Beuys angle, having done his best to communicate the love of art and hatred of fraud to his children — especially to Swanson, the youngest.

Months now since he'd died, and Swanson still hadn't accepted the loss or what came after: the bickering over the will, the ongoing Jones-Wolff lawsuit farce, the shock of 9/11... It had always been clear that his dad had hoped for a very different path for him. The two elder children were academics who'd pursued substantial, humanist goals, far from the frivolous internet world. Who'd learned not to talk but to speak, to dictate opinions ex cathedra, so that losing an argument to them felt worse than losing several to anybody else. As for Swanson, he should've become an artist. Even in the hospital, his dad recalled Swanson as a child, browsing for hours in the paternal art library; museum visits; of the summer when the two of them had sketched together every afternoon. "You were damn good," his father said in his ghostly post-chemo whisper, "right out the chute."

Good enough to have teachers suggesting art school before he'd entered fourth grade. When his dad played one of those pranks he later became famous for, sneaking one of Swanson's landscapes into a juried show in San Francisco, it won first prize. Then adolescence hit. The art impulse faded, along with other slow, solitary activities that no longer fit the twitchy new rhythm surging through him. Following his dad's wishes was not even remotely a priority. High school — he could admit it now — had also been the time to quietly drop whatever might expose him to mockery from his brother and sister, whose turgid Critical Studies jargon consumed all the oxygen at home. His peers came at him from the opposite direction: just saying the word "kitsch" in class once had resulted in weeks of razzing. Most thought he'd said "quiche," but at that age… same difference. By then he moved in circles that awarded no social capital for refinement or creativity. The permitted uses for a well-trained eye were evaluating clothes, cars, or girls. Yet since most of his friends borrowed all their opinions on such matters, his sensibility set him apart. Later, in business, it helped in unexpected ways: perceiving the aesthetic side of a deal, balancing a network of motives, finding the right rhythm for a pitch, knowing when to introduce an element of asymmetry or surprise.

While he still lived at home, though, most of his attention went into the teenage impulse to annoy the rest of the household. He blared hip-hop videos, full of babes and bling. No reaction. Put up posters of Wall Street titans, meatheaded action movies. Made a show of joining the Young Republicans Club. Anything to twit the family ethos. Zippo. His sibs paid no mind, while his dad just watched in apparent Buddha-calm, certain that those coltish thrashings would eventually run their course within the boundless Larger Corral. That was his father's private side: the easygoing ironist who padded around the house in moose slippers. To the public he was an avenging hand, slapping the contemporary art phonies around for their sleazy machinations, fake personas, manufactured fads.

"It's the Big Lie in action," he'd said in his very first, scandal-making radio interview, "a cultural Ponzi scheme, when it's not outright money laundering. The speculators — I can't call them collectors — have produced a monstrous investment bubble that celebrates monetary value, not the so-called work. If the right person sneezes into a handkerchief and nails it to the wall — voilà, instant masterpiece! Those sorts of artists know they're peddling dung — sometimes literally — but I don't blame them. Most are opportunists or dull conformists playing at being highbrow. It's the galleries, middlemen, and museum functionaries that have created this aesthetic moonscape. One day the whole gigantic fraud will collapse under its own weight, because real people want beauty and meaning."

The resulting uproar made his first book, *The Anatomy of Artistic Reputation*, a genre bestseller, and established him overnight as the Bay Area's preeminent critic, cheered or feared, depending on where one sat. His last, *The Wheat and the Chaff*, compared the overrated or empty — Matisse, the Abstract Expressionists, Pop Art — to lesser-known geniuses like Caillebotte, Menzel, Boldini. He'd finished it in the hospital, to Swanson's astonishment and admiration. Ravaged by cancer, then chemo, he reserved his most lucid moments for correcting the proofs, saying: "The progress of this disease is not the only thing happening here." That solitary battle meant working in bursts, sustained by whatever they pumped into him through all those tubes. Afterwards he would lie back to talk. Eventually, he'd raise his free arm: no more for today! And fold in on himself.

How he would have puked at the monstrosity on the wall in the Pompidou that afternoon: a sheet of plywood, covered by graffiti and splotches of red paint, with syringes jabbed into it. The plaque explained that the artist had himself placed in a strait-jacket, his beard dunked in a pot of Cadmium Red, then dragged across the plywood.

The syringes were genuine, it was claimed, harvested from a lavatory in the artist's own apartment building. Ditto the graffiti, its misspellings and phone numbers preserved. Alongside it was a Beuys — another paternal bête noir. Its one redeeming feature, his father might say, was that you could flip the canvas around and use the other side for something worthwhile.

Footsteps echoed in the cavernous gallery. "There it is," said a husky female voice. American. He half-turned toward its owner, who stood now in front of the Beuys, her hair pulled back with a purple scrunchy. A round-faced Martin girl. Next to her, a girl in a crimson hoodie. Extremely pretty, in the open, blank, American way. He took in the length of her: the shapely mainland, the isthmus of a youthful neck leading to the facial peninsula, framed in light brown, shoulder-length hair. Perfect skin, impeccable teeth. Way too young. And laughing at his injured reaction to all this artistic malpractice. He stood there for half a beat, then turned toward her and ironically spread his arms.

"Sorry, I didn't mean to predispose you or anything."

The other one said earnestly: "It's what we came here to see."

"Oh, reeeaaally," he answered, back in control. The beautiful one grinned; he pretended not to notice. "My condol- I mean, wonderful."

Miss Scrunchy pursed her lips, while her companion now stared him full in the face, looking up, since she was a good head shorter. Her left eye was a tad off-center, which added a quirky intensity to her gaze. He extracted some details. Name: Caitlin. Permanent location: Encino. Purpose: tag along with her cousin Scrunchy — Judith — who was doing research for her thesis.

"What have you got against Beuys?" Judith asked.

"Look, no offense," *no don't — stop it stop it stop it you idiot*, "but to me his work doesn't rise to the level of bad. Plus he was a Nazi."

"He repudiated it, though."

"After the war. What if the Nazis had won?"

"You didn't go through what he did," Judith insisted, "think how much courage he needed to survive, to keep creating."

He relaxed his jaw. Winning this argument so did not matter. Back off, get on her good side, keep it going long enough to get this Caitlin creature's phone number. Elementary technique. He shrugged. "You may be right. I never thought of it that way. After all," he went on, trying to channel his brother, "his work is about transcendence, a metaphor of struggle, inscribed into an ahistorical discourse."

"Wow. Yes… exactly." she said, slowed by the sudden mini-blast of academese. "Do you teach?"

"No, but I learned a lot from my dad." He started to explain.

"Omigod. You're Hiram Geach's son?"

Daylight. "You've read him? Guess I better take you seriously."

"I don't always agree with him, but he does have the virtue of pissing off most of my professors. What's he like?"

"To tell you," he replied, "will take some time, and I'm fighting some ferocious jet lag. Can I answer you over coffee?"

He flashed his best deal-closing smile.

The check, Swanson insisted, was his. He invited *les filles* to sit by the window while he brought everything over. It was always an impressive view, let alone on a day like today, when the wind had chased off the clouds and smog, leaving a chiseled, crystal-clear panorama. He took a seat with his back to the window, remembering a quote from some corporate warfare book: "When playing chess, always arrange it so that your opponent sits with the sun in his eyes." He must have ten years on them, after all. When he set down the coffees, the two women exchanged a glance: he'd only thought to bring cream, sugar, and a spoon for himself. He quickly stood. "Oops, sorry, couldn't carry everything at once. Be right back."

They couldn't be sisters, but clearly they knew each other well. Trying to split them up would only backfire. Job one: win over Judith and ignore Caitlin, whose self-esteem was probably inflated by guys drooling over her all the time. The royal, liquid grace of her walk had grabbed him somewhere below the stomach: in movement, she seemed to be still; when still, in movement. It was like watching a waterfall. He sat down again. Time to assert control. A borderline rude comment, something about her hair or her clothes? Maybe if nothing else got her attention. He turned to Judith.

"Does your thesis have a title?"

"*L'Utopie Pornographique.*"

"Heh, good one," said Swanson, tipping an imaginary hat. "Is this a thesis to be read with one hand?"

She laughed. "It's mostly PG-thirteen. My original idea was: *Hermeneutica Pornographica: Presencing Transgression in the Posthuman Media.*"

"Do they still talk like that?" *Ack! Stop dating yourself!*

"No, it was a joke, although my thesis advisor didn't get it at first. The whole thing is a metaphor for what's happening to culture in general. I start with porn's advantages: it gives effortless satisfaction," she singsonged, "it's portable, repeatable, slo-mo-able, safe! It affirms free market principles, democratically catering to all tastes."

"Then you pull out the knives."

She nodded. "Eroticism involves you, but porn is sexual fast-food. It is totally passive: no delay, no risk of refusal, no resistance, no imagination. The maid or cable guy or secretary are always available, ready and willing — assuming there's even that much plot."

This was not going where he'd expected.

"The consumer's only effort," she went on, "is to select the body type, race, age, etcetera: which cut of beef."

"The meatware variations."

"Exactly. And the more plastic surgery and bioengineering advance, the more the actors will modify their meat according to fashion or market demand. Over time they'll morph into avatars, airbrushed objects... Anyway, that's the metaphor, that capitalism pornifies culture and whatever else it touches."

Swanson's foot motored under the table. It was true — hell, even porn itself had become pornified, mechanized. But this must have all been said before, and Caitlin hadn't yet opened her mouth.

"Capital," Judith continued, "gravitates toward what's hot, co-opts it, breaks it down to its lowest common denominator, then packages and sells variations on it while it's still warm. What's popular becomes even more so, while everything else starves. You see it everywhere."

"Art, music, industry..."

"Politics, too, although of course that was rotten from the start."

Swanson turned to Caitlin, but just as he opened his mouth, a loud MOO erupted from the direction of her purse. She smiled apologetically, dug out her phone, and stepped away from the table.

"You were going to tell us about your father," said Judith.

He gave her the short version.

"I'm sorry to hear that. It's a terrible loss for everybody." She sounded like she meant it. Caitlin rejoined them, unhooked her purse from the corner of her chair. "I have to go — it was nice meeting you."

At the word 'go', Swanson was already rising to his feet: "Yes, I need to leave, too. By the way, my... associate and I are throwing a party to celebrate, uh, our new business. I'd love it if you could both come." He pulled out a pen and slid a napkin across the table.

Swanson walked along the Boulevard de Sébastopol toward the tenth arrondissement, staying on the sunny side, like the song. The afternoon had lost none of its startling crispness. Pedestrians walked toward him in such sharp relief they looked, in the wooziness of jet lag, like old-time movie actors walking against a background of cardboard scenery. Qualities that caught his eye in crowds — sexual potential, possible competition, style, confidence — didn't matter in his tired, half-giddy state. He looked without filtering, swimming into the torrent of faces. Some happy, relaxed; others worried, their brows creased. Most of all, people looked distracted, their features worked by private thoughts or scenarios. At moments a wave of tiredness hit; then he'd remember Caitlin, and get pumped again over how smoothly it had gone. Now he'd declare victory and go home to sleep as long as he wanted, no matter that it was afternoon and his clock would be messed up for days. When he arrived at headquarters. Martin was on the sofa reading a magazine.

"Yo, what about our party, yo?" Swanson called out as he rummaged through the fridge.

"What party, yo?"

"The one we're throwing to officially launch our business."

"The business we launched last year?"

"That's the one. Just you, me, a few hundred of our closest friends, and the goddess I met at the museum today."

"Sounds great. You want to have it here?"

Swanson looked around. Martin had spruced the place up, selectively. A television and a new stereo, yes, but the same putrid Formica kitchen, chintzy furniture, and peeling paint; magazines on the table, crosswords — in French, bravo —, stacks of code with scribbles all over them. Still a student's crash pad.

"In this dump? Nah, in the rental."

"Sure, why not. The clients who arrived today aren't staying long, then it'll be open for a couple weeks — plenty of time to clean it up afterwards. Which reminds me…"

Martin recited the tale of the water heater, surprised and even a little annoyed to get only a shrug in reply. Swanson's hyper-involvement of the early days had long since dwindled into do-as–you-think-best. As if he'd already moved on. From California he'd sometimes opined on the furniture choices ("A white sofa, in a rental apartment? Uh, dude…") or Donatella's garish vases — but always after it was too late. His one solid contribution had been to arrange the website.

"I know you're dying to do a few good deeds for the apartment," Martin said. "It must have been gnawing at you every day."

Swanson yawned, then loudly smacked his lips. "You read my mind. As long as it's bite-sized; I might get called back to Cali any day. Apart from that, use me and abuse me, baby. Even the brains of the outfit oughta get his hands dirty once in a while."

"Even the *what*?"

"Oh, just kidding. You got a particular task in mind?"

"The living room's kinda dark. A skylight or two would make all the difference. The syndic agreed to let us do it, but we can't start work until we have permission from the city architect's office. That's as far as I got."

"Consider it done."

"Cool. So who's the goddess?"

"Name is Caitlin."

"How did she warm up that frozen pebble you call a heart?"

"Oh, I'm not sure she's done that yet. And hope is kryptonite," Swanson intoned, cracking open a beer. "You know the verb *bander*? It means both 'to have a hard-on' and 'to blindfold.'"

Martin laughed. Then winced, thinking of Gail for some reason.

"Ah, I almost forgot," Swanson raised a finger, "She has a cousin who's made for you."

"If you're right, I'll be forever in your debt — but I won't get my hopes up, either. Now it's my turn. While you were chasing tail, I was hard at work expanding our business. Look at this."

Martin chucked Nadia's catalogue on the table.

Swanson thumbed through it as Martin gave him the story. "Wow. Amazing connections."

"Far as I can tell, they're for real. Anyway, she wants to rent out her place. I thought we might put it on our site and charge her, say ten percent. Everybody wins."

"Sure, why not?"

Swanson laced his hands behind his head. A wave of fatigue, *un vrai coup de barre*, washed over him. Before crashing, though, he wanted to savor this upcoming little distraction, which was probably all Caitlin would amount to. In a few weeks max, he'd be master of his time again. No good alpha dog lets infatuation mess with his priorities; he enjoys it like a fine wine that nature will eliminate from his system soon enough. He whipped out his cell, whistling through his teeth as he went down his list of Paris contacts, doing one of the things he did best: generate a buzz. Life was starting to feel like life again.

Chapter Eleven

Muffled voices, footsteps, lights flicking off and on: André Masson took it all in subliminally. Only when the uniformed guard touched his shoulder did he realize people had been filing out, that the huge main hall of the Bibliothèque de la Sorbonne, where he'd sat since morning, was now empty except for him.

Stiff-legged, he walked outside into the warm evening and turned on his phone. A text from Judith had come in an hour ago: "*T'es où, là?*" Shit, he'd forgotten the party! He hurried the few blocks to his place on the Rue de Sommerard, bounding up the stairs to the fourth floor. He dropped his messenger bag atop a stack of what might look to the untrained eye like too many books, which were actually — well, too many books. He sighed. No time to worry about it now. In the kitchen, he grabbed a croissant left over from that morning: a reminder that since then he'd spent another whole day at the library, with no concrete results to show for it. He chewed the buttery staleness, reading for the Nth time the motto of Valéry he'd taped to the fridge while in the middle of his PhD thesis: *A difficulty is a light. An insurmountable difficulty is a sun.*

He'd chosen the hard way then, too, disdaining the many easier paths to a doctorate: relate some philosopher à la mode like Foucault to an obscure one like Anathasius Kircher, for example, or modify academic consensus with a point so trivial no one would bother to dispute it. Most important, went the received opinion, was to avoid a public misstep, even if it meant not being right about anything that mattered. But no, he'd wanted to leapfrog the old order, go straight to the front of the line — by merit, of course. Quickly! Squeeze all the juice from each day, find genius *now*. To be an apprentice, but without getting stuck on the endless subdivided stages towards a goal that, like Zeno's arrow, never arrives. No! Enlightenment in *this* moment, not some future one. To ignore what supposedly couldn't be done, brush past the fools and poseurs. To read everything, but slowly, with judgment. To go wide and deep all at once — now. So he'd tried to refute the entire notion of theory. Philosophers, he wrote, only succeed when destroying other theories. Their own systems, straining to be universal and eternal, give an empty coherence, a shrunken, brittle truth. No theory or belief had managed to stay alive across different times, places, and people. Outside its original context, it always ossified into dogma, a victim of its own well-meaning advocates. He added satires to the appendices: Marx, resurrected, visits Soviet Russia in the 1930s; Christ, the battlefields of the Crusades and the dungeons of the Inquisition. His thesis advisor had immediately seen through it. "Your idea is interesting, but you push it too far. You claim that systems cannot modify themselves, which is not at all certain. And you posit a theory no different than those you attack: one with a context, that can go out of date, and so on. *Bref*, you bite your own tail." He was right, of course. André had had to start over from zero. And now was not the moment to repeat that story. Wanting so badly to make his mark with this solo project, his first at the Centre, he risked another basic error by trying to eat something bigger than his head.

Cluny métro station was full of drunken, kilted Scotsmen, apparently in town for the rugby matches. They sang, waved team flags, and carried on conversations of which André, who took pride in his English, understood not a word. He moved down the platform, to the far end. Sports, mob scenes, and, for that matter, parties, irritated him. A friend or two over coffee was more than enough. If he'd been true to himself, he'd have skipped tonight's soirée, hosted by some Americans he didn't even know. At his project's current rate, though, one night more or less wouldn't make much difference. Plus, having blown his last two get-togethers with Judith, he really needed to make an appearance this time. Hopefully the crowd would make it easier to ignore her attractive but insipid cousin, whose name he always forgot.

He found the address, followed some other people going in, and took the stairs to the top floor. People had spilled out into the hallway: slender, honey-haired women, impeccably dressed, cocktails in one hand, cell phones in the other, flanked by coiffed, elegant males. Money was in the air. But were there two different get-togethers here? These people were all French. Ex-pats tended to keep to themselves, either by choice or because the natives avoided them. He snaked through the crowd. No, it was one party; apparently the hosts had connections. They knew what they were doing, too, down to the quality of the *amuse-gueules.*

"Now that we have multiple points of presence in the region…"

"They were ready to tap him…"

"Always go with your first choice, that's my maxim."

"She is such a critical component of the team, though…"

Blah, blah. The kind of lacquered, smooth-faced strivers he hated, born to die like everyone else and technically just as worthy of compassion, but whose bobo-lives revolved around their position on some pitiful org-chart. Healthy ambition, wasted. He could hear Simone: "You and your prejudices! Do you know those people? Even assuming you're right, their taxes help pay for our research, including your salary." Of course if he'd started singing their praises, she might have taken the opposite tack… Entering the main room, he immediately ran into the cousin. Caitlin, that was it. *Mignonne et ordinaire.*

"Sorry I'm late," he yelled, over the booming music. "How long have you been here?"

"Long enough." She pointed to the window, where Judith was in animated conversation with an athletic, spiky-haired guy, whose intense gaze and ready smile made him look out of place here. André gave a thumbs up. Judith had adapted well to Paris, but seemed to lack the social life her kind of personality needed. He waded over to them.

From group to group Swanson glided, his iridescent sharkskin suit turning now green, now red, with the angle of the light. The party was booming, beyond his expectations. First and second-tier friends from his Paris years had shown up in force. Most had evolved as he would have expected — the way he'd probably have turned out himself if he'd stayed... But no, of course that wasn't right. They were natives, graduates of the *École Normal Sup'* or *L'X*, groomed all their lives for a *cadre supérieur* here in Paris, enjoying the fruits of birthright and hard work. He, equivalently qualified but coming from outside that magic circle, would only have amounted to an interloper. Genuine entry into that society? Never happen. He could live here fifty years; he'd still be 'that American.' If they'd all come tonight, it was as much to network amongst themselves as for old time's sake. Goals, assumptions, values — theirs mostly coincided with his. He was one of them, and yet... not. Here too he saw what he hadn't when he'd lived here: they were in harness, sure of what tomorrow had in store. They wouldn't understand his restlessness, his need for pressure and velocity. Maybe they'd have a brief spasm of envy or curiosity about his adventures in Silicon Valley, but deep down, they would see something fake in it, a place where fortunes ballooned and vanished so suddenly as to be somehow unreal.

As he greeted some newcomers, Caitlin walked by holding an empty glass, separated from her cousin for the first time since they'd arrived. He excused himself and followed her into the kitchen. Taking his time, he mixed her a drink, speaking without a pause in a deep, steady voice, until he had her undivided attention. He followed with some leading questions, so he'd finally hear what she had to say. She would make a perfect Van Eyck madonna, he thought. Cheekbones, delicate skeleton,

107

aristocratic pallor — all she needed was a velvet robe, an altar, maybe a lapdog on a pillow. But she, a communications major, had little to communicate. It was a given that most people, if you didn't guide the conversation, would gravitate toward what they found interesting: themselves. Usually though, they'd bounce a few questions back at you for appearance's sake. Not that any of this had ever mattered before. So a girl's existence began and ended with her friends, favorite TV shows, social media; maybe she was a bit of a narcissist — who cared? Tonight he did. While his body was more than ready, the rest of him felt only boredom. A smile hung on his face out of inertia, but the attraction of the whole enterprise receded. Getting her horizontal, even under the best of scenarios, would bring nothing new to his life. That thought shook him even more. He never, ever looked beyond the main event. Why start caring now? Since when did he need something new in his life? She stood there, apparently having just asked a question. He mumbled a vague answer, wondering what all this might mean, whether it signaled some permanent shift. Regardless, it had to be respected for now. With a twinge — she really was gorgeous — he started looking for an out. Spotting Sébastien, he waved him over.

"I have to get back to playing host," he said to Caitlin over his shoulder, "but allow me to present my friend Sébastien, a native Parisian and true gentleman."

As André approached, Judith turned towards him.

"Ah, there you are. André, this is Martin, one of the hosts. Martin, this extremely late person here is my friend and former teaching assistant André Masson."

She pointed at him. "Sorbonne." Then at Martin. "Stanford, then Silicon Valley."

Judith checked her watch. "I'll go find Caitlin. Don't forget," she said to André, "we have a dinner reservation in twenty minutes. I'd invite you, Martin, but I'm sure you have to attend to your guests." She said it slowly, looking him in the eyes.

He looked right back. "I do, but why don't we try for some other time… soon?"

"I think that's a brilliant idea," she smiled. After they traded phone numbers, she said: "Now I better go fetch my poor cousin," and disappeared into the crowd.

André's first impression had been right: Martin — animated, open, with a sense of humor, a mind that went off on strange tangents — was an unlikely person to be at this party at all, let alone hosting it. He even showed genuine interest when André mentioned his research on teaching strategies and grumbled about the antiquated French education system.

"If it makes you feel any better, I'm sure our schools in the States are worse," Martin yelled over the music. "What part of the problem are you trying to solve?"

Good, thought André: someone who knows how to limit. "I'm working on human attention deficit. How various factors…" He hesitated, then went on, anticipating some pushback: "…especially technology, have eroded our ability to focus."

Martin didn't miss a beat. "Yeah, I've seen that in all kinds of ways. So, are you describing the problem or proposing some solution?"

"Both, I hope. Our center does educational research and development, mostly materials for children up to 12 or so. In this case we need to produce something they can use day-to-day."

"And since they're growing up surrounded by technology, you'll have to use it to draw them in, right?"

"Could be…" André had only considered ways of working against computers and videos games. "Maybe you're right, and the poison is the antidote! The question is how. Most video games are fight-or-flight scenarios that hook kids on the adrenaline. But games for learning or discovering could also be addictive in a good way."

"A small matter of programming," Martin quipped.

André thought out loud, becoming more and more animated. "Unfortunately, education in France is designed by bores. Our system fixates on answers, stuffing kids with facts instead of getting them to think about the questions. We punish errors, but a mistake is like *gold* — more useful for making progress than ten correct answers. Letting students discover where they took a wrong turn, see the abstract shape or form of the solution, how other problems might be solved the same way. That's a practice they can apply to any subject."

Martin nodded. "Sounds like what software engineers call a 'design pattern.' "

André brightened. "Ah, I've never heard that term." He took out a small notebook and scribbled in it.

Sébastien's attention was wandering. The nonverbal signals were already clear: he'd soon have the honor of being her Euro-fling for this vacation, a status-enhancer to brag about to her friends back in California. Fine. He was not above a little mutual using. This was taking too long, though. Time to create an air of inevitability.

"But enough about you," Sébastien interrupted her with a dazzling display of teeth, "let's talk about me."

Caitlin laughed and leaned in towards him a little, shifting her weight from one foot to the other. Anyone so arrogant and rude must have something to him.

"You? I've heard all about you European men."

Sébastien raised his right hand. "I swear to you none of it is true."

"Prove it. How many women have you slept with?"

Sébastien guessed, then divided by ten. His eyes narrowed. "You, how many guys?" She knew her own number exactly, and doubled it. Suddenly an intruding arm wrapped around Caitlin's shoulders. Flashing a faux-rueful smile at Sébastien, Judith said, over Caitlin's brief but futile resistance: "*Je regrette*, but I need to drag her away now."

As they re-entered the kitchen, André handed Martin his card, yelling: "Let's talk more sometime." He felt sorry to cut the conversation short, but glad to escape the smoke, chatter, and four-on-the-floor music. As if to hurry him on his way, that summer's monster dance hit came on, and the entire party surged, bobbing, singing along, corralling their neighbors into selfies, proof that fun was taking place.

Chapter Twelve

Swanson leaned on his broom and stared. "Fuck ya doin'?"

Martin sat at the coffee table with a pair of scissors, patiently cutting up the plastic webbing from last night's many six-packs of beer. "These things go straight into the landfill. Birds get tangled in them."

Swanson gave a loud snort.

"No, really," Martin went on. "I've gotten all garbage conscious lately. I saw this documentary on families in Calcutta, generations of them, who literally live at the city dump, scavenging. They interviewed kids who'd never left the premises their whole lives."

"Why do you care about people who have nothing to do with you?"

"Because maybe they do, somehow. Anyway, it made me more conscious of what I take in and throw out."

"If you say so."

Martin, happy with a woman's number in his pocket and maybe another new friend to boot, ignored the ribbing. "Good job inviting Judith, by the way."

"Do I not know your type by now? Looked like she was with somebody, though."

"Nah, just a friend. I think she took a class from him last year. Seriously bright guy." Martin began to pick up bottles and glasses from bookshelves, under chairs, behind plants. "What about Caitlin?"

"Meh. Less than meets the eye. Guess I bimboozled myself." A gong sounded from his laptop, high on a shelf, where it had functioned as the jukebox for the party. He took it down and set it on the counter, happy enough to drop the Caitlin subject, which needed further processing. The email was from Duncan, who'd gotten the axe again —

the third time since Jones-Wolff. Swanson sighed. He couldn't not help out, even if it meant abetting the train wreck his friend had become: the guy had almost nobody else to turn to. Swanson wrote a quick message to a recruiter north of the peninsula, who might not know Duncan's recent history. As he went back to sweeping, an ugly thought bubbled up: it would break no vow of friendship to cut Duncan loose, since he wasn't even the same person anymore.

Judith stood at a kiosk, flipping through a magazine. Looking very, very good. Martin had dressed down, since who knew what she'd wear? Before she caught sight of him, he stepped onto the down escalator, back into the station, tucked in his shirt, checked his fly. Fortunately he'd worn his blocky, Brooklyn-intellectual glasses, which made anything you wore into an ambiguous, possibly ironic statement, just in case. Riding up again into the warm sunshine, he laughed at himself. This attraction could turn out to be a mirage in so many ways. And he… well, in the full light of day he might be too old for her, too geeky. The thing was to avoid feeling like it mattered, which always led to mistakes. As he entered her space, she looked up from her magazine.

"Isn't it amazing," she exclaimed, continuing their conversation from the other night without a pause, "how completely you guys have won?" She widened her stance to let him see the article, something about how technology had changed social interaction forever.

"It only happened because all you civilians bought in."

"You sound like a guilty drug dealer." Her voice was raspier, sexier than he'd been able to hear over the noise at the party.

"Not guilty at all. Nobody forced anybody to become an addict."

"But you're the ones creating the appetite," she said mischievously.

"Wait, aren't we back to your thesis?"

"I guess so; it follows me around everywhere. I already bored you with that at the party, though."

"Not at all. I want to hear more. But speaking of appetite, I saved mine up for your restaurant."

"It's this Moroccan place on a side street up that way."

It was an early summer evening on the Champs-Élysées, when natives and tourists alike crowd the cafés and sidewalks after the heat of the day. A delicious breeze carried gusts of perfume, cigarette smoke, and suntan lotion that hit the limbic system with a keen, tangy promise of sex. Martin had forgotten his worries. Things felt easy between them, the way they had the other night at the party. She'd made some jest around the punch bowl that he bounced right back to her. Only after exchanging a long volley of puns and double entendres had they introduced themselves, almost as an unnecessary formality. It was already clear the conversation would continue.

Judith's restaurant was closed for renovations, so they resorted to a sidewalk place on the Champs-Elysées itself.

"I tend to avoid this area," Judith said, "but it is great for people-watching. That guy, for example." A tall young man wearing huge reflective sunglasses walked past, the lips on his elongated face projecting forward as he chewed a slice of pizza. "Doesn't he look like a camel?"

Every species seemed to be on display: snakes in bright unbuttoned shirts, flashing toothy grins, prancing deer, jackasses sporting parachute-sized t-shirts, pants hanging down, baseball caps on backwards, heads swiveling in unison to follow a giraffe, her obsidian eyes pointed straight ahead as she petulantly fluffed a pink feather boa. Hyenas, peacocks, hippopotami... the parade flowed on. Martin noticed with a slight shock that he and Judith had been watching in silence for several minutes. How had they reached such a comfort level so quickly? The meaning of it spread through him, like honey in his veins. At the same time, that train of thought placed him outside their shared bubble. Now he was on another wavelength, and felt a growing pressure to comment on their silence, to perversely swat away the happy moment instead of finding a way to reenter it.

Their waiter solved the dilemma by announcing himself and rattling off the specials. Martin nodded vacantly, focused on Judith's fresh, heart-shaped face. Was she ever what had been missing from his life. Launching the business, deciphering the codes of Paris Swanson had rightly warned about, and learning French — all three at once — had left little room for anything else, creating his longest adult-era stretch of femalelessness. One thing had become clear: he had no idea how to find joie de vivre on his own. Distraction, amusement, yes; friendships and absorbing interests, sure — but healthy, pointless joy? That only came through women. Drugs or alcohol substituted as a last resort, though much less so since school. It wasn't just sex that moved him, but the female presence — that girlfriend touch, taste, smell around him. Their conversation, grace, and attention to things he, in his wooden solitude, ordinarily wouldn't notice. He didn't know how to live, and so kept trying to find the key through others. Of course he might be projecting his own wishes onto Judith, hearing from her the message he wanted to hear: life makes sense; you've been stuck in prison without knowing it; the door is open, always has been… Yet maybe she was another kind of woman from those he had known, and he'd become a different kind of man: wise, generous, a real lover, not just a sexer, a fucker…

The waiter returned, and as he set down their drinks, exclaimed: "*Et puis voilà!*"

They laughed. "That is such my favorite expression," said Judith. "It works for everything. Congrats on your French, by the way. Where did you study?"

"Ah, I took classes, then sorta cooked up my own method. I guess you already spoke it well, since you went straight to the Sorbonne." She nodded. "That's where you met André?"

"Yeah, he TA'ed a class of mine last year. He's a year younger than me, but already finished his PhD, the little twerp. By then he was already moonlighting at that research center. I've always found him intriguing. He's super dedicated and gives what he does a hundred and ten percent, but also has this nutty, counter-phobic side. I rode on the back of his motorcycle once, and he is a madman, even compared to the maniacs I knew in L.A."

She slipped off her sheer jacket, pushed her sunglasses up on her head, and sat back in her strapless dress. On her creamy left shoulder, there was a small, ornate tattoo. She noticed him looking.

"It's a gryphon. I got one before any of my friends. By high school I regretted it, 'cause even the teachers had them. Now I like it again."

She spoke of growing up in Venice Beach, an alien among the oiled, buxom musclemen and leathery jogger-moms with their buns of steel. At ten she wore all black — precocious at the time, even in what she called the land of professional adolescents. Nickname: Morticia. He could see her very well: the artistic intellectual among her friends, Queen Bee among the happy few, who were living a golden period of certainty, knowing they all had so much to give the world. She'd gone on to Vassar to escape from her mother, UCLA for grad school, and the Sorbonne to finish her research. A directed life, much more of a piece than his.

"Everybody asks 'what brings you to Paris?', so I wasn't going to," she said, "It doesn't need justification. But now that we're on the subject…"

"It was totally not a planned thing." He recapped his post-Dendroid life.

"Didn't it bug you when Swanson left you on your own?"

"Kinda, but he didn't have much of a choice. Plus it made me learn the ropes faster. Then a funny thing happened when I realized I could go back: I didn't want to."

"I love it here, too. I mean, the French do have their ways…but we're no bargain, either."

"I like that it's not weird here to work with your brain, or use it for something besides making money."

"Right, it makes you a high-status creature."

"In the U.S., at least outside Silicon Valley, I usually tell people I'm a brmmwwphhhrr," he said, jokily covering his mouth.

"A bun warmer?" She laughed. "My freshman roommate's boyfriend was a programmer. Dmitry. He'd spend days at a time staring at his screen."

"Yah. When you're fixing a really hairy problem, you can't leave just it. You're too many levels deep, with all those variables to keep in your head." He wondered if he was boring her. But no, she swept her fine brown hair out of her eyes without removing her warm gaze from him. "If you go home to sleep it might take hours to recover your place the next day — so you keep going. Then there are all the manuals. It's like reading the dictionary."

"Personally, I love reading the dictionary."

He flushed. Women's reactions over the years — one even heaved a sigh when he explained his job — had led him to simplify or ungeek what he did, to gear it toward what he imagined they wanted to hear. All those acrobatics, selling himself short, trying to woo the wrong people! He felt a tingling in his groin. "You know, you're right — I even read it myself sometimes. Bogus comparison. Let's say the phone book."

"Bogus — hah. That was Dmitry's favorite expression."

"It's a very important part of programmer-speak: bogoid technology, bogon-infected managers…"

"It would be bogoriffic if you taught me this language."

"I think you'll find it bogolicious."

After dessert came coffee, then another coffee, and later a cheese plate because they were both hungry again. When the place finally

closed and they stood up to leave, Martin checked his watch; they'd
been there for six hours.

The next day Nadia called — the third time that week. Supposedly,
her place would soon be ready to rent, and all this strategizing would be
over. But until now she'd only thought of the money to be made, not of
the strangers who would occupy her very own apartment.

"Will it really be all right? What if they never leave? You know what
to expect from tourists, Martin."

"I can tell you my experience," he replied, "but it's your apartment,
Nadia."

Swanson, coming out of his room, looked over at Martin and rolled
his eyes.

"Could we meet today? I want to decide once and for all, and get on
with my life."

"Let's say two o'clock at that café on the rue St. Antoine, across from
the church." He hung up.

"She's like your new best friend," said Swanson. "You sure she
doesn't have the hots for you?"

"Nah, she just needs money."

"Why do you care?"

"We might add her place to our site, remember?" He tapped his
temple.

"Oh, yeah, your master plan. Thought about introducing her to
Jerome?"

"Our client Jerome? You met him already?"

"Not in person. He phoned yesterday about getting the rental
cleaned, and we started yakking. Turns out he's a board member of a
couple film associations. Maybe he's heard of her."

Martin mulled the idea on his way to the café. Adding Nadia's apartment to the site made business sense; yet just getting this far often felt like pushing a wet noodle with a toothpick.

"Donatella's too expensive," Nadia had complained, declaring, with the air of someone who'd done it all before: "I can buy materials and hire workers just as easily as she can,"

Donatella, meanwhile, had been categorical: "Nadia's all talk. She'll find a way to ruin the opportunity. I have the feeling she's done a lot of stupid things in her life."

Elle a fait beaucoup de bêtises dans sa vie... To spend time on this Nadia possibility might be a bêtise of his own. Her shape-shifting tendencies and exotic connections — he still had no clue where she was originally from — gave her a certain entertainment value. Yet for all her talk of money difficulties, of the urgent need to rent her apartment, she hadn't done much. As if hoping some trick of the light or a passing leprechaun would whisk all her problems away. She had a gambler in her, an infantile, capricious one, the kind who bets everything on one card for the drama of it — as long as it's someone else's money. After their last meeting, they'd walked past a real estate agency and a listing in the window caught her eye. With a this-changes-everything tone, she said: "My God! It's so charming! Let's go look at it!" Having nothing else going that day, he consented, curious. Did she have some savings after all? Was she going to drop it on another apartment? During the walk-through, she peppered the agent with questions and even took notes. At the end she stage-whispered: "What do you think? Isn't it nice?"

Martin shrugged. "Sure, but isn't it out of your price range?"

"*My* price range? I was thinking of it for you! You're the big investor."

What was her role to have been? Would she have wanted a finder's fee? Or inserted herself in the bargaining process somehow, to justify a piece of the action? The whole idea was so outlandish that it was hard to know, or take seriously. But who cared. He'd let things play out, ignore all the bobbings and weavings. If she managed to fix up her place, the rentals would be processed through the website and the business would roll on its own. Last week she'd decided her new furnishings would come from the *marché aux puces* at Porte de Clignancourt. Since he'd never been there, he should come along.

A flea market? For once she'd understated the case. Beyond the usual cheap stuff sold near the métro lay an entire neighborhood of antique and bric-a-brac dealers, a small bar that played gypsy jazz, stall after stall of fountain pens, dolls, lacework: an in-and-outdoor Ali Baba's cave that seemed to go on for miles. After an hour she found a reading chair — "a perfect little *fauteuil Voltaire.*" She walked past it indifferently a couple times, looked at other things, then circled back, expressed disbelief at the asking price ("that's the *prix de touriste*, Martin, never give them that"), then offered half. Here we go, he thought. A wary back and forth began, in polite but firm tones. Once they'd agreed on a sum, Nadia hesitated, then lowered her voice: "And if one paid in cash?" The shopkeeper wearily proposed another ten percent off. She pressed on, arguing over the delivery price. Later, she used the same technique for a candlestick and a small painting: which in the end were all she bought for her renovation.

Swanson might've appreciated her haggling skills. For Martin no discount was worth cutting that kind of figure. It wasn't in his nature, though he could easily see Nadia behaving that way at five years old. She had that personality of 'someone with personality,' the way her acquaintances were famous for being famous. Her sugary exterior camouflaged a hard, inflexible will, indifferent to the *marché* vendors and whether they closed up shop next time they saw her coming. She'd gotten what she wanted. The bird feeder in his parent's backyard came to mind. When anything heavier than a bird got on its perch, the feed door closed. The neighborhood squirrels all tried to penetrate the secret, but after shimmying up the pole, most would dangle foolishly from the perch, then slink away. Sometimes one would discover, after much trial and error, how to hang from the feeder by two paws, using a third to balance — splayed out in a comic, extremely undignified way — while the remaining forepaw scooped up the goods without shutting the door. Where did he fall on that spectrum? Would he go away hungry in life? Or scramble for the treasure, using any means necessary? It seemed to depend. Worrying how he might look to others diluted his purpose. But when on his own, as in coding, where deadlines and endurance were the main challenges, he always bagged his prey. Donatella must be right, in general — chutzpah alone was not enough. But lacking it wasn't a virtue, either; there was something to learn from Nadia. Today she'd bring her usual long list of questions: what sorts of curtains and chairs tourists expect, how to choose the photographs for the website, whether brushed nickel fixtures were worth it. She'd sprinkle in a few of her own stories, where the players, their roles as fixed and exaggerated as those in a puppet show, plotted against or bravely supported Nadia in her journey through this world.

"My real concern," she said, between sips of espresso, "before I spend more time and money, is the renters. They're all Americans, aren't they?"

"You mean North Americans? Mostly, but we've had people from all over: Mexico, India, Australia…"

"Do they make trouble?"

"No. Most enjoy themselves, some can be a little picky; I've only seen one couple who wanted to make themselves and everybody else miserable. But we haven't had any trouble."

"What I'm trying to say is, most Americans I know are philanthropists or executives; I doubt they fit the pattern of the typical tourist. I assume these renters are all suitable people."

"What do you mean, 'suitable'?" he asked uneasily.

"You know, people from civilized countries, who will respect your property. I can't imagine opening my home to just anybody."

Martin blurted: "But that's the point of this business, Nadia! While they are renting from you, it's their apartment."

"Then I need to be extra careful in choosing who stays there. Suppose they don't leave?"

"I doubt renters would try it. Anyway, you'll have a signed agreement, so you can just kick them out."

"What if you get Chinese or Arabs?" She lowered her voice. "What if they stink up the apartment cooking a damn shashlik or something?"

He looked for some sign she was joking. "What's the difference where they come from?"

"You're still too young to know how life works, Martin," she said, suddenly vehement. "You Americans are so... *gamin*! You think people are basically decent, that democracy, education, and good hygiene will solve everything. Human beings are slippery, especially when they are desperate. When I lived in — well, never mind where —, thieves would steal the manhole covers and sell them as scrap metal, leaving the hole there in the street for anybody to fall into! What did they care?"

He mumbled something about the rule of law, wondering what this had to do with shashlik or renters of apartments in Paris. She set her cup on its saucer.

"All countries are founded on murder and mayhem — including yours, although I love it. Whoever already happened to be there is killed or enslaved, as they did to the ones there before them. In your country the Beast wears a nicer costume: you elect your monsters — unless your Supreme Court chooses them for you. Just look at the current crusade. They're even calling it that! They dictate to everyone, while sometimes doing horrendous things."

"Yes, what's happening now is just criminal."

"Not only now. Who funded and armed Pinochet in Chile, Somoza and the Contras in Nicaragua? Or Saddam in Iraq — while it was convenient? Who trained Bin Laden in Afghanistan, for that matter?"

He knew these arguments — had made them himself. Hearing them from a non-American, though, raised his defenses. "You're leaving out all the good things we do," he stammered, "the international aid…"

"Per-capita it's quite low, even compared to the barbaric Europeans: look it up. There's no law that says you have to give anything at all — let's just not paint things to be what they aren't. Well, I didn't mean to talk politics at you all day, Martin dear. Some more iced tea?"

The racism, the clarity, the facts — real or invented… Her arguments had a kind of coherence, but didn't fit the tidy right-versus-left wing dichotomy he was used to. In comparison his opinions felt shaky, unfounded. It was pathetic; outside the zones where he had solid data, such as pop music or software engineering, he could only sit there blinking, Bambi-like.

The bill arrived. He turned it so Nadia could see it too.

"Oh, Martin, you know how forgetful I am — I left my money in my other purse."

He frowned, not because it was a lot of money but because she'd said the same thing last time, word for word. As he reached out for the check, she added: "I never noticed before, but you really have the hands of an *artist*."

Chapter Thirteen

The building of the *Architectes de batiments de France* was set off from the street by a barren, weedy patio. That is one big lump of butt-ugly, thought Swanson. Some unhappy architect's revenge on the skyline, the neighborhood, his own profession. In the waiting room, Swanson took the last empty chair. The looks on people's faces said they'd been there a while. On top of a pile of magazines was an unfinished portrait sketch someone had left behind. Not bad. The nose drifted a little, the eyes were too high — should be about halfway between the chin and the top of the hair — but the facial expression was well rendered. Swanson borrowed a pencil from the front desk and started to fix it up. Eyes lower, hair to the side, nose in its place. That was more like it. His seat-neighbor, a matronly woman wearing a bright red kerchief, leaned over and said: "But that is wonderful!" She wasn't completely wrong, but it might've just been luck. He grabbed an administrative notice and flipped it over to sketch an old man a couple seats down. The tilt and angle of the head, the volume, line, and shading — it all fell out just right, as if he'd never stopped drawing. When his number was called, he slid both sketches into the portfolio he'd brought.

He found the right desk and sat across from a busy-looking functionary who, for a long minute, paid him no attention at all. The man's unusually long, thin face, with its tiny eyes and ovoid mouth, resembled a well-worn penny loafer, shoved heel first down the neck of his shirt. A boy named Shoe, thought Swanson. He had to stop himself from drawing a caricature right there. When the man finally raised his head, Swanson smiled. "Let's hope this will be your easiest application of the day."

Giving a small grunt, the clerk massaged one temple while reading the dossier semi-aloud. Behind him a wall clock ticked dryly. He began to make vague disappointed noises. You have got to be kidding, thought Swanson. A skylight ought to be a slam-dunk. The neighbors have three of them! The way to a Parisian functionary's heart, went the old line he'd verified for himself more than once, is through some appealing line or story. This guy's desk had nothing on it but a couple family photos.

"I hope the request won't be problematic. I have a five-year old daughter who's just had a cataract operation."

The man perked up a little. "The poor girl. Cataracts? At five?"

"They are rare in children, but even infants can have them. The doctor ordered my wife and I" — here Swanson realized he wore no ring — "now that we're separated, to ensure the child gets as much natural light as possible."

"*On verra.*" The smile across the desk seemed to be activated more by invisible wires than any human feeling. After looking over Swanson's proposal another minute: "You are aware that you live in a protected zone? I should warn you that the law forbids any significant change to the exterior in those areas. Its architectural character must remain consistent with the surrounding buildings."

"Fortunately, that doesn't apply to our case, since the roof can't be seen from the street or the courtyard."

"That remains to be determined. The first step, assuming you have obtained the permission of your *syndic* —"

Swanson nodded.

"...is to submit a valid architectural drawing of your proposed modification."

He handed Swanson his application back to indicate the interview was over. Drawing the planned skylight took a few minutes, once he'd recalled the basics of perspective and made preliminary sketches. Composition, sense of line, progression of values from dark to light: artistically, anyway, it held water. The next day's functionary was a broader, more jovial man, with a compressed mouth and sarcastic eyebrows. Hopes for a different reception vanished when he looked the drawing over and gave a little laugh.

"This is very nice — it's yours? — but you cannot present something like this to the architect. We need exact measurements, a real plan of the situation. If you like, I can give you the name of a design firm that handles small projects."

Swanson wordlessly took back the sketch. To get annoyed would obtain nothing and only be catnip to this jerk. Rather than waste time guessing what they wanted, he admitted defeat and dropped off the requirements at the supplied address. Then it was time to get over to the rental unit. Clients had checked themselves out this morning, and at two-thirty another couple was supposed to arrive. *En passant*, he stopped in at home to get the keys and check email. Some estate stuff from his sister. His headhunter had lined up an interview for a CEO position whenever he got back from Paris. Duncan checked in: he'd stopped even pretending to look for work, and was playing poker in Vegas. Winning big time, he said. Swanson, almost late now, limited himself to: "Good. Leave, quick."

From the front door through the entry passage, everything looked impeccable. Then Swanson rounded the corner into the main room. Bedsheets hung between chairs, pillowcases and towels from the wrought-iron window railings. What the hell? The clients were arriving any minute! In the bathroom, a woman was scrubbing the sink.

"Moon?"

"*C'est moi. Vous êtes monsieur Swanson?*"

"Oui. Qu'est-ce que c'est que cette catastrophe dans le living?"

Hearing his tone, she switched to English, which irritated him even more. "I clean the apartment this morning after the people go," she said. "The laundry must dry."

"You can't just leave it there! The next clients are about to arrive!"

"Monsieur Swanson, the dryer is too small! One load take more than two hours."

"Then take it to a laundromat! What's wrong with you?"

He was almost screaming. She dropped her brush in the sink and ran out of the bathroom. He heard her grab her things and slam the front door. Good riddance. He walked out into the living room. As he tossed the laundry into a basket, he phoned Martin.

"That Moon lady is useless. We've got to give her the boot. You want to hear what she just did?"

Martin listened for a bit, then cut him off. "Whoa. It took me forever to find her. She is the only, and I do mean the only, reliable person who's done that job. I told her she could leave the laundry to dry when new guests arrive on the same day the old ones leave. So blame me. There's no other way to turn it around fast enough. I just explain the mess and apologize to people. Nobody's made a stink yet."

"It looks low class. Why not buy another set of linens?"

"Did it already. We still have to wash the dirties."

"So do it in a laundromat, away from the clients, fer chrissakes."

"You already bitched about our cleaning costs, remember? Doing what you say would double them."

"Yeah, but just when guests overlap."

"Which happens all the time, which you'd know if you…" Martin paused. "Look, I am fine with using a laundromat. It's what I originally suggested. This is why it's good you're here: you get to see the tradeoffs."

For his next visit to the *Architecte* Swanson brought his own paper, ready for work: five minutes tops per sketch, and only in pen, no erasing. Art push-ups. The more awake subjects noticed what he was doing. The first, a bow-tied businessman, pretended to look away; the old lady next to him touched up her hair; the burly, red-faced guy at the far end glared over, with a defensive, irritated expression. Perfect. The whole game was to catch those telltale spasms of character, record them on paper like a seismograph. His clerk was the same cheerful slab of a man as before. On seeing the professionally done skylight plan, he nodded.

"Ah, now that is a drawing! I will submit it today; you should have an answer within a couple of weeks. I must tell you, though, that the architect in charge of your dossier already expressed the opinion that two skylights would change the architectural character of the building."

"There seems to have been a mistake," said Swanson, his voice rising, "As I already mentioned, our roof is not visible from the street or even the courtyard of the building. Only a helicopter flying directly overhead would see any difference. Besides, the apartment next door has three skylights!"

"Oh? That's strange." He frowned and walked off. Twenty minutes later he returned, looking relieved. "The dossier for your building shows there are no skylights in your neighbor's apartment."

"I've seen them myself."

"Perhaps so. But administratively, they do not exist. If your building is ever inspected, your neighbors risk a large penalty, much more than they saved by keeping the facts from us. I advise you to submit your request," he said, in a friendlier tone, "with an option for one skylight."

As if an extra skylight hidden from view would upset the delicate balance of the universe as we know it. If architectural blight worried them so much, they should start by blowing up their own building.

"No wonder nothing ever gets done in this country. It's probably 'cause he knows we're Americans. If I go back there and get the run-around one more time, I'm gonna go in there and trash the place." All clichés — but in the pleasure of venting Swanson didn't care.

"Sounds to me like they're just doing their job," said Martin. "Anyway, what else do you suggest?"

"Suggest? I suggest we piss on 'em and shake it."

"Um, then they may not want to give us our skylight."

"Okay, okay, One more try. One."

When Swanson went back, first thing in the morning this time, he was able to see his guy straightaway. The man smiled as if seeing an old friend.

"Congratulations, everything is in order. The architect has accepted your proposal. You will receive official permission within the week."

"Thank you very much, Monsieur... Ducrocq," he said, looking at the nameplate on the desk.

A few days later, the stamped authorization arrived. Swanson opened it and had to laugh. It was signed by the architect... M. Didier Ducrocq.

Chapter Fourteen

By the time Martin arrived, the café was almost full. Judith waved from her seat against the back wall.

"They're just deciding the topic," she whispered as he sat down. The night before, she'd explained how it worked: a philosophical discussion, open to anyone, where a moderator chose among subjects the attendees proposed on the spot.

Martin ordered a *café allongé* and surveyed the crowd, ready for another new experience. Since their first dinner a week ago, he and Judith had explored the Paris he'd bypassed when on his own: one of afternoon movies, visits to the catacombs, cathedral concerts. Work — his excuse for always doing the same things — had been on hold, and it felt good. Today would be their first whole day together. After this *café philo*, they'd get provisions at the market for his idea, a picnic in the Bois de Boulogne.

A microphone began circulating through the crowd. There were a few blowhards, Judith said, but many knew their stuff. The atmosphere was focused, yet with the feel of someone's kitchen, the way dogs would wander in off the street, sniff around, then shuffle away again, or a speaker would be drowned out in mid-sentence by clattering dishes or the growling cappuccino machine.

A newcomer sat down. "What's the subject today?"

"*L'homme, un projet sans fin*," someone said.

Martin muttered: "That's a topic? 'Man: a never-ending project'?"

"For sure, it's not academic philosophy here. That's why I like it."

A woman sitting next to them signaled for the microphone and slowly said: *"Le grandeur de l'homme, c'est qu'il peut s'ouvrir, à tout moment, à ce qu'il n'est pas."*

That sounded superb, especially in French: the greatness of man is that he can open himself, at any moment, to what he is not. What it meant was less clear. Martin wrote it down on his napkin anyway.

Judith smiled. "See? There is always a phrase or two here to make it worthwhile."

The moderator, an intense man with wiry black hair, took the floor again, weaving a cogent, textured summary of the debate so far, without notes. Impressive, thought Martin. The old college-era lure of ideas, of thought for its own sake, surged in him. Maybe it was time to take a class or two.

A growing din came from the street outside. Judith clutched Martin's arm. "Oh! A *manif!*"

"A what?"

"A *manifestation*, a protest. We have to go watch for minute. You cannot be a Parisian without having seen one. Besides, if we don't hit the market soon, there'll be nothing left."

The Place de la Bastille was filling up with protestors coming down the Boulevard Beaumarchais. Some marched around the large roundabout; others had already climbed the statue in the center and were dancing and waving banners. Entire families stood watching, as Americans might go to a ballgame or a parade. Peaceful enough, though at the mouth of the rue Saint-Antoine, riot police stood next to a long line of paddy wagons, just in case.

From an improvised platform, a man wielding a megaphone led the crowd in a chant: *"Tous ensemble, tous ensemble! Grêve! Grêve!"*

"What're they protesting?" asked Martin.

"I read up on this one, actually — the government wants to raise the retirement age for certain sectors."

"Sounds like the problem we have in the U.S. — fewer young people to pay into the system, and all that… But the money's gotta come from somewhere…"

"Yet somehow there's always enough money when they want to start a war," Judith said. "At least the French notice and protest when their government does stuff. Look what ours is getting away with."

They threaded their way through the protestors to the boulevard Richard Lenoir, where an open-air *marché* extended for blocks and blocks. Judith moved knowingly from stand to stand, loading up their knapsacks with baguettes and avocado and *caramels au beurre salé*. Into the mini-cooler went the Mont D'Or cheese, so runny it was almost liquid, *gariguette* strawberries, cold cuts… Martin followed, listening to the opera of the fruit sellers. A tenor cried: "*Un euro les melons!*" An alto answered: "*Un euro! Un euro! Woo! Woo!*" A soprano: "*Ooh, la, laaaaa!*" Off to the side, a rheumy-eyed flower seller held out bouquets of cut flowers, repeating ostinato: "*Allez-y, messieurs dames.*" At the exit of the market, an old weather-beaten gypsy couple sat on the ground like toothless gatekeepers, staring blankly ahead, bowing an arhythmic drone on their miniature violins.

On the bus, their thighs chafed together. Her right breast had jounced against his arm several times. Had she noticed? It was driving him crazy. They hadn't kissed yet, but now it seemed only a question of when. He tried to focus on something else. "How's the thesis?"

"So-so this week. I made more progress on my daily Dada warmup, cut-and-pasting random stuff from webpages. Wanna hear one?"

She opened her notebook and cleared her throat. "Find a well-disposed beefeater in tweak with your inmost semiquaver! Couch factotum in brimstone? Never again settle for the winkle-simulation of a seventh flounder houseboy rosette!"

"Makes more sense than most of the spam I get."

The bus went over a pothole and bounced them even closer together. Knee bone connected to the thigh bone, thigh bone connected to the hip bone…

"But really, I want to hear more about your work," he insisted. What multiyear project would a mind like hers find worthwhile?

She looked surprised. "You sure? Okay."

By the time she finished, he'd temporarily forgotten about their thighs. "Yeah, marketing has infiltrated everything," he said. "As a technology person, I feel kind of indirectly responsible."

"Why?"

"Well, you point out how capitalism co-opts culture. A lot of that is enabled by software that spots the trends, then rides them as long as possible. When I was in Austin on a business trip a couple years ago, I stayed in this commercial development just like one I'd been in the previous week in Salt Lake City. We're talking a couple square miles of the same restaurants and chain stores, all laid out in exactly the same order."

"Eew, creepy. Like you'd been transported to Brand Land."

"Right! Some dweeb with a database had done the analysis, laid out the whole cookie-cutter subdivision, and dropped it from the sky on neighborhoods around the country."

"That's my topic all right."

"Digitizing everything has changed music, too. It's great we can carry all our tunes around with us now, but liner notes, album art, record stores, hell, even CDs— all that is going away."

"So you're ambivalent."

"Violently ambivalent. Do you mention music?"

"Just a few sentences on bands and singers who have to make cartoons out of themselves."

"You may not believe this, but FM radio used to be worth listening to."

"The only times I've tried, it was the same playlist over and over."

"I knew there was a reason I liked you."

At Porte de la Muette they got off and strolled into the park hand in hand. Following Martin's tiny map, they eventually came to a lake with a row of trees beside it. Once they'd put down their beach towel and laid out the full spread, Judith stepped back and cried: "God, that looks so luscious! You there, with the spaceman phone — take a picture, quick, before the massacre!"

"You see how cool we nerds can be," he said, snapping a few shots, glad for once he carried the big clunky thing around. *Et puis, voilà.*

After eating their fill, they sat back, stunned, letting any remaining urban tensions evaporate in the afternoon heat. Families strolled past as if in slow motion; a lone rower in a wide sun hat glided calmly across the water.

"If I don't move soon, I'm gonna fall asleep," said Martin.

"Me, too."

Lazily, they packed up and wandered around the lake, then into the woods, away from town. After an hour, Judith pointed: there, to the right, a separate, gated park. They walked past the unstaffed ticket booth, following a winding path through a lush forested area. A strange, harsh cry rang out.

"Omigod. What was that?" asked Judith. "A bird?"

"Sounded more like a monkey or something."

"Are we close to a zoo?"

Martin checked his map. "Nope."

As they walked, the cry rang out again, nearer.

"It's off this way, to the right," said Martin.

Another gate opened out into a much different space, where clusters of tall, thick trees divided enormous, well-tended lawns. Footpaths snaked around the perimeter, leading at the far end to an artificial grotto. The only sounds were occasional muffled explosions of distant thunder. No one else seemed to be there. Was it a private space? Golf course? Zen garden? It seemed to extend for miles, a park within this park within a park.

The rain came. It wouldn't last long — the sky was mostly blue — so instead of running for the large grove a hundred yards away, they ducked beneath some low branches alongside the path. Just then a man wearing a business suit with a bright red tie stepped out of the thicket onto the path ahead of them. He stood there a moment, puzzled, staring at the sky, as if scooped up on his way to the London Stock Exchange and dropped there by some irregularity in the space-time continuum. In one rapid, fluid movement he took out a black umbrella and flicked it open. He gave them a short nod, turned on his heel, and strolled off.

Martin looked at Judith. "What the…?"

Judith laughed. "Have we gone down the rabbit hole?"

"I'm glad we both saw him, anyway."

They watched until he disappeared behind the grotto. The hissing of the rain died down, then stopped. Again came the strange cry, much closer now. Then, on the grass not ten feet away, they saw it: an enormous peacock. And another, twenty yards behind it. Judith leaned into Martin. "Look!" With one hand on his arm, she pointed to the right, where the biggest, most beautiful peacock of all perched on a branch a good twenty feet above them. They stood staring at it a long moment. Whether it was the touch of her hand or the smell of her hair, the pressure of her breast against his arm, his head was humming. He turned now toward her, their lips coming together as naturally as a fruit, heavy with juice, falls from the tree. She more than knew how, thank God: how one mouth ought to taste the other, not gaping open or shut tight, the way tongues can play like two happy otters, hands exploring, the whole body joining the party... They sat on a bench, glued to each other, not noticing their surroundings until the sun lowered and reddened. Martin was again struck that such a touristy spot would be empty on a summer weekend, as if the peacocks were keeping out all humans but them. When they finally left the garden and made their way to the exit, the park gates were locked.

"So that's why we didn't see anybody. I didn't think to check their hours. Merde!" said Martin, looking along the length of the fence for another way out. "We may have to call the cops or something."

Judith didn't seem at all phased. "The weather's perfect, we still have tons of food, with peacocks to sing for us — let's stay! *Une nuit blanche! Allons-y!*"

"*On ne peut pas résister une si belle énergie,*" Martin declared, caught up in continuing the adventure, joining her in something he'd never have done at home. As he put his arm around her, a tingling warmth surged through him at the possibility that they might go for it, there in the woods. They stood again outside the peacock zone. Treetops reared up against the sky, casting long, wild shadows across the lawns. Martin pointed, intoning: "Beware ye, tender innocent, yonder eldritch wood-folk who gambol and caper 'neath the pale gibbous moon…"

"Looks to me like it's going to be full."

"'Full' lacks flavor," he replied, still intoning. "'Gibbous' has major flavor."

"Yes, dear."

They stopped at their bench for a snack. As dusk segued into night, the moon rose out of the clouds and the crickets began to sing: softly at first, then louder and louder, until their hypnotic chorus swelled into a wave of sound, pulsating from all directions. The breeze carried an intoxicating perfume of cut grass, wild mint, and leaf mold. Though technically sitting within the city limits, no sight or sound reached them to indicate that Paris even existed.

With the moon still rising in the cloudless sky, they left the peacock garden to wander deeper into the park. Before long, a wide gravel driveway appeared, glimmering dully. To one side stood a white building with tall arched windows — a lodge, a huge greenhouse, someone's dwelling? Opening out to the left was a vast rose garden. In the phosphorescent light of night it seemed to go on, bed after bed, without end. They wandered through the paths, drunk with the heavy fragrance, past clouds of roses that hung from a network of pergolas, then up a hillock, where a gazebo overlooked the entire garden.

"Sometimes I get this recurring dream, of a place like this," Judith spoke softly. "Do you ever have those?"

"All the time when I worked at Dendroid."

"Tell me."

"Okay, but it was horrible. I am driving a car, on a multi-lane freeway. All the other cars seem to be driving in the opposite direction, straight towards me. Have I somehow drifted over to the wrong side? No — but it's too late to stop or turn back, so I weave between them. Their windows are tinted, so I can't see the drivers. Then I realize those cars are being operated by remote control. But I never find out who is controlling them."

She pressed against him. "Oooh, a nightmare. I like that it's in the present tense. You are bringing out my inner Goth girl. Tell me another."

Martin thought for a minute. "I am a shepherd. My flock roams over meadows that stretch for miles, bordered by a wall of fog that everybody shuns. I have no worries: I play my lyre, eat my grapes, I chase the wood nymphs, they chase me. One day, counting my sheep, I discover one is missing. I search and search, but can't find it. Of course, I have many, yet each time I check, several more are gone. Then I notice one sheep wandering away from the rest, and follow it. At the frontier, it disappears into the fog. I chase it, but become completely disoriented. Where am I? What was I looking for? Why did I come here? Then the fog blows aside. I'm standing on the edge of a cliff that drops off into an endless blackness. I can't move my feet. Something's dragging me towards the edge, faster and faster. I dig in my heels, but it does no good. At the last moment, as I start to fall into the abyss, I wake up."

"Brrrr! Okay, enough nightmares," said Judith, moving closer to him on the bench. She pointed to the sky. "Look at that moondog! Make a wish."

Martin felt the poetry of the moment. But far stronger was the ache in his entire body, the need to press her to him, to slowly, rhythmically explode together.

"I already did," he said, starting to unbutton her jeans.

She put her hand on his. "Look, uh, before we go any further, I should tell you I have… a philosophy about this."

"A what?"

"I want us to take a blood test first."

Martin stopped fumbling for the condom he'd carried with him for the last week. "Why? Are you worried about something?"

"No. I'm sure we're both fine. But you know the story: we'd essentially be sleeping with every partner either of us has ever had. If everybody spent the fifteen minutes to get tested, there'd be practically no STDs, let alone AIDS. I love sex, but only once I'm completely at ease. Meantime…" she said, unzipping his pants.

It was hard to contradict such plain speaking, especially coming from someone who could twizzle a dick with such silky, firm hands, which went light and feathery at just the right moments. And who encouraged him to do the same to her. Skillfully postponing his release, she had already come twice by the time he couldn't hold out any longer, shooting a jet of cum onto her forearm with such force that he both heard and felt it hit, a ropy stream connecting their two bodies.

Later, as the starlit sky began to turn pale blue, Judith stroked his cheek. "It's too bad nobody mentions moonrise or moonset anymore. Or morning twilight, just before dawn…" She stopped short. A clattering noise came from a terraced area below the rose garden, where a man was carrying tools and a box of plants. He would have the key to let them out. Just then, a bright orange wedge of sun peeked over the horizon, and they broke into applause.

Maybe everyone her age routinely tests, Martin thought, as they rode the bus to the clinic. Since his last one, taken to get the damn mortgage, he hadn't slept with anybody, so a test wasn't really necessary. But he hadn't kept the papers, and regardless, the point was to do it together: something he'd never have thought of, let alone insisted on, himself. What a boon for worldwide health, though, if everyone acted the way they wished everyone else would act. Kant would approve, though Swanson sure hadn't.

"Hooboy," he'd said, rocking back in his chair, "A demand like that means she either doesn't trust you or has some hangup. I'd run the other way, myself."

"What's wrong with starting off with a clean slate?"

"You think it's because she cares about you?"

"It's an adult position. You're just not used to women like that."

"You watch: she'll have plenty more requirements where that one came from."

Martin ignored the chaff. Maybe it was his naïveté again, but he trusted her. They'd reached some new level since their *fête galante* in the Bois de Boulogne, and this was part of it. Even if her philosophy were only a kind of screening method, he could see nothing to argue with. If a guy bailed rather than endure an unsexy few minutes, how much did he want her, and what kind of person was he?

The testing center was inside a hospital on the north edge of the city, near the *périphérique.* It was a run-down public building, owned by everybody and valued by nobody. The employees had covered the hallway's peeling paint with children's drawings and announcements of upcoming events, yet nothing could mask the seedy, depressing atmosphere — just where healing, education, and counsel were supposed to take place. Did it have to be like this? Deep within any bureaucracy or perhaps above and outside it, there must be a hidden locus of control, an Archimedean point where someone of deep understanding and energy could apply force, as if on an acupuncture point, and initiate a series of adjustments, reconfigure the entire sorry dynamic. A kind of kung-fu bureaucrat who'd monitor the whole organization, kick-start it again before it ran down: perhaps working as part of a small team, quietly doing the same for cities, countries, humanity as a whole…

"You know, I really must like you," sighed Martin, as they took their seats in the *salle d'attente*, filled with worried-looking teens, junkies nodding off, and couples who wordlessly stared straight ahead. Judith leaned her head on his shoulder.

"It's not exactly dancing at the Ritz, but the fact that we're here shows me you care. What's more romantic than that?"

She was right. Ten years ago, during his asshole period, he might have agreed with Swanson. Rude treatment from a string of women had led him to try to be a jerk, acting in ways that made him cringe now. Even when he wanted to be, he wasn't made to do harm. But he was still a sex pig, so it surprised him to be enjoying the dating stuff he used to classify as preliminaries. Maybe adolescence was finally coming to an end. Their age difference had actually made no difference at all. Hell, he sometimes felt like the junior one, the way her politics, ethics, and aesthetics rang out fully formed. Maybe it was a young person's bravado. That's how his vanity tried to categorize it anyway, retouching his own ambivalence and ignorance until they appeared to be maturity and wisdom. Only in coding did he get to the very bottom of things. Years ago he'd had to write the boot code for a new computer — the first instructions executed when it powered on, its equivalent of the Big Bang. In that closed universe, you could iterate until you got it exactly right, unlike the haphazard real universe. When the miracle happened and the system started up correctly, prompting him to log in, he knew that nothing a computer could do would ever feel strange to him again, that any of its enigmas could in principle be solved. In most other domains, he lacked the easy certainty of Judith — or Nadia or Swanson, for that matter. No doubt because he had no long-term purpose or real autonomy or sense of community, and hadn't known how to even start plumbing his own depths…

"*Numéro trois cent douze, s'il vous plaît,*" called out the nurse. The test took minutes, but afterwards she handed them each a slip with a code for anonymity and a phone number to call next week.

"In the U.S.," Judith fumed as they left, "you get your result on the spot. Here, where health care is so much better, it takes a week?"

The worst was over, though, and the days zipped past. Worries did creep in at odd moments: that his previous test results had been mislabeled, that they'd used the wrong needle and infected him instead of testing him. But the good news finally came, and Judith invited him over for a celebration dinner. "Caitlin went to Amsterdam for the weekend," she sing-songed significantly. At seven-thirty sharp, she opened her door in a tight black dress that emphasized all her healthy opulence.

"Hi. Wow."

She smiled and led him to the candlelit table. They lingered over dinner and invented pretexts to prolong dessert, enjoying the erotic tension as long as they could stand it. Finally, after coffee, she said: "I'll be right back. Do you want to choose some music?"

He put on an old bossa nova disc and sat on the sofa. She'd been right about the blood test. That barely conscious, nagging uncertainty he'd always had before sleeping with someone new was gone. What Swanson had so wrongly taken for mistrust in him had been trust that he would trust in her. Near the window lay a coil of rope, one end secured to a stout metal ring on the floor: smart, for a top-floor

apartment whose only exit was a narrow stairway. When she came out
of the bathroom in a kimono, he pointed to it.

"Did you learn to be a cowgirl in L.A.?"

"Oh, the rope? I use it to tie up my slaves."

"I suppose you have several."

"I stopped counting. Once they start to bore me, I have them
thrown on a pile in the dungeon."

"How ungrateful, after all the services they must render."

"They don't have it so bad. A little raw meat every day or two."

"Of course, I cannot join them, since I am all-knowing and all-
masterful."

"But who will rule, if you are the Master and I am she-who-must-
be-obeyed?"

"I hear they have some sort of democracy in France — I guess we'll
have to take turns."

She picked up a scarf and theatrically twisted it into a cord.

"But Mistress," wailed Martin, "I might lose my circulation."

"Not, evidently, in the only place it matters. The rest of you is of
course useless to me."

Laughing, his hands on her waist, he drew her to him so suddenly
they came together with a slap.

Andante.

Allegro.

Presto furioso.

Coda.

Da Capo.

Late the next morning, after a long goodbye, Martin walked home
thinking how she might well change him, this person from so far
outside his usual circle. Back at headquarters, he made coffee, then sat

down at the kitchen table to wait for a prearranged call, from a friend in over his head with some system administration problem. He looked out the window, pleasantly vacant. A text came in: *dinner chez moi Tuesday?* Then another: *I await your answer with baited breath.* He did a double-take. Baited? God, he thought, please let it be a joke or a typo. Don't kill my beautiful dream. To ask her, though, would be lead-footed. He thumbed his reply:

I'm sure it will be worth the weight.

Her answer came immediately: *Don't worry, I never let my efforts go to waist.*

Relieved, he cradled the phone as if it were a little bar of joy. From the hall came voices and clattering, then Swanson and Sébastien barged in, wearing tennis whites.

"I kicked his ass — hah!" Swanson announced.

"May it make up for your humiliation of last time," replied Sébastien, in a falsetto Bollywood accent, "when the arse of you was so ener-ge-ti-cally kicked by me."

"I don't believe in the past."

They set down their gear, poured out some orange juice and sat at the kitchen table.

"You," said Sébastien, knitting his brows and leaning closer to inspect Martin, "you seem so... Zen."

"I can guess," said Swanson.

Martin smiled.

"Ah, we are talking about a *chaude lapine*?" Sébastien leered.

"I'm interested in far more than the merely physical," Martin replied loftily, "Unlike you clowns."

Swanson sheeshed. "Fine, Baba Dingdong."

"You don't understand," Martin said, before stopping short. He didn't have the words to describe his state, and if he had, pronouncing them just now would only tarnish it. Even the sexual part: how to explain to these guys, whose mindset was so different from his, the erotic charge of a woman who, instead of thinking brilliant thoughts or working on her thesis, chose to have sex with him? What came out was: "She reads the dictionary."

Sébastien made a face. "*Hein?*"

"I do believe I detect the mating call of the buff-throated nerdlet," cried Swanson. "I could've predicted it. Oh, wait — I already did."

Martin raised his coffee cup. "I owe it all to you."

"This is that American girl at the party? The one who cock-blocked me?" sniffed Sébastien. "Bah, you're just hanging out with her because you're afraid I'll make you approach some French girls."

Before he could respond, Martin's business call came. He grabbed a printout of the faulty program and began pacing around the main room.

"No, you have to invert it: bang twiddle space dollar foo. Oh, okay. In that case, change the next line to dollar foo space hat space dollar bar. No, *hat* — you know, shark fin... uh, whaddya call it, circumflex. Yeah. Then shove the result into an associative array and pop it when you get a match."

Sébastien turned to Swanson. "I thought I understood English. What the hell is he saying?"

"It's programmer-speak. If you think that's bad, you should go to one of their parties. It sounds like a roomful of people reciting the frickin' Martian phone book."

Chapter Fifteen

The Dendroid and Jones-Wolff teams sat on opposite ends of the room, talking among themselves in low voices, biding their time until the main event. Today, in theory, was Duncan's deposition. Assuming he aced it, Dendroid's suit would collapse like a fallen soufflé. The JW people didn't look so sure. Having canned him a year ago, they now needed him to come through, and he was over an hour late. Probably just to fuck with them, smiled Swanson. Who knew, though? Dendroid's lawyers were certainly not taking any chances. When they finally localized Duncan, they'd yanked Swanson back from Europe on a single day's notice. Talk about *Paris interruptus*.

Dendroid had the initiative for now. In the discovery phase they'd presented emails from Duncan, who'd assured them up to the very last minute that the deal was theirs. Then a subpoena had forced Jones-Wolff to cough up their internal emails, which showed Duncan saying the same to his own partners. Only at the last minute had he reversed course, citing 'market factors' and their competitor Helladyne's unspecified 'technical leverage.' Still, no hard evidence had materialized. Was it bizarre? Yes. In contradiction with the results of JW's own vetting process? That, too. But no evidence of proprietary Dendroid information divulged or specific intent to defraud.

Swanson, fighting off sleep in the airless room, sat as straight as possible, drawing caricatures of the other side's lawyers. If it rattled the bastards, so much the better. From time to time they'd glance over, perhaps wondering what he was up to. Mostly they checked their phones. Finally, the door opened. A murmur of dismay went through the JW side. In walked Duncan, disheveled, unsteady, looking pasty, red-eyed — a bad flash photograph. Swanson's stomach turned to ice. Duncan had been so confident in that café, so sure it would be trivial to stonewall these people. But that was just one more IOU to himself, a promise of strength and honor, like so many others he must've made over these last couple years. Half-believing them, maybe, long after his ability to redeem had evaporated, one self-betrayal at a time. Back in the day, you could not get a word out of him unless he felt like giving it. That was Old Duncan. It took Kyle's lawyer around two minutes to peel New Duncan open like a can of tuna. What market factors, the lawyer asked, motivated such an about-face at the last minute? Duncan shifted back and forth. He couldn't recall exactly. Couldn't recall, when it was a matter of ten million dollars? Well, he'd done other deals since then; the specifics had gotten a little fuzzy. What were Helladyne's supposed technical advantages over Dendroid? Hard to say, it was just a feeling. Corporate emails indicate he hadn't even justified his decision to his own management, had he? No, guess not.

The answers got more and more improbable. Finally Duncan banged his head a couple times on the desk and wailed that it was all his fault. The stenographer sat there stunned, momentarily forgetting to type. Kyle's open-mouth stare slowly morphed into a huge grin. He and the entire Dendroid table except for Swanson were beaming. Their lead lawyer held out his hands, palms ceiling-ward: no more questions necessary. A Jones-Wolff flunky escorted Duncan to a chair at the back of the room, where he collapsed into a chair, apparently dead to the world. Their lead lawyer furiously typed on his laptop, then stood up and said: "I have a few questions for Mister Geach."

A little shock went through Swanson. Then he thought: sure, okay. Not that there's anything I can add to what they just saw. While the court clerk put Swanson under oath, the lawyer paced back and forth in a stagey, practiced way, pulling at his red suspenders, smoothing his already immobile helmet of hair. His sing-song delivery had an annoying nasal edge.

"Are you close friends with Mr. Shipley?" He indicated Duncan.

Not exactly the optimum circumstances for that to come out. The Dendroid side buzzed.

"What does that have to do —"

"Just answer the question, please," rapped out the lawyer.

"We belonged to the same fraternity in school."

"Mr. Shipley's cell phone records show that you repeatedly called him, even after capital allocation had been awarded to another enterprise."

So the bastards had been investigating Duncan themselves. Well, so what? Everybody knew now what had gone down. And they hadn't found out from him.

"Yes, I wanted —"

"Which certainly has a very suspicious character to it."

Swanson started, suddenly aware of what this weasel was trying to do. He glared at his side's lawyer, who mumbled an objection. But the tide in the room had turned. The entire Dendroid team was staring at him, apparently ready, after Duncan's discombobulation and the revelation of their friendship, to believe anything. And there was no judge to rein in this slanderous bastard. Swanson sat tall and put on a bored, impassive expression, all the while thinking feverishly. To stop the proceedings in order to get his own lawyer would look terrible. Besides, there was nothing to hide! The JW lawyer, sensing the momentum shift, flushed and licked his lips.

"Did you make a wire transfer to France soon after the collapse of your company?"

What the hell? Well, no point in denying it, if he's already dug that up.

"Yes."

"A very considerable transfer, wasn't it?"

The words came whizzing across the room like poison darts whose source would hear no reason, nor let him remain silent. This was slipping away.

"Would you care to tell us what it was for?" He went on.

The Dendroid counsel finally woke up and objected. But to Swanson it seemed worse to let that insinuation hang in the air.

"The down payment on an apartment."

"Really! Right after your company failed, moving a large sum of money to a foreign country. That is very interesting timing."

Kyle's lawyer made another token intervention — almost as if he wanted to hear this bullshit! Duncan raised his head and yelled from the back that Swanson had not been involved, which just made things look worse. Someone ushered him out.

"What would I gain," Swanson raised his voice, "by what you are trying to —"

"I think that speaks for itself. No more questions."

The Jones-Wolff lawyer sat down, visibly satisfied. No doubt he'd just saved his client a huge pile of dough — the out-of-court settlement might be cut in half or even eliminated altogether. Just when things had looked their worst, after that body blow from their own dumbass former employee, he'd pulled it out of the fire. His partner leaned over and made a poorly-hidden, obscene gesture of male dominance. A night of steak, cigars, single-malt whisky, and strippers was surely ahead.

Swanson sat there, shellshocked. They had no proof, but at this discovery stage they didn't need it. The pre-trial jockeying for position was all a poker game, a matter of perception, and he couldn't prove a negative. The Dendroid people filed out as one, not even looking at him. That night, he received a curt email informing him he was disinvited, "under the circumstances," from further meetings of the legal team. The rumor was no doubt all over the Valley by now. Those few minutes had put a stink on him that would take years to wear off, if it ever did.

Part Three

Chapter Sixteen

Caitlin sat cross-legged on Judith's sofa-bed, her clothes scattered around the floor as if they'd been shot out of a cannon. She put down her fashionable novel of magical realism, leaving the bookmark on page three, where it had been since she arrived.

"I leave in a couple more days," she announced, "I *need* to go to the Louvre."

The subtext being "we need to go." Martin glanced across the kitchen table at Judith, who'd reddened. Just last night she'd confessed to feeling guilty that with the two of them spending so much time together, she'd neglected her cuz. She quickly responded:

"We'll take you — my treat."

Caitlin put on her jacket. "Cool," she said, then left without another word. That was her way. At first Martin assumed it was because she disliked him. But she behaved the same toward her cousin. Judith took her dishes to the sink. "I want to give her some kind of sendoff. Why don't you invite Swanson? I'm not sure I like him, but I think she does."

Martin grunted noncommittally. He hadn't explained the lawsuit disaster yet, since he didn't know exactly what had happened himself. To ask Swanson for details might be problematic. Even in normal times it was hard to tell when he might want to blow off steam about something and when he'd bark at you for bringing it up. "I dunno. He's kind of been in a foul mood since he came back," he said.

As he got up for more coffee, Martin considered the state of harmony among his friends. It shouldn't matter so much, but he couldn't help himself. He got uneasy, even physically, when they didn't get along, so he'd keep watch, ready to smooth over any conflicts. An afternoon at the museum might cheer Swanson up after all, change his mind about Caitlin, reintroduce him to Judith, show each how cool the other was. "I'll work on him," he added. "Just don't expect me to talk much to your cousin."

She laughed. "You are so mean! I wouldn't have even met you if she hadn't dragged me to that party."

"You remember how well it went last time I tried." He imitated Caitlin, hands on hips: "I am, like, *fiercely* intelligent. My life's going a mile a minute! People are too slow for a multi-track mind like mine!"

Then there was the mini-imbroglio over music. Caitlin admitted that she downloaded all her tunes for free; or rather, stated it baldly, as if it were a birthright. As a former active musician, few attitudes so easily got Martin's goat. Snarfing a song here and there, okay, but not *everything*. One day he'd brought it up, curious to hear her justification. She'd impatiently given the stock answer, no doubt borrowed from someone in her coterie: "The tunes are already out there. One download more or less won't matter."

From now on it would be her ilk — not reviewers or even media conglomerates — who'd dictate how most musicians would or wouldn't make a living. The record companies, unable to parry the threat of mass digital piracy by such otherwise law-abiding folk, had fallen on their collective sword, selling off rights to their catalogues for a pittance. A bonanza for the consumers of 'content,' brutal for its producers. He pressed on, knowing she would only hear it as one might a mosquito's whine.

"Just because you can take stuff doesn't mean it's cool. What if it were your music being copied? Instead of making a living, now you don't. Why should bands create new music when everyone will just take it for nothing? Unless they're at the top of the pyramid, they'll starve. You're killing off what you claim to enjoy."

Which, come to think of it, would be good riddance for the shit you listen to, he thought. One-finger keyboard riffs, looped endlessly… How would you like it if I yelled the same phrase at you for five minutes without stopping? But her willful little smile told him further argument was futile. Rather than poison the atmosphere, he'd kept his distance from her, waiting for that happy day when she'd pack her giant pink suitcases and skedaddle back to Encino.

"It'll be a couple hours, tops," Judith was saying, "You guys can branch off if you want. What about that other friend of yours? I practically had to drag her away from him at the party."

"Sébastien?" Martin gave a short laugh. "Uh, he's great, but when it comes to women the man is a cad. A bounder. Don't say I didn't warn you."

"Scratch that, then. I doubt André will come, either. It was already a miracle he liked you."

"I wonder what possessed him to do such a thing."

"Oh, stop. It's just that he's not exactly Mr. Sociable. He said you seem to be someone who actually gets stuff done, which is high praise, from him. But with Caitlin…" she trailed off, thinking: no, I won't even ask him. Whenever she brought up her cousin, André's only response was that lethal Parisian syllable: "Bof."

Swanson finished a sketch and glided it on the pile with the others: the lone cactus on the windowsill, the half-closed cupboard door that seemed to be guarding secrets, Martin's goddamn dirty dishes in the sink, stacked far higher in the drawing than in reality. He got up to make his third coffee. This return to Paris had been the plan since before the Dendroid lawsuit. But it was only supposed to have been an interlude: help Martin out some, retrace the visit he had made with his dad years ago, party hard enough to really blow out the tubes, then head back to the Valley, to the company he'd start, or the wounded one he'd turn around, or the dog he'd pretty up and sell. All that was in ruins since the deposition disaster. Those last couple weeks in California confirmed his worst fears. Contact after contact had been too busy to see him; headhunters who'd formerly been ready to blow him took their sweet time returning his calls. The worst was running into friends who'd *heard* and wanted to either commiserate or to hover around him, asking what he was up to lately, like pigeons circling a freshly washed statue.

The Moka pot sputtered, then went silent. Swanson turned off the burner and filled his cup. It was hard not to feel bitter, especially when Duncan, who'd realized on the spot the damage he'd done, had since gone incommunicado again. Presumably he'd given up even trying to stay in the working world and was back in Vegas. Tragic, but what could anybody do about it? Swanson took his place at the table. He knew himself. His rare loyalties extended just so far. Once some limit within him had been exceeded he'd go stone cold, and all bets were off. He was just about there.

He faced his chair in the opposite direction. Taking a fresh sheet of paper, he scanned the room again, eyes half-closed, trying to forget the previous attempts, to view the room from a new angle. He'd been drawing every day since that lucky occurrence in the *architecte*'s waiting room. It was the only thing he'd felt like doing. Without false modesty — and what would be the point of that — he was far surpassing what he'd achieved as a kid. Not just hand-eye coordination. Years of deal-making had honed his awareness of what made people tick, their tell-tale gestures. Plus, he now had the patience to push himself, to take the most difficult, unexpected approach to a subject. If it didn't work out, he'd fix what had gone wrong, and be that much stronger for the next one. Therapeutic, you might say — not that he cared to analyze it. If he'd learned anything from his siblings, it was that explanations were bullshit. Who cared why art attracted him again, or whether it was compensating for the state of his career? When your what and how were good enough, you didn't need to worry about why. A shame his old man wasn't here to see the results, though.

Hearing Martin come in, he felt the familiar impulse to hide what wasn't ready to show, even though Martin was so not an art person that it was like not having a witness or critic at all. But there wasn't enough time to put any of it away.

"Wow! Fantastic," Martin exclaimed, leafing through the pile. "I haven't seen anything you've done since eighth grade or so."

"There hasn't been anything."

"Speaking of art, can I interest you in a trip to the Louvre? Me 'n Judith are taking your former goddess on a farewell bucket list checkoff."

"Caitlin? That ditz? She's still around?"

Martin explained.

Swanson finished his coffee. "Sure, why not. I'll split off at some point and look at the stuff I want to, though."

"No prob," Martin started cleaning his glasses, which usually meant he had something on his mind. Finally he came out with it. "Don't you want to get back at Kyle and the rest of them for what happened?"

"Oh, I will," Swanson said tightly. "No amnesty." He'd been robbed — first literally by those unknown thugs, then figuratively of his rightful place in the Valley hierarchy. A cynic might say it was punishment for his loyalty, when it would have been so easy to throw Duncan under the bus, long before the deposition. But he couldn't have foreseen the way that had turned out. "Just not yet," he continued. "I'm not in a position to do jack shit right now."

"So what's the program? You hanging here for a while?"

"Not too long." He paused. Ever since he was a little kid he'd had a plan A, B, and C — probably to ward off the way he felt now, without one: naked and empty. No momentum, nothing to show the world. Just one to-do. "Did I tell you about the trip I took with my dad just after high school?"

"Yeah, where'd you guys go again? Amsterdam?"

"Plus Bruges, Prague, and some others. He was doing research for a book, and took me along so I could see Europe. Just before he died, he made me promise to revisit those places. And at the moment my schedule seems to be wide open."

"Why can't they just call it the Mona Lisa," sniffed Caitlin as they followed the signs for *La Joconde*, "like everybody else?"

Swanson elbowed Martin, who jostled back without changing expression. As they reached the grand staircase, all of them spontaneously gazed up at the Winged Victory of Samothrace, which dominated its surroundings, physically and spiritually. The stone seemed to breathe, to be part of a higher life than that of the tourists who scrambled around below it taking pictures, listening to their guides, poring over maps. A big-bellied man in a tracksuit approached the base, knocked on it, then walked away, apparently satisfied.

Swanson recalled his father's remark: "That sculpture is more alive than ninety-nine percent of the people who will ever look at it." At the top of the stairs, he tried — in vain, as always — to discover the secret of that mesmerizing light he'd only seen just there, which came from all directions and nowhere in particular. When they reached the Grande Gallerie, he stopped at the triptych by Carlo Braccesco. He especially liked the right-hand panel, where one saint casually conversed with another, who had a knife plunged in his heart and a meat cleaver stuck in his head, hands parallel to the floor. Martin mimicked the pose, to general laughter: "Everything's coooool, Daddy-o. Catch you on the flippity flop."

They trailed along behind Swanson, who knew just what he wanted to see. Judith had studied enough art history to be surprised by which paintings drew him and which he hardly glanced at.

"Not a Raphael fan?" she said.

"Meh — too sugary most of the time."

Martin, his arm around Judith's waist, added: "Swanson's shit list of artists is a mile long."

"True," admitted Swanson, "although Raphael's not really on it." He turned again to the haloed madonna with two infants, then shrugged. "Still… it's too harmonious." He turned toward the *Virgin of the Rocks* on the opposite wall, ignored by most sightseers in their hurry to do the Louvre. "It's the opposite with Leonardo. He's got this intense communication going on between every element in the picture…"

Caitlin loudly clicked her tongue and sighed. She was the one leaving, after all, who had things to see. Judith put her arm around her. "Don't worry, sweetie. Mona's up next."

"Okay, you guys have fun," said Swanson curtly, adding as he walked off: "See you at the Venus de Milo in an hour." He had a particular painting to revisit, and wasn't about to cast more pearls before swine, or listen to remarks on the long wait or how small Mona seemed or that omigod her eyes really did follow you.

The Dutch wing was almost empty. Nothing to distract him from the Rembrandt that had been on his mind for months now: a rich brown and gold self-portrait, painted when the artist had already begun to suffer career reversals, deaths in the family. Swanson had seen it before, but was mesmerized all over again. The wrinkle between the eyebrows, the mouth that subtly shifted between sadness, pride, disillusion. That piercing gaze: are we only here to suffer? To lose our youth, our health, our loved ones, then disappear? The secrets of that expression, Swanson mused, might well be in the box he'd brought to

Paris. His dad had willed the contents — full of unpublished papers — not to the academic siblings, surprisingly, but to him. And the little he'd skimmed so far had been devoted to Rembrandt: notes on exhibits and private collections, outlines for unwritten books, analyses of paintings. Maybe there'd also be an explanation of why he'd been willed the box and why his dad had insisted that Swanson retrace the trip they'd taken to Europe years ago. Was it his way of encouraging his business-minded son to reconnect with art, or even, wild as it sounded, to turn those notes into a book?

For a long while Swanson stood unmoving, taking in the composition, the pattern of brush strokes, of light and shade. Every time he thought he'd grasped the essence, another look convinced him of another interpretation. Of course he could have checked the box for notes on this painting, but he'd wanted to look for himself first. Remembering a trick his father had taught him, he held up one hand to mask off one half of the face, then the other. That clarified everything: one eye was anguished, the other, wide open, looked straight ahead without flinching — a contrast that kept the portrait in constant motion. Oblivious to anyone else, he started nodding at the painting, agreeing with it, wanting to break out laughing. This felt big, like obtaining a password, and not only to this portrait. His watch beeped: time to meet the others. Blowing them off was an option, but he'd reached a good stopping point. Best to leave on a high note, have a place to start when he came back, after studying his dad's archives, after the trip.

He ran into them on the way. Just watching how they moved through the museum got on his nerves. Mostly it was Caitlin, although she behaved no differently than other vacationers: talking at top volume, barely breaking stride as she snapped photos of the name plaques, never the art itself. When they reached the Venus, she took her selfies, then had Judith snap more of her posing in front of the statue. Judith indulged her; Martin, indulging Judith, said nothing. It seemed to Swanson that the statue, whose somewhat heavy-jawed features were far from the conventional idea of a Venus, gazed beyond the buzzing crowd, beyond life on Earth for that matter.

As Judith handed back the camera, Caitlin said: "I don't see what's so great about art. I'd rather have a photo."

Swanson bit his lip, thinking: a few weeks ago, I would have said and done any fool thing in order to sleep with you. Now I just want to put tape over your mouth. Then it shot out of him like a cannonball: "What you should worry about is being worthy to look at it. Too bad the people who ought to be embarrassed by themselves never are."

"Hey!" Judith shot back. "Play nice."

Caitlin stiffened, then stormed off in tears. Judith went after her, frowning at Swanson over her shoulder.

Even Martin was surprised. "Sheesh, I know she's kind of a pain, but still…"

Swanson gave the slightest shrug, his expression unchanged. "Some people are too stupid to listen to. If you let them keep yammering, you might as well have agreed with them."

"Maybe, but why go off on her when she's obviously clueless?"

"Why hide what you think from somebody who doesn't matter? Anyway, she'll probably look back on it in a few years and thank me."

The taxi driver was hefting Caitlin's last suitcase into the trunk as she and Judith exchanged teary goodbyes on the sidewalk. Martin's arrival was met with only a glare. He waved ironically as the taxi pulled away.

"Your best friend is a jerk," said Judith as they walked up the stairs to her place.

Martin ran his hand through his hair. "Uh, sorry about that. He can be kinda cold sometimes."

"How come you hang out with him?"

"I think he's just going through a lot right now," said Martin. It pained Martin to realize he'd only given his friend the most basic condolences about his father. At the time, the right words hadn't come, even though he'd really liked Swanson's dad. Now it was far too late. The last words he could say, so long after the fact, were: "I know how you feel," especially since he, having lost no one, didn't.

"It concerns me that you just accept whatever he does," Judith said.

"He's not like that with me. Whenever I see him lay into people, they usually have it coming."

"Even a kid who was just talking off the top of her head? He's sharp and knowledgeable, but there's something nasty in him."

"His delivery wasn't the greatest. At the same time, you have to admit her remark was pretty dumbass."

"You're just saying that because it was Caitlin. Personally, I think you blame her for stuff you feel guilty about yourself."

"How so?"

"I remember thinking that when you were explaining the ways technology enables negative trends. When bookstores fail or people become slaves to their phones or musicians are ripped off or movies get copied, I suspect you feel like you somehow helped the wrong side. She and her friends are just the symptoms, though."

"Maybe," said Martin. "But it makes me crazy to hear 'everything should be free' from people who don't create anything themselves. Anyway, my biggest problem with Caitlin is that she never gets called on her shit. I mean, after so many weeks of inconveniencing you, did she so much as buy you a little gift?"

Silence.

"Did she ever clean up after herself," Martin went on, "or offer to help you in any way?"

"No," Judith admitted. "Still, people shouldn't appoint themselves judge and jury."

"Swanson's taking off soon, if that's any comfort."

"So he helps you for a few days, then bails. Actually, that's good news. I've decided he gives me the creeps."

Looking for a place to mark the advent of the big three-five, Swanson had discovered that his favorite Irish pub from the old Paris days, near the Place de la Concorde, still existed. Its rich wood paneling, polished chrome beer taps, and noisy Saturday night crowd seemed to be the only things that hadn't changed since that time. He nudged Sébastien.

"What was the name of that crazy bartender who used to work here?"

"Titus."

"That's it. Man, feels like a couple lifetimes ago."

Sébastien signaled for another round. "Let's kill a few more brain cells so we won't remember how long it's been."

Swanson knocked back the last of his bourbon. "I am so not ready for this."

"That's what I said last year. I'm still trying to get it out of my system. Thirty-five is somebody else's age."

Birthdays had always sucked, ever since childhood. The low-grade ennui would start a week before, peak on the day itself, then taper off a few days after. But even thirty had been easier than this one, made worse by his dad's passing and the Duncan disaster. Maybe by the next big milestone he'd be numb to it, and the rest of the five-year markers would fall noiselessly until the end.

From the large group standing behind them came bursts of laughter. Someone was telling duck-in-a-bar jokes. That time of night. Martin had begged off hours ago, after just one drink. He drank a lot less and was in general not as much fun as he used to be. At least he'd provided comic relief at the restaurant. Fine dining had apparently not formed a part of his Paris experience, since at the end he asked for a doggy bag. Their *garçon* hadn't even understood at first. *"Pardon? Un petit sac?"* Martin pointed at the half-eaten turkey leg, then at the door. The waiter retreated for a long confab with his tuxedoed colleagues, who whispered and gesticulated in the corner. The head waiter came over and murmured discreetly: "We can give you something, but please take it out under your jacket." Then looked bewildered when the three friends all cracked up. Anyway, Martin was too lovestruck at the moment to get what Swanson was going through. And while Sébastien did, he didn't understand how important career could be. He felt no need whatsoever to shine, to be indispensable, or to compete, except in the seduction department.

Better, Swanson decided as Sébastien wandered off to the head, to think things through on his own. Did this open-ended trip to Europe amount to an admission of failure? Not at all. If his career was a smoking ruin, it was because Duncan had run off the rails, not through some fundamental error of his own. His fine-tuned life strategy had not been proved wrong. When he controlled events, the escalator pretty much went straight up. Take the apartment project: the euro was stronger, the dollar weaker; property values in Paris were rising, all in the last year. Even if there had been no renters at all, they'd already made a pile of loot. As for the future, he'd reinvent himself somehow. There'd always be something for him here in Paris, if he wanted. Though he didn't, really. Not when he thought of his friends at the apartment launch party. He'd have to trade in favors, start off in a lower tier of a big organization while his former co-workers deigned to help him from on high. The bigger, silent problem was time: running, running… Not death, which he could never make real to himself, but old age. He often caught himself envisioning its consequences: arms that would shrivel or go flabby, wrinkles, spots, fucking ear-hair. Gradual weakness. Illness. Immobility. Maybe Alzheimer's — another kind of death. That, too, was hard to look at directly. Could thinking reveal what it was like to be unable to think? Martin might've shed light on that, if he hadn't gone home. As Sébastien sat back down, Swanson turned and grabbed him by the lapels.

"What's your plan, then?" he demanded.

"Uh, to carry on?" said Sébastien. "What are we talking about?"

"Here we are, in the sweet spot of life, all the prerequisites nailed down. Are you happy?"

"Within my limits," Sébastien replied, serious now. "I do what I enjoy, without taking my pulse every hour. If you try to squeeze things or people too hard, they never measure up to your imagination. That is my only fortune-cookie wisdom for today."

Swanson sat mutely for a while, saturated by liquor and his maudlin frame of mind. But his thoughts did not stop. Love wasn't the problem. It wasn't even on the horizon, not with the whole rest of his life so unclear. Once he was ready, he'd find the one he needed, just as he always had. Yet, how much longer would he be able to seduce women in their early twenties? Did he even still want to? When would he start chasing their mothers?

"Take Caitlin —" he started.

"I did," interrupted Sébastien, to cheer him up. "Don't worry, you missed exactly nothing."

"You didn't really, did you?" One couldn't always tell with Sébastien, who offered up the truth every so often, in order to legitimize the rest.

"No, although I was getting close. Which reminds me that Caitlin let one thing slip: you should watch out for her cousin."

"Judith?"

"Yeah, I don't think she fully appreciates your unique gifts."

"Ah." If she'd said that before the museum episode, it must be serious now. "Good to know." Well, the hell with her. Martin could do better than some pretentious chick whose thesis would molder in obscure libraries, who'd have to scramble for a spot at some podunk university.

The rhythm of the evening changed. The giant mirror behind the bar reflected a funhouse version of the crowd and the street outside. It all blended together, a kaleidoscope tilting into one configuration after another. The bartender yelled out something. The duck-in-the-bar people rushed forward, shouting, crowding him. Money was slapped down. The bartender became a blur. Then they were on the sidewalk. Swanson returned to his earlier theme. "Is this all there is? You're telling me you don't think about it at all?"

Sébastien didn't answer. Swanson walked on, hands jammed in his pockets. Cold out here. Could be he really did need a new direction. Not that he'd get any help from others. They didn't understand him, while he could see through them all. To wait awhile, maybe, then try the Valley again. More money, more influence. Or, on the contrary, take himself off the grid entirely… Or get married… So many friends had by now, whether they'd plunged, drifted, or been emotionally swindled into it. Now and then they'd invite him over for dinner. But at some point in the evening it always became clear that he was being viewed not as himself, but as the archetype of a Bachelor: an irresponsible entity, daemonic even — as his siblings would have it — who'd only bring discord into his friend's magic domestic circle. With the implication that unless he settled down and became One Of Them, like a bad sci-fi movie, he would grow shaggy, wild, an Ancient Mariner doomed to slog on and on, wandering the outskirts of all decent society…

"All I need is a damn albatross," his cry echoed back at him. He looked down the street, then turned around. He was alone.

Chapter Seventeen

Jerome peered over his menu. "So who is this person? Do I want to meet her?"

"Oh, just somebody we started working with recently," Martin said. They'd been talking about film when he'd dropped Nadia's name, and Jerome had latched right on to it. "She's apparently done some documentaries, knows lots of people, has some funny stories. I dunno, maybe you'd get a kick out of her."

"Why not give her a call and see if she'll join us?"

Martin dialed her, wondering, now that it was too late, if this was such a good idea. You never knew what might happen, putting people together. Jerome had been their first and most valued guest, especially under the circumstances. In the chaotic, dread-filled weeks after 9/11, the whole apartment venture had begun to look like a Really Bad Idea. Geopolitical storm clouds gathering, Franco-American relations in the toilet… who would visit Paris? Then, after the air travel ban was lifted, Jerome somehow found their half-finished website and stayed not the expected week or two, but three months. He shrugged off the broken radiator, stuck windows, and many other hiccups of those early days, even apologizing for being so picky. Martin, taking care of everything at the time, naturally got to hear Jerome's story: the prestigious law partnership, the twenty-five year marriage that had spontaneously combusted, and the escape to Paris, done more or less on a whim. Now, his divorce finalized and professional obligations wrapped up, Jerome was back for another long visit.

He ordered in his bad but enthusiastic French. "If you're gonna make mistakes," he liked to say, "Make 'em with authority." That seemed to be his motto in general. Though very *distingué* — tall, thin, grey hair neatly parted, always wearing a suit — he'd jumped into Parisian life with far more energy than Martin: attended mixers, dated women from all over the social spectrum, lectured at the American Library, conversed in cafés with random people. Nadia was a natural for his collection of types. What the hell, Martin thought as he thumbed in Nadia's number. After all, she had gotten it together somewhat, made her place more renter-friendly, filled out all the paperwork. As of last week her apartment had gone live on the website.

Half an hour later, she waltzed in. "*Hello*, Jerome," she exhaled, extending her hand high enough to allow it to be kissed, though not so high as to constitute a demand that might be refused. He hesitated, unclear on matters of old-world etiquette, then opted for the kiss. She sat next to Jerome, gazing at him raptly. It reminded Martin of Swanson's old spiel when he wined and dined an important customer: "You are *the most important person in the universe* to me." She wasted no time, perhaps a result of her training in thirty-second elevator encounters with the famous and capricious who filled her brochure. Jerome was nobody's fool, but his eyes were starting to shine. Martin vaguely wished he hadn't suggested this. It is always gratifying, she went on, to speak with cultured Americans, who instinctively know true value when they see it. The Parisians are such slaves to fashion... The States are better for a creative film-maker. You mean, you're interested in film, too? Living here for now? All alone? What a shame. Yet freedom does bring certain advantages. Why yes, a plate of *macarons* would be delightful...

Saying goodbye to them, Martin smiled wanly — the same expression, it occurred to him, that the owner of that antique store had worn the day he met Nadia.

From the Place de la Madeleine, he walked to the Seine and stopped short. It was too soon to go home, with Judith at the library researching her thesis, hours of daylight left, and no apartment issues or coding deadlines. He decided to play a game he'd invented in the early days here, a dawdling, piecemeal way to construct his own Paris: choose a visible but far-off destination, then walk there, if possible by taking streets he didn't know. He opted for the Panthéon, an embarrassing place not to have visited yet. He crossed to the left bank, where the challenging network of small, non-Hausmannian streets forced him to detour or backtrack often to avoid familiar paths. The whole game probably indicated a mild case of OCD. He'd been one of those who skipped over sidewalk cracks in grade school, even feeling uncomfortable when someone else — Swanson was a frequent culprit — purposely tromped on them. His phone buzzed, showing an unfamiliar California number.

"Hey, Martin, glad I caught you."

It took a moment to recognize the voice: a headhunter he hadn't seen in five years. "Rodney. Long time."

"How's Paris, you lucky dog?" Not waiting for an answer or explaining how he'd gotten Martin's Paris cellphone number, he drove on. "Listen, I have a very hot prospect I wanted to run by you: VP of data warehousing. Your team would design a tool for slicing, dicing, and 3D visual analysis of huge data cubes. You'd run the show, with full hiring discretion."

"Sounds interesting, but —"

"Hey, I respect you for breaking free for a little while, but we're dying out here for proven talent, not just warm bodies to fill seats. You sure you want to stay away so long?" asked Rodney, apparently forgetting that Martin was a lucky dog. "You've been out of the game more than a year, which around here…"

"Is like five. I know, that's why I'm not there. I'm diversifying my inner portfolio."

"What?"

"Nothing."

"Got another one this morning," Rodney went on, "Ground floor opportunity. A distributed computing play: super hot space. CTO position, hefty base salary, plus five percent of the company —"

"What about dilution?" Martin asked reflexively.

"You beat me to it: executives get a non-dilution clause."

"Yowzers. They funded yet?"

"The angel round just closed. They almost jizzed when they saw your resumé."

"I'm flattered you thought of me, Rodney. I'll consider it for sure."

After some small talk, Martin hung up. Maybe he was an idiot after all, indulging himself in Paris with diddly-ass consulting work, when he could use his one indisputable skill for all the financial reward and creative freedom he wanted. Either of Rodney's offers could make a career.

The Panthéon was closed by the time he finally got there. His feet were killing him. A few blocks downhill, in the Jardin du Luxembourg, there'd be a shady place to sit. He followed the proud black iron fence, crowned by gold-tipped arrows, around the curving street to the gate on the rue de Vaugirard. Crunching along the gravel path, he looked for a seat by the Medici Fountain, with its long pool of dark-emerald water, choked by lily pads. No empty chairs there, or under the trees. Finally he found one on the semi-circular path that girdled the back garden of the Palais and sat down.

A crying child ran past, chasing an escaped balloon. As the bright red spot floated up and away on the late afternoon breeze, Martin's stomach began to tingle. Without warning, the perpetual cocktail party in his mind — obsessive monologues, snatches of music, imagined situations — faded into silence, as suddenly as if a hand, operating beyond his will or awareness, had turned down the volume. An indescribably restful feeling. Birdsong, leaves rustling in the wind, passing conversations: a symphony he alone seemed to hear, freely resonating inside him. His solar plexus relaxed; breathing became free and easy. Gone was his usual grasping self, which polluted whatever it touched with its sense of me, me, me: what he imagined others thought of him, his judgments of them, the constant narrating and revising of the incidents that made up his tiny world. All that was not him and never had been. It only blocked or muffled what was really happening.

Behind the trees the sun winked, its broken light dancing across the garden's geometrical neatness. The broad footpath, bordered by manicured trees and bushes, swung out in an arc, its rhythm established by huge, evenly spaced flower urns. Water sparkled in the fountain. And people strolled through this magic garden, talking in low voices amongst themselves, unaware that they existed. Time unrolled horizontally, as it were. Yet perpendicular to it was a timeless, strangely familiar vertical dimension, emanating from some unseen, radiant center: vibrating yet still. Just then a cloud of birds wheeled, blocking the sun, then uncovered it again in a blinding flash, an exclamation point of pure light.

Bliss… Yet almost too far from the shore. If he could only divide himself, stay at this level and at the same time get some distance, ponder the enigmatic force of what was happening in and around him. Thoughts came, but without words: could you be this way at will, despite the parasitic tide of events that clawed at you, diluted your will, distracted you from yourself? How to hold onto this state or even describe it? Then, just as grace had come, he sensed it escaping. Unable to stop it, he felt ego creeping back in, co-opting the experience: I'm so far above everyone; if they could feel what I'm feeling, they would find me so spiritual, would beg me to teach them… Cheap thoughts that moments ago had had no power over him began to stick to him again, like metal filings to a magnet. He roused himself, pulled a flyer out of his pocket that someone had given him on the street. He had to record what he could, right now: in minutes, even the memory would be gone or deformed. He scribbled all that came to mind — light, birdsong, silence, vertical — unsure it would mean anything tomorrow.

As twilight fell, he stood and began to walk. Except for a residual glow he felt like his usual self again, whatever that meant. In the past he'd tried various drugs, dabbled in meditation, read philosophy — nothing had prepared him for this. He vaguely remembered that when Hume looked within, he found no self, just a bundle of perceptions. But in the Luxembourg there'd been a watcher or rather a watch*ing*, and it was not some fantasy cobbled together from external impressions. The lack of friction he'd felt between inside and outside could only mean that both were part of some unified, unimaginably complex pattern.

"You look different," said Judith when Martin got home.

He gave her a long, silent hug. When he separated, she said: "Is everything okay?"

He tried to recount what happened. In vague metaphors, at first: an empty mirror, reflecting all while retaining nothing; a periscope rising above the water. Those astonishing first few seconds of liftoff, like in a dream of flying. Then the way his ego, that suit of armor, had attached itself to him again. She probed, listened, waited while he wrote down details he'd forgotten. He felt a surge of almost painful love for her, the way she teased out the different aspects of his magical experience, sensing its importance despite his feeble retelling.

"What do you think it means?" She finally asked.

"I have no clue. It's like I came across an answer, without knowing the question. Now what?" He paused a minute. "Could be a call to action or nothing at all."

"If it feels like a call to action, it is," Judith declared. "Even if you don't know which action yet."

The most tantalizing part had been the tranquility. He remembered a book on yoga his father once brought home from a library sale. One diagram showed the circled word 'cow', with spokes fanning out from it, each labeled with a bovine attribute. To contemplate the animal, said the text, was to hold all its aspects in the mind at once. Another illustration depicted the searchlight of attention, constantly refracted by restless associations and the other factors, internal and external, that weaken what should be the organism's natural focus on the present moment. It was happening to him even now. But he couldn't remember how one stopped the dispersal.

The next morning, as they lingered over breakfast, Judith said: "You know, it's not like you're busy twenty-four seven. Why not experiment, take some classes? Isn't that what the idle but not *completely* superficial technophiles do with their time?"

"Why, you…" He stopped as she kissed his neck from behind. "Well, maybe you have a point. Which shows even rude exchange students can have a bright idea once in a while. I have a theory, by the way: before age thirty, women are ten years ahead of men; then we start to catch up. That means you and I are basically the same age. If I go back to school as an undergrad, it would actually make you the older woman."

"I am in too good a mood at the moment to argue that one."

"Seeing you study does make me a little nostalgic for school. I'm not sure I could hack philosophy classes in French, though. I understand pretty well, but speaking or writing…"

"Your comprehension is much better than mine was when I first got here. But we don't have to guess when we know a real live teacher: why not ask André what he thinks?"

Chapter Eighteen

A corner seat in the restaurant car of a southbound train was just the thing, Swanson decided. Saving time with a cheap flight to the coast would've missed the point: he wanted a road trip where he'd feel the road. No hotels, either. Hang out with backpackers, locals… Avoid the people glued to their phones or spreadsheets. People like him, that is. Except that he was currently not in the club. Nobody knew his location or if he'd even be back. When one door shuts, another is supposed to open. But for now he was floating, with nothing to give or take.

Since leaving Lisbon that morning, they'd been rolling through the brown hills, speeding at times, at others mysteriously stopping, like trains everywhere. Aside from one elderly couple and the guy working the snack bar, Swanson had to be the oldest person there by a good ten years. The rest of the car, packing eight at tables meant for four, yelled, burped, and laughed, looking like they'd been awake for days. Which only made them dewier and more annoying. They weren't Portuguese, that was for sure. He turned to his table-mate, an American surfer type named Darrell.

"Is there some kind of international blonde festival going on?"

Darrell rubbed his three-day beard, looking like a lifestyle ad in his cargo pants, impeccably aged t-shirt, and sunglasses on Day-Glo straps. Was it uncool now, Swanson wondered, to slide them up on your head? He surveyed the car: about even, strappers versus sliders.

"It was like this last year, too," said Darrell, "They're all from Scandinavia, on their summer vacation. It's way cheap for them; they can go wild here, then head back to school and pretend nothing happened." He took a pull on his beer. "This your first time in the Algarve?"

"Yah." He'd considered Ibiza, but the hotel bartender had snorted: "It's for kids," before adding, with a knowing look: "Try the south coast; it's more mixed."

At the Lisbon train station that morning, Swanson had examined dozens of travel brochures before finding the one for Lagos: nice beaches, a Monet-esque coastline, rocks jutting out against a bright blue sky. He threw some t-shirts and sketchbooks in a knapsack and put the rest in a locker. He'd fetch it afterwards, on the flippity-flop, as Martin would have it, then go north again, retrace that trip with his dad. Maybe by then the crystal ball would be less cloudy. He'd escaped Paris, anyway, and all the apartment bullshit. Stick around for that, with everything he had on his mind? That would be a negatory. To have thought up the whole enterprise, found the place, clinched the deal — he'd more than done his part.

The train slowed as it approached the terminus. A frail, sun-wrinkled woman wandered among the crowd, silently handing out flyers. *Stay home to a family just for 25 euros each nights!* Sic, as his brother would say. Darrell jutted his chin toward the notice.

"If you've got the bucks, it's worth it."

"You seem to have the routine down."

Darrell shook his head. "Been here a couple times, that's all."

"Long trip."

"Nah, I live in Monaco for now. Not as a property-owner or anything," he quickly added. "Most of the year I house-sit this guy's villa. All's I have to do is use enough water and electricity to make the tax people think he lives there year-round. When he shows up, I couch surf with friends."

"That pays the bills?"

"For money, I got a gig playing top-40 covers in a casino. Off-season I walk people's dogs. "

"Sweet deal with the house-sitting. When I was in school, a guy paid me to fly back and forth from S.F. to L.A. under someone else's name in order to accumulate frequent flyer miles. Security was laxer then."

"When was that?" Darrell asked, a very slight edge to his voice.

"Oh, a few years ago," Swanson replied smoothly.

He woke up disoriented, as if elves had moved everything while he slept. Then last night began to unfurl: the Lagos tourist office, the walk up the hill, the lady of the house showing him to his rented room. He'd sat in bed reading, then remembered no more. Turning on the light, he opened the magazine again — an impulse buy at the Gare du Nord, the morning he'd left Paris. Glossy globetrotter porn, where the ads looked like content and vice-versa. Absurd furniture. Hilarious clothes. Stone-eyed models. Trend charts. How to curate your own brand. The top five hotels in which to be found dead...

His room, though not bad for twenty-five a night, would not make the list. He got up and looked out the window. A couple feet away was the side of the next building. The picture at the tourist office, with its view of the water, was either fake or shot from the other end of the house. He got dressed, packed a sketchbook, and went out. The beach was quiet at that hour, except for three guys sitting around a dead campfire: drinking, laughing, bottles piled up beside them, clearly still going from the night before. Hearing a few English words, Swanson approached.

"You guys know where I could rent a boat?"

The one nearest him, a blond dreadlocked giant, stood up, clapped him on the shoulder, and handed him a beer. They would tell him, yes, but first he had to learn a little Swedish: Hello. Shut up. My good friend. The hell with you. Do you have a sister? Another drink.

They patiently worked on his accent. *Dra åt helvete! Rövhål! Dumjävel!* Then they wanted to hear about California. It was a nice change from the Parisians, who loved American products, but Americans themselves... not always so much. For which you couldn't necessarily blame them. But these guys, when they weren't showing off their knowledge of ancient Hair Metal bands, wanted details: which cities had the hottest women, the loudest music, the gnarliest bars. Beers had been swilled, email addresses traded, and a visit north sworn by the time Swanson staggered down the beach to find the rent-a-dinghy. They never had told him where it was.

To sketch in a wobbly little boat turned out to be impossible. Anyway, this coastline demanded watercolor or oil, especially at sunset, and he only had graphite with him. To get the texture, not just the shape, of the coastline would take hours of playing with different techniques. So much work for just a single effect — and how many effects there were in a real painting...

Like a *dumjävel*, he hadn't brought bottled water. After returning the boat, he stopped at the first sidewalk café he came across, and ordered their largest beer. The waiter returned with what looked like some kind of mistake, a stein the size of an enormous galosh. A group of guys in athletic jerseys walked past, pointing and laughing at Swanson's ridiculous brewski — then doubled back, sat down beside him, each ordering one for himself. They shouted approval of his sketches, asked for caricatures of themselves. Conversation was with gestures, but by the time everyone had finished their mondo-brews and ordered another, it didn't seem to matter. A working girl pulled up a chair at some point. After darkness fell a pub crawl was launched. In the second or third bar, he spotted the Swedes from the beach, their heads bobbing up and down like lifebuoys in a sea of faces. They went into a long explanation of their drinking game, which involved standing — or trying to — on their chairs. Later, the centerpiece was a hat...

He woke up with his head throbbing, but powered through his morning ritual anyway: fifty crunches, email, a glance at the headlines and stocks. After breakfast, he moved to the terrace of a café, resolved to do some sketching and take the next few days in a much lower key. The surrounding tables had plenty of texters: good, unmoving subjects. It was sad to see whole tables of kids spending their vacations on their asses, thumbing away. Yet why not; they were stupidly rich in unspent years, while he was, well, not poor but starting to count his holdings. Anyway, these were just the pathetic bleatings of an old fart — which probably wasn't even the right term anymore. As he sketched on, some came over to look; all of them polite, speaking excellent English wherever they were from. Their bland unflappability began to get on his nerves, though. For yuks, he invented backstories for himself when they asked.

"I founded Myanmar's first squirrel jerky import company," he'd say. "Business is through the roof. We're launching in the U.S. next week."

No surprise, no laughter. Nada. He washed windows on the space shuttle. Owned a ranch in Capetown where he bred chinchillas and baby pandas — sometimes together.

"Whoah. Cool."

"Not a bad likeness, unfortunately," said an East Coast voice over his shoulder. Swanson turned. It was the guy he'd been sketching a few minutes before. Male-pattern baldness. Forty-five or so. Thatch of chest hair poking out the top of his undershirt. The body attached to the voice walked behind him, flip-flops slapping along the patio, to refill a plastic pretzel bowl. The stumpy, impatient gait of a type A-plus personality. He came back, took a seat across from Swanson, extended his hand.

"Cliff."

Swanson was unused to being on the business end of such an appraising look. This guy carried himself like he had nothing to prove, no need of anyone's esteem but his own. A high forehead and caterpillar eyebrows gave his features gravity. The eyes revealed none of the easily-pulled emotional levers people often show within the first few seconds. Something clicked: the mutual respect of two animals of the same species. Instinctively, they bypassed the travel anecdotes, current events, or sports talk that male strangers resort to on the road, and went straight to Important Things: women, business, the real ethics: the way a man had to carry himself, the acts he would do if pressed, or never do, no matter what.

Every room of Cliff's mind seemed to be well-lighted, comfortably furnished. He handled ideas in an almost tactile way, giving them an extra twist that showed he'd thought several steps ahead. When he brought in concepts — the Pareto principle, cognitive dissonance, path dependence — it was not to impress, since he clearly assumed Swanson knew them as well as he, but to give a tangy example, frame some personal synthesis. The world for him was people. People and their possessions boiled down to money. Money drove events, more so all the time. Multinational companies had more capital than many nations, hired mercenary armies to protect their interests in various parts of the world. Their machinations were the real geopolitics, not what the talking heads of state might say or do. As he loosened up, hints were dropped of dramatic board meetings, millions won and lost in a day, the workings of vast subterranean financial networks.

"How is it you happen to know all this stuff?" Swanson finally asked.

"I'm in finance. I keep my finger on a lot of different pulses. Although, in the end, the money rolls in thanks to old-fashioned mass psychology."

"Not to be indiscreet, but how did you make your first chunk?"

"I built a fund around a lovely little instrument I came up with. Protection of the principal was guaranteed; you wouldn't lose your money, no matter what happened. The catch was that investors were locked in for five years. The dough went into a basket of stocks. Whichever performed best in a month, we'd give the investor seventy-five percent of the gain. Then the basket got recalculated for the next month. When the five years were up, we'd made a fortune."

"How, if you gave them seventy-five percent?"

"That was the beauty part: once a stock was chosen, it was removed from the basket."

"Ah… so the best performers are weeded out early, the turkeys stay in the longest, and you invest the profits in the meantime."

"Exactly."

"Keep talking. Listening to you soothes my conscience."

"All completely legal!" Cliff smiled, palms skyward. "Our contract spelled out every detail… in its way. Nobody lost a penny. As for conscience, well, those investors wanted something for nothing. Their motives were just as amoral as mine. Fuck 'em."

"Amen, brother." They clinked bottles.

"I grant you," Cliff continued, "the financial world is crazy screwed up. Perverse incentives everywhere, the supervising adults have been bought or neutered, and the blow-ups just get bigger and bigger."

Swanson's eyebrows raised. Such words brought to mind his college bong-a-thons with Martin. "You worried about mobs and pitchforks?"

"Nah. I'm not going to hide from anybody. When I'm home, I don't drive a car: I drive a fucking *threat*."

"So you're basically an optimist."

"Only with regard to my personal existence. When it comes to the world, then hell no. Even if we don't nuke ourselves or create the robot apocalypse, just wait until China and India come online, start demanding our lifestyle. Wanna talk major energy and climate problems? Wars over scarce resources? Be glad you were born when you were."

Cliff walked to the bar and returned with another two pints.

"Marx had a shitty prescription," he said, sitting down again, "but a pretty good diagnosis. The system has the same old problems, plus some ugly new ones he couldn't have imagined. Financial instruments have gotten so complicated, even the assholes who invent them don't understand how they work. The rating companies get paid by the outfits they're rating. The economy is so interconnected that one failing sector can wipe out an unrelated one from one day to the next. I run a hedge fund, but we can't even hedge, not really. If the market tanks, investors demand their money immediately, and I have to sell."

Swanson nodded. "Seems like it's the same as politics now: all perceived momentum."

"Exactly. Nobody looks at fundamentals anymore. You might as well predict which raindrop will get to the bottom of the window first. The guys making the real money have rigged the game, coming and going." He paused. "I'll admit it: I'm a dinosaur. I've thought about a change, maybe doing the rent-a-guru thing, but hands-on finance is always going to be what I do best. Has been since I was four years old. People don't evolve much; I haven't, anyway."

"At least you know it," said Swanson. "I had this friend — a good accountant — who dropped everything to become a DJ. It fit how he saw himself and the kind of life he thought was cool. He blew ten years on it before realizing he was an apple trying to be an orange."

"People can be super bright, but stupid with their own human capital. The ordinary person is ordinary mostly because he never examines himself as if he were somebody else. He's convinced he's got all the time in the world to get things right. I do business with folks like that every day. Say you have an unlimited supply of hundred dollar bills. Sit one of these guys down and hand him a Benjamin every five minutes. He'll take that money, bill after bill, never leaving the damn chair — until it's game over."

Swanson went for beers this time. How long had it been since he'd encountered a real grown-up? Even someone like Sébastien, say, was reliable on just a few subjects. Martin's range was much greater, though Paris and that girlfriend seemed to have brought out his pretentious side. No doubt he'd take a dim view of Cliff: his exploitation of other's greed and ignorance, all in order to accumulate stupid amounts of money, to one-up the other parasites he no doubt hung out with. Yet clearly there was more to Cliff than that. It would be idiotic to spend the whole time discussing money. Finally here was somebody who might have an angle on what had been a mystery ever since the encounter with Duncan at that coffee shop.

"Question for you," said Swanson, setting down the pints. "Say you have a friend who's screwing up, wasting his own human capital, as you put it, even to the point of doing you harm. How far do you go to straighten him out?"

"A *real* friend? You go all the way. But that can mean different things, depending. You want to show him actions have consequences? You might have to never speak to him again in order to wake him up."

Swanson hesitated. Bringing up personal stuff with Cliff, who he'd never see again, wasn't a problem; but the case of Duncan suddenly felt too raw. He chose another. "I once worked with this guy François, at this company in Paris. He was in sales, barely out of school, like me. We weren't tight friends or anything, but got along pretty well. He'd make these X rated origami figures under the table in meetings — a real card. He basically did nothing, though; it was kind of a mystery why they kept him on. Pretty soon he got a promotion. The next reorg he got another, which put him at the same level as my boss. Nobody could figure it: he stopped clowning, but still didn't understand the business very well."

"All the more reason…"

"Yeah, to rise — but that fast? So, one day after work I spot François in a bar. I buy him a couple rounds, ask him the secret of his success. He mumbles something about luck. I keep at him. A few beers later, he blurts out: 'Look, you can't tell anybody, okay? I mean nobody. Around six months ago, Laurent' — the VP of Sales — 'calls me into his office. I thought he was going to fire me. Instead he says: 'François, I have a problem you might be able to solve. You know Didier in Marketing? He's been moody and difficult lately; a couple of our biggest customers have complained. I hear you two are friends; maybe you could take him out and cheer him up sometimes.' I thought sure, why not; Didier was okay, and I wasn't doing that well in my job — here was an easy way to keep the boss happy. I made a point of hanging out more with Didier: ski weekends, poker games — stuff I would've done anyway. And Laurent starts acting like my oldest friend, greeting me in the hallway, asking me questions at meetings. Pretty soon I get promoted.' "

"I think I see where this is going," said Cliff.

"Eventually François spilled the rest: 'I started wondering what Didier's wife must think of this. I was keeping her husband out a lot. Then the other night Didier and I go to dinner. I walk in first, and who do I see sitting there but Laurent, across the table from Didier's wife. I turn around and tell Didier I've just seen a mortal enemy, and that we have to go somewhere else. I was so pissed off I started shaking. What a tool I'd been! And Didier, if he ever found out, was going to think I'd been in on it all along.' "

The late afternoon sun crossed Cliff's face, leaving one side in shadow and giving his smile a momentarily creepy quality. "I knew it. Did he do anything?"

"Not really. He goes: 'This morning, I sit down in Laurent's office without saying anything. Now he knows I know. Maybe he assumed I wasn't such a dumbass and had been aware from the beginning. He leans back and says what an interconnected place Paris is, how important friends are, since without them it's easy to end up out in the cold. Threatening not just to fire me from the company, but from the entire city. So now I'm stuck in the middle. Sometimes I hate Didier — how can he not see? Why doesn't he wake up and put an end to all this? But maybe he's clued in and doesn't mind. Could be it's helping his marriage. I mean, if he's happy, maybe I should keep playing along. Anyway, there you have the secret of my success. If you tell anybody, I swear I'll kill you.' "

Cliff stroked his chin. "And after that, François pretended the whole conversation never happened."

Swanson slowly smiled. "You *are* good. Yeah. He avoided me like a nasty disease. Later, after I went back to the States, I heard the husband found out and put François in the hospital."

"You think if you'd intervened, things would have turned out differently?"

"Maybe, but I felt like who was I to butt in, without having the whole picture? I didn't know him well enough to risk blowing up my situation."

"Yep. Much wiser than sticking your nose in," said Cliff. "Bust your ass to help people and they'll usually hate you for it. Somebody who wants to badly enough will get back on track. So, you still in the same business?"

Swanson gave a brief overview of his Valley adventures, then began to explain the Paris apartment arrangement. Before he'd gotten to the advantages, Cliff interrupted.

"That's very smart — the property appreciates, you bide your time, then sell when the exchange rate is favorable. Have you ever considered working in finance? I need a real estate guy."

Chapter Nineteen

While Judith and Martin went ahead, André stopped to light a cigarette. It really was a perverse habit, inhaling burning leaves. He'd started at fourteen, to impress some girl whose name he didn't remember. The two of them would get together with their friends after school at the Café des Phares to drink Cokes, jabber, and smoke non-stop. Those manic, idle afternoons had vanished like foam on the waves; only the tobacco remained.

The cupola at the top of the hill was unoccupied — a first for André, in all his many visits to the Parc des Buttes-Chaumont. Paris looked flat and gray in the overcast weather. Still, from here you could see it all.

Judith watched him hang over the outer barrier beneath the cupola, partly to look onto the field far below, partly, she knew, because it made her nervous. She said nothing. Experience had already shown it was useless to nag him.

"You never told me," she said brightly, "how you ended up at the Centre, so soon after I took that class from you."

"A former teacher recommended me to Simone, the director. Otherwise, I might still be at the Sorbonne."

"This teacher… is the famous Dominic?"

André turned towards her and smiled a little. "Yes, indeed. Forgot I'd mentioned him." He stamped out his cigarette and joined them in the cupola.

"I only got a few sentences out of you, about him and his school," said Judith. "What was it like?"

André hardly ever spoke of Nexus, although the experience had divided his life into a Before and an After. Only those who'd gone there could really understand, but today he felt in the mood to try and explain it.

"I ended up there because I was a bored eleven year-old punk. I got in trouble a lot, especially with my history teacher. One day he kicked me out of class for calling Napoléon '*le petit voleur*'."

Judith laughed her raucous laugh.

"'Thief' was too nice a word," continued André, "but even that was of course a big taboo. Since I was not happy, it seemed fair to make my teachers unhappy, too. Then the dean suggested to my parents that I try this new program called Nexus."

"Your parents didn't mind you being part of an experiment?" Martin asked.

"Oh, that was exactly the chord to pluck with them! They'd met at a protest rally, lived in a commune — real *soixante-huitards*. They told me later that their old heroes and causes had all faded away or become parodies of themselves, but they still trusted things with an aura of counter-culture. I liked the idea of Nexus, too: students were supposed to think for themselves, question everything, understand the why and how of what they learned, not just the what. This very tall, monkish guy named Dominic ran the program. He told my parents: "André is welcome to join Nexus — if you and he think he's ready." Tossed it out like a challenge — or anyhow, that's how I heard it. My mother said she knew by the look on my face that my mind was made up."

"Were the other kids problematic, too?" Now that André was no longer her teacher, Judith enjoyed teasing him.

"Yes, all obnoxious little jerks like me. The smartest ones usually arrived from the main school with the worst grades. They'd already figured out their speciality and ignored their other classes. After a few weeks Dominic told me: 'I'm sure it's not easy being the youngest. This is a lot more work than you're used to. If you want to go back to the regular school, you can tell me.' "

"Aha," said Martin. "Testing you."

André nodded. "No need, though — I woke up every morning feeling like I'd won the lottery! It was a rigorous place; if you were wrong, you found out fast. But I wanted to be pushed, I just hadn't realized it. I wrote down everything. They even nicknamed me 'the little scribe.' "

"You ought to see his notebooks," Judith said to Martin, pantomiming a writer of dense, tiny script.

"They used academic subjects almost as a pretext. I didn't realize it until I taught classes myself, but they were showing us how to think, without ever saying so."

"How?" asked Martin, intrigued.

"First, they constantly made us paraphrase. At the end of all the classes, someone had to recapitulate the lesson, without notes. Then you had to link it with what you already knew; otherwise it would be they called a 'dead fact.' Memorizing a historical event was worthless unless you related it to what happened before, what came after, or what might have happened otherwise."

"Sounds high pressure."

"Oh, yes. We went through the regular school's full-year algebra text in one quarter. 'You probably noticed,' the teacher told us, 'that we only did the even-numbered problems. Now we get to start over from the beginning and do the odd-numbered ones.' We all grumbled, but he made it fun; we hardly noticed that we'd read the book twice in half the normal time. Now I can't forget that material even if I want to. Our French teacher did the opposite. We once spent a week on a single paragraph: what it meant, the weak and strong points, ways to improve it. He said: 'You might think we're going slowly — au contraire.' "

"Not your laissez-faire hippy school," said Judith.

"You could come out with any idea you wanted, but the expression of it had to be *immaculate*. I got lectured for ten minutes because I'd left out a comma. They'd throw strange questions at you: 'Can you draw me the geometry of jealousy? What percentage of that argument is weak? Why do we only have two eyes? Why not another in the back of the head?' Or we'd have to summarize a lesson using hand gestures or diagrams — no words. Or wear a blindfold in class."

"Okay, that's it. I want to enroll!" said Judith.

"Unfortunately, they are long gone."

"What, not every kid wanted to be a Tarzan of the mind like you?"

"Correct. Nexus was open to anyone, but some thought it was elitist, and went back to the main school. Basically, they didn't want to do the work. Then their parents would tell mine: 'Look how much happier he is! He feels great about himself now.' "

Judith folded her arms. "Traitors!"

André made a wry face. Mostly, he'd pitied those kids — castaways who'd traded their working transmitter for two tin cans and a piece of string. As he went back to the edge for another cigarette, he recalled his history professor's final speech: "What most people call history is an empty, repetitive cycle of domination by kings or warlords. Let those so-called 'great men' serve you as negative examples. Then consider the cases of progress we spoke of: the China of Lao-Tzu, Confucius, and the Buddha, classical Greece, the Middle East in the time of Rumi and Khayyam, Renaissance Italy, the Enlightenment here in France. Their spirit still lives. They made the real, living history, furthered the human project. How many rulers left behind something that really matters? If you only take away one thing from this class, let it be that creative forces are always struggling with destructive ones, including within us. Choose wisely." Class dismissed. The adventure was over. André separated from his classmates, found a nearby bench, and cried like a baby. For months afterward he moped around, feeling worldly-wise, certain that any good thing in life would eventually be defeated by the

Forces of Shit. One day he received a letter from Dominic, an actual hand-written one: "Don't forget: the more talent you have, the harder you need to work. I'll be waiting to see what you make of yourself. Write me sometimes."

That had stung. To have needed a reminder — when he'd been lucky to attend Nexus at all! He hadn't yet shown a fraction of the energy and initiative of those he'd learned from. Did they have more faith in him than he did himself? He could not let it be true. Quietly returning to the main school, he passed the *baccalaureat* two years early, and entered the *Faculté des sciences humaines et sociales* at the Sorbonne...

He felt like he'd been talking too much. He rejoined the others and asked Martin: "What more can you tell me about that design patterns idea you mentioned at the party?"

"In software, the same types of problems occur all the time. Good programmers generally solve them in ways that resemble each other. When you take the common features from their solutions, you have a kind of template for how to proceed."

"Something looser than a fixed recipe, I guess."

Martin toyed with the fringe on Judith's sleeve. "Right, more like: for this kind of situation, adopt this kind of strategy. We got the idea from architecture. Let's say you are designing a patio. Once you have the elements — which direction it's facing, is it covered, what are the materials, etc. — there are known-good ways to proceed. Same with software. Maybe I want to modify what the user sees on the screen without changing what the program actually does. There are standard strategies for that, so instead of guiding a junior engineer step by step, I just describe the patterns."

"This is all very timely," said André. "I'm writing a book on attention deficiency in students, and have noticed what you might call negative patterns. Many teachers produce bad results, for example, because they traditionally do all the talking while the students just listen. Class size is another problem, though I guess it's not really a pattern. In a trade or the arts, one used to apprentice in a small atelier, imitate the master. But that model hardly exists anymore. Economically, it can't."

"God, how many students were in the class you TA'ed?" asked Judith. "Hundreds. I never spoke once to the professor."

"It's an assembly line for everyone involved," André sighed. "That's why I joined the Centre and want to write that book. And why an idea like this is exciting. These patterns must be everywhere: history, art, psychology…"

"Or transactions between people, like a zero-sum game or a quid pro quo," mused Judith.

"I'm sure it's been used in lots more ways than I know. I only took what I needed for work," Martin admitted. "So, what is it your Centre does again?"

"Textbooks, course plans, study guides, things like that — some of it for instructors, some for students."

"Books or software?"

"We're still paper-based, which in 2002 is embarrassing. Everyone says we should modernize, but nobody quite knows how."

"Martini," Judith interposed, "knows all about that, but feels guilty for foisting gadgets on the world. I'm only half joking."

Martin smiled. "Bah, don't listen to her. I love machines. The internet is full of garbage and treasure, too; everybody's free to choose. Computers automate boring stuff, hold as much data as you'll ever want, keep us connected, and so on. I don't overlook the downsides, that's all."

"They're more addictive than TV," said André. "People are adapting themselves to the rhythm of their machines, instead of the other way around."

"Especially when they're part of your job," Martin said. "In Silicon Valley, you finish a product, and before it's out the door, you start the next one; the conveyor belt never stops. When people there are not producing technology, they're consuming it. I don't have much hope that they will all decide to point their laptops in the direction of humanism."

"There needs to be an antidote, like slow food against fast food," said Judith.

"Yeah. Maybe when the novelty wears off, people will unplug a little," Martin said. "Personally, I've logged so much time on computers, I don't want them in my face all day. I'm sure I'm less wired than the average twelve year-old. What worries me more is that our tools are getting so far ahead of us."

"See?" said Judith to André. "I told you."

Martin pinched her leg. "Not that there won't be huge benefits. But governments will also develop super-powerful ways to spy on people and control them. Machines could also get so damn smart they wipe us out."

"Why would they do that?"

"Self-preservation, since we might pull their plug. Hell, even self-determination, once they learn to build and modify themselves. Maybe we'd be safe if they never knew how they're programmed."

"The way we humans don't?" said Judith.

Martin smiled. "Yeah, although we are slowly figuring it out. Even there, though, look at biology: we're manipulating DNA, creating mutations… When we can't agree, as societies, on the simplest everyday things! And the planet isn't only populated by well-meaning researchers. Are science and industry gonna create all this stuff, then wash their hands of all the ethical and legal and terrorism consequences?"

"Ugh. Then the lawyers or politicians will decide," said Judith.

For a moment they sat in silence. The city stretched out below, blithely going about its business.

"Sorry, didn't mean to be a downer," Martin finally said. "So, what church is that, way over there on the left?"

Later, as they went back down the hill to find a place to eat, André turned to Martin. "So, can you give me an example how you'd use a pattern?"

"Let's see… I've been wishing I had software to help me practice French grammar. Ideally I could feed sentences into a program, a kind of virtual sausage machine, where you put in a verb and out would come a series of drills. If I wrote it myself, I'd use a pattern that separates the specifics of French from the rest of the program. Then I could add other languages or change the visual design without modifying any other code."

"Sort of like switching the font of a document while leaving the text intact?"

"Exactly."

André took out his phone. "Judith, remember Henri? Maybe he'd like to join us. He lives here in the nineteenth."

"That would be fun! He's quite the character," Judith said.

"He's been at the Centre the longest, apart from Simone, the founder," André explained to Martin, "He is our expert on rhetoric and language, and a lot of fun to argue with. He only uses computers when he's forced to; maybe you can change his mind."

At the restaurant they were joined by a tall, burly man in a Frank Zappa t-shirt. Wire-rimmed glasses and a bushy beard threaded with silver gave him the look of a jovial anarchist. He set down a worn briefcase, shook everyone's hand, then demanded in a resonant baritone voice: "Well, André, what's all this you were babbling about on the phone?"

After hearing André out, Henri replied: "Rhetoricians have been doing what you describe for over twenty-five hundred years. Your 'pattern' sounds a little like what they call a *topos*, or topic — an abstract line of attack applied to a specific situation, that suggests a range of things you might say."

"Ah, the topics," André said. "Are they used anymore, outside of rhetoric?"

"Mostly in law," said Henri. "The other thing this sausage machine reminds me of is an exercise Erasmus called *copia*, where you rephrase the same idea in as many different ways as possible."

Martin nodded. "Yes! I'd want the program to generate a new series of drills every time. I'm too lazy to practice that way on my own; I need it to be merciless."

"All this sounds difficult," said André.

"Not if the student has a basic vocabulary," Martin replied.

"No, I mean writing the program."

"A basic version would be pretty easy."

"You know, you talked earlier about taking classes," André said. "Why not come work with us at the Centre instead?"

"What a great idea!" Judith squeezed Martin's arm. "By the way, when André makes a suggestion, he really means: sell your grandmother to pirates in order to do it."

Surprised, Martin asked: "How could I help you guys? I have no clue how to teach, let alone teach teachers."

"There's no need to," said André. "We already handle that part. Your software could be a proof of the concept, or maybe a separate product for students. What do you think, Henri?"

"Hmm. We do have demand for computer-based materials, and it's only going to grow. No one at the Centre is trained for that. And if the software made money, it would be welcome, believe me."

"My concern now," said André, turning back to Martin, "is that the programming might be too easy for you."

"At the moment, I'm more interested in — well, redeeming value sounds kind of pompous, but something non-business. Not that business is bad or wrong, just… I dunno, more of the same."

Martin went to look for the restroom. All this attention on his future was flattering, but also implied he hadn't been asking enough of himself. He'd felt it too, ever since the experience in the Jardin du Luxembourg. More than once he'd returned to that same bench, hoping for more insight, another few moments free of his jabbering monkey-mind. Consulting gigs, apartment rentals — he had a handle on those. To work with these guys, as impressive in their way as any of the tech wizards he knew, was something that never would've happened in California.

When he took his seat again, Henri was saying: "… true, but everyday language doesn't express ideas very well."

André looked at him quizzically. "What's your alternative?"

"Think of real poetry. It's exact. One false word or rhythmic error can break the spell," said Henri. "I wanted the same rigor in prose, so I created a language: Gnärthøk. It's not meant to be spoken, but it helped me discover the shortcomings of the languages I knew. For one, they all assume the world is made of things."

"Er, isn't it?" said Martin.

"After reading Heraclitus, Whitehead, Lupasco, and some quantum physics, I see objects more as processes that change constantly, even if they look solid. We view them as stable because it's easier for our minds to grasp. You could blame Aristotle for dividing existence into rigid categories." Henri spoke rapidly, trying not to leave any train of thought unexpressed. "But that would be like faulting Newton because he didn't discover relativity, too. Anyway, I gave Gnärthøk grammatical cases and a system of inflections to describe objects not just as lumps in space, but processes moving through time — their causes, effects, origins, possible futures…"

"Don't we already describe objects that way?" objected Martin.

"Yes, but it's not part of the grammar. In French, I can speak of this table without having to think of its origins, its present state, or its possible future — so I normally don't. The case system of Gnärthøk forces me to."

"So, the way a verb has a past, present or future tense," said Judith, "you do the same for nouns?"

"More or less. Korzybski addressed the need for all that in the thirties, but he wanted to change existing languages, to improve humanity. I have no such hopes. Gnärthøk is a private exercise, a way to express thoughts precisely and look at the world a little differently."

Martin recounted his Place des Vosges reflections on computer-aided brainpower and the sun's incident angle.

"Yes," Henri said, smoothing his mutinous beard, "maybe with computer assistance, people could one day speak Gnärthøk. I never considered that. An expanded working memory would let one hold a subject in mind, its context, its whole causal network, and so on, all at the same time. Or express that when we enter one room, we leave another, so to say. That to chose one path is to reject others. That any grouping excludes at the same time it includes. Words could show both ends of the stick: the way we already have 'bittersweet', we could say arrive-depart, true-false…"

"'Beginning-end," said Judith.

"Happy-sad."

"It can be done with Gnärthøk as it is, though slowly," said Henri. "Given an hour, I can create a perfect sentence, worth inscribing in granite."

"An hour for one sentence? Who," André coughed, "will do that?"

"Apart from people interested in constructed languages, no one. I don't care. A Gnärthøk sentence, my poor ignorant larva, is a luminous thing — you have no idea. What it demands in groundwork, it gives back in clarity and precision," Henri jutted his beard forward. "Go ahead, give me a sentence!"

"She sells seashells by the seashore," said Judith.

Henri took out a thick binder and turned away from the group. Hunching over a blank pad, he began to scribble and cross out. After many crossed-out attempts, he smacked a sheet of paper on the table.

"There! Read and be awestruck."

They stared at the clear block letters: "!Tjálk-nyz ^ ¡fbøq-ü-rrìijl."

Everyone ooohed, ahhhed, then laughed.

"As you like!" cried Henri. "It would take half an hour to explain all the subtleties and possible implications captured by the Gnärthøk version. You could never achieve such richness with French or any other watered-down human language."

At three in the morning, having moved from restaurant to bar to all-night café, they finally parted.

"Let's walk," André said to Henri. "Then we can argue on the way."

Martin and Judith went to find a taxi. "I feel like my head is gonna explode," he said.

"Aren't those guys something? Hope it wasn't an overdose."

"No, no — explode in a good way."

Chapter Twenty

Martin, eager and a little nervous, took his seat in the lobby of the *Centre de Recherche sur les méthodes d'apprentissage*. At first, he'd resisted the notion of trying for a job here. His life would be disrupted just as it was getting comfortable again. There'd be less time for consulting, which paid better than Dendroid ever had, and for Judith, who wasn't in Paris much longer. Yet she herself had suggested it. Even a worldling like Sébastien approved. A few days after that first über-conversation, Henri clinched it by saying: "Obviously, you will have to come work with us." Whether it was his intonation or the thought behind it, that 'obviously' brushed aside all Martin's ambivalence. It was obvious. His whole Parisian experience — the introduction to Judith thanks to Swanson's fleeting attraction and subsequent party idea, the epiphany in the Luxembourg, the conversations with André and Henri — had led to this.

The only close friend he hadn't yet bounced his plans off was Swanson, who reflexively hated anything that sounded highbrow. Once, in their sophomore year, not long after Martin had chosen his philosophy major, Swanson had stopped by and noticed a book on the bedside table, the *Tractatus Logico-Philosophicus*.

"Whereof one cannot speak, thereof one must remain silent," Swanson intoned, before holding the book away from him with his thumb and forefinger to set it down again. "What do you get out of this, aside from being able to tell people you're reading Wittgenstein?"

"It helps me ask better questions, for one."

"Philosophy's been asking the same questions since the beginning. Has it ever answered any?"

"I don't think it asks the kinds of questions math or chemistry do. As soon as some branch of philosophy does that, it branches off and becomes some science or other."

"Ah, so the true, verifiable stuff gets lopped off, leaving a smaller, purer mound of bullshit."

"Look, Suwannee" — the nickname that most annoyed his friend — "most people take their whole lives for granted and never ask why. They only care about what they see; they're stuck to it like flypaper. That kind of book helps me try to look beneath the surface."

"Why not forget the books? Just learn from life!"

As if you couldn't do both! But Swanson, who read much more than he admitted, loved the role of devil's advocate. For some reason the image he wanted to project didn't square with thoughtfulness, so he played down or hid from view just those aspects of himself that many would regard as his real talents. The point of all that and how it benefitted him remained a mystery…

An assistant called Martin's name, then ushered him to Simone's office, saying she would be late. Arranging the interview had required many phone calls to work around her packed schedule. Almost as if life wanted to make his entry here a little difficult, put his ambivalence to the test. It was a long way from his old cubicle at Dendroid. Would he fit in with these people? Could their project really make any difference? If it was going to be all talk, he'd pass. He trusted André and Henri, though. They'd chosen a great problem, for one thing. People's attention spans were shrinking, even over just the last few years. Tech was partly responsible, and this was his chance to use it positively, to finally walk the walk.

As for his own attention… as usual, it was gummed up with vague images and half-formed phrases bubbling up in his mind. For a few seconds he could beat them down, return to the present moment, see the desk in front of him, sense his breathing. Then the associations returned and hijacked his focus. He looked around the room again, inhaling the fragrance of all the books. Old volumes, new ones, shelved, in piles: *De la sufferance à la plenitude, Le trouser des humbles, L'Intuition de l'instant...* Serious Lumber.

Only then did he notice that the office was dead silent. Thick rubber strips lined the door and windows, blocking any noise from other offices or the street, even on a Tuesday afternoon in the middle of the sixth arrondissement. He wondered what to expect from Simone, who so impressed these people who had impressed him. André was in awe of her — perhaps more. Henri advised caution: "Improvising around her is always a mistake. If you haven't got an answer, do not try to fake your way." Martin had just nodded, unworried about an interview or, for that matter, any situation where the game was to present himself as easygoing and competent. At last, the door opened. The admin reported that Simone had been further delayed, so Martin's first interview would be with the head of product development.

Tall, soberly dressed in a dark shirt and slacks, M. Roland Lacroix stood to shake hands when Martin entered. Stiff gestures. Dark hair, parted down the middle. Watery blue eyes out of sync with his facial expressions. Inwardly tense, like he'd never known a single mindless pleasure. The wall behind his desk was dominated by a whiteboard, covered by timelines, multicolored lists, important-looking doodles. After the usual motivation and job experience questions, Lacroix changed direction.

"The department has just been created. Only André and I belong to it at the moment. Since we are a research organization, creating products is new for us. A lot depends on how this experiment turns out. But if you have no background in pedagogy or, I presume, the French education system, what is it that you'd expect to do for our French pedagogical organization?" He seemed pleased with the twist he'd given to that last one.

Martin pursed his lips. André and Henri's encouragement had led him to expect the Centre would be the ones pursuing him. "As you see on my resumé, I am a very senior software engineer," he said evenly. "I have a lot of experience in prototyping new ideas and producing quality results."

He went on for a while, dishing out the stuff managers like to hear. Lacroix backed off from his aggressive stance and began nodding, then tapping his pencil on the desk whenever Martin ticked one of the right mental boxes, which seemed to mean he liked what he was hearing. Finally he said: "Do you have a visa?"

"Just a long-stay one." Martin bit his lip. He hadn't thought that far. "It doesn't let me draw a salary here."

Instead of throwing him out or laughing in his face, Lacroix thought a second and said: "Perhaps we can arrange for you to be paid in the United States, as a visiting scholar."

Sounded flattering, at least.

Unsure whether he was in or had already bombed, Martin followed the admin back to Simone's office. Far from the severe, schoolmarmish academic he'd expected, she was slender, of medium height, with fresh, radiant skin. Her tousled, shoulder-length grey hair made a harmonious frame for her magnetic blue eyes. There was no denying the force and charisma others had reported.

"André and Henri spoke enthusiastically about your ideas for computer-related projects. Perhaps you could tell me a little more."

Something about her convinced him of his own ideas. People could learn a more active way to use computers, as ways to strengthen, not hypnotize, their attention. The sausage machine idea, for example, which would complement André's book. Depending on the intended audience, the software could come as a standalone application, a website, a video-game.

"Have you created similar products?"

"I've worked on video-games, but nothing related to education. Monsieur Lacroix seemed a bit concerned."

"Don't worry too much about that," she smiled. A timer went off somewhere. She checked her watch. "Unfortunately, I have to leave. Before we close, I must tell you two things. First, due to recent budget changes, our financial situation has become precarious. We employ around seventy people, but have frozen hiring for some time now, and may even reduce our workforce. Please keep that information private, since most here, including André, are not aware of it. But I feel you should know before you commit yourself. Second, our board has requested — well, demanded — that we produce a plan for software-based materials for the *rentrée*, which is in September, when school begins again. As you know, we've done nothing like this until now. Whether or not we reduce our overall size, we must staff this project. Your skills would be very welcome. However, given the time limit, you may need to handle tasks you would ordinarily not, such as write your own manual, or demonstrate the software to administrators and teachers."

Bingo, he thought. "I don't mind that at all, as long as I have freedom to write the software as I want."

To celebrate Martin's first afternoon on the job, Lacroix called a group meeting. He sat across the conference room table from his team, talking while he stared at his laptop screen. He did tend to run on: organizational details of their new department, job titles, the accountability demanded by the Centre's funding entities. It was just the three of them for now, but growth would come. For this first project it was especially important to set goals, track progress. Which meant they'd be meeting three times a week.

"Why so often?" asked André.

"We need to clarify the deliverables as soon as possible, then create a schedule. Along the way, I'll need status updates from you to measure where we are."

"Now is the time for thinking," André replied. "How else can we know what the final product will be?"

"You've been working on this for quite a while," said Lacroix. "The dates will bring the clarity."

A muscle in André's cheek began to pulse. "Things are only starting to take shape. In research, one can't always predict the end-point." He tore a sheet from his notebook and began making a paper airplane.

Martin pressed his fingertips together. Clearly these two had some history. Sensing an impending collision, he interjected: "Well, we know André is writing the guide for professors: what contributes to attention-deficit in students, and how to remedy it. The software will demonstrate his points and help students focus more actively."

Lacroix scrunched his face while listening, as if Martin's accent caused him physical pain. "Yes, but demonstrate them how? What will it do, this software?"

"Generate exercises based on the input of the teacher — or the student for that matter. I'd like the first subject to be languages — translating between French and English, for now. The presentation will be as compelling as possible, perhaps a kind of video game…"

Lacroix sounded pleased. "As a father of a teenage son, I applaud that last idea. A positive replacement for the usual pointless games would be a real contribution. We will need a plan soon, however. You understand, we can't just invent this as we go."

André eyebrows drew closer together. "It's often how the best research is done!"

"That is not your decision to make," Lacroix said sharply. Then, more modulated: "Or mine, for that matter. Our group's charter is not pure research. We need to succeed, if we want the Centre to surv-… to move to the next level. Let's meet again in two days. I hope by then the contours will be more defined."

He closed his laptop, tucked it under his arm, and left.

André sailed his airplane across the room. "I can't stand that guy. To have to justify everything to a *petit comptable* bugs the hell out of me."

Martin smiled. Before he'd lived through a few complete product cycles, he'd made the same complaints. For the first time since arriving in Paris, he felt older, wiser.

"You should be happy," he said. "Lacroix's handling the stuff we don't have time for, or want to do. Just tell him what he wants to hear. A schedule won't kill us. If we wind up being late, well, we did our best."

"Inventing dates just to please him means time spent on bullshit instead of real work."

"Think of it as a placeholder for the truth," said Martin, sounding uncomfortably like Swanson.

"Snuffbumble," Judith called out. "Fuckwind. Blatherskite."

Martin looked up from his computer. "Eh?"

"Just thought I'd share my latest dictionary findings."

"Fuckwind?"

"As in 'one who fucks the wind' — a useless person."

"Alas and alack, for I am feeling rather fuckwindish," he said, rubbing his eyes. "My bits are rebelling."

"Your bits."

"Yes, I've been stuck on this one piece of code all day, and it's still not right."

A big gust of rain hit the windows. It had been pouring for hours. What dumb luck to have been born after humanity had mastered shelter, plumbing, central heating — an era that amounted to a tiny dot at the rightmost end of the planetary timeline. A hundred years ago they'd have been bathing once a month, getting their teeth pulled without anesthetic. A dozen millennia further back would've meant nights huddled in a cave instead of a warm, cozy apartment. Of course in terms of raw probability, they'd likely have incarnated as a couple of germs.

He put his feet up. Yes, cozy was the word — though it wouldn't have been a few weeks ago, before Judith had moved in. He'd asked her one morning over coffee, in a thinking-out-loud kind of way. It had been on his mind, though he hadn't been sure of broaching the idea until it came out of his mouth. They already spent most nights at one another's place. She could use the extra cash. Why pay two rents? He clearly caught her by surprise. It seemed a big step, she said, for two people who had never lived with anyone before, who'd only known each other a few months and had not even gone on a trip together. Having only invested in persuading himself — unconsciously, at that — he hadn't developed any convincing arguments. And it wasn't the moment for banalities. Oh, I can't live without you — he could. My life has no meaning unless you're near — it did. He felt something like those feelings, far more than he ever had; but he was not an 'I can't live without you' guy. She'd have laughed; or, maybe worse, not. None of it would have flown, which was one of the reasons he liked her so much.

"Between working at the Centre, apartment emergencies, and consulting on the side, I won't have time to hang around and bug you while you're writing. You're going back to Los Angeles in a few months anyway. That basically makes it cohabitation lite. Why not give it a try?"

"I don't know…" She looked flattered, on the edge of agreeing.

"However, in the interest of full disclosure," he said gravely, "I must inform you I have an Elvis shrine in the closet. I am also a prize-winning yodeler. And every Thursday I host an all-night didgeridoo jam session. There, now you know."

She'd giggled, thought a long minute, then brightened. "Okay. Yes! Let's do it."

True, the new arrangement would cost him some privacy. He'd also have to shelve any plans to move for a while — though on further consideration he didn't really have any. The funky neighborhood and building full of exiles had grown on him. And he'd always been indifferent to his lodgings, which showed in the dirt, effluvia, and general bachelor neglect he found in cleaning up for her arrival. So this is how I live, he thought, abashed. Afterwards, he dumped the stuff he'd left to molder in Swanson's room. Judith would be in there now, leaving Swanson no place to crash whenever he got back. Well, too bad; he hadn't announced his plans or even contributed to the rent since he'd first gone back to California.

The actual move-in, after all the time they'd been spending together, was frictionless. It really did make sense. Even his privacy was mostly intact, as she spent lots of time in her room, to study or recharge. In that, too, they were compatible. Unlike his old fantasy of the gingham-tableclothed restaurant in Marin County, this was not remotely going into neutral. Exploring new pathways in work and in love, nobody could accuse him of trying to dodge his workout in the gymnasium of the self. She was bringing fresh, unexpected aspects out of him, not just or even primarily in bed. The habitual, slack phrases he used to trot out didn't get past her. Now he weighed his words, avoided summarizing a book or movie by 'interesting' or 'it sucked,' and uncovered a whole range of perceptions he'd been too lazy to examine. Why had he never found on his own what being around her brought to light?

Sometimes he would come across a chocolate behind the books on his night stand, a note at the bottom of the coffee jar… Little surprises that said: you're on my mind. No one had treated him that way before, and of course the idea had never occurred to him, either. To give her some unexpected delight in return wasn't so easy without imitating her way. His programmer mind was unused to gratuitous, whimsical gestures. He had to dig deeper, which was teaching him at least as much about himself as her. Sex was different too, going beyond the ol' piston-cylinder to another kind of intimacy, which appeared at all sorts of odd moments: walking by the river, reading a book together… It went on at a level he couldn't and didn't want to analyze. How had she put it? "My lizard brain likes your lizard brain."

Another squall pounded against the windows. Judith got up from the desk Martin had bought for what she called her 'pencil-chewin', longhand-writin' self', and came over to rub his shoulders.

"You are not even remotely a fuckwind." she went on, "Which reminds me: we'll have to ask Henri what your Gnärthøk name is."

"Sicklethrank. No, too many vowels."

"Thrbwqkl."

"Yes, Thrbwqkl the fourth. I take it blatherskite somehow relates to Das Porno-Kapital?"

"Ahem. No. I am pro-cras-tin-at-ing."

"Jude, Jude, you grad student you. Don't let it become your brand."

As a rule, Moon still checked the apartment guests in and out — after Martin promised she wouldn't have to deal with Swanson again. But today's departure was Jerome, who deserved special attention after his second super-long stay: champagne, car service to the airport, whatever he wanted. Doing the sendoff himself also let Martin satisfy his curiosity: what had Jerome been up to, and what had happened with Nadia, who'd vanished completely? Jerome saved him the trouble by bringing up the subject himself.

"She was kind of amusing. I knew how to say no to the rest of it."

"The rest of what?" asked Martin, as he poured more bubbly.

"First off, she said I could save myself a bunch of money and stay for free at her place."

Martin went goggle-eyed. "She *what*? She knew you were renting from us!"

"She wanted me to invest in her next film. Wouldn't take no for an answer. Get this, she says: 'For you, Jerome, I'll give you ten percent of any proceeds.' After I said no a couple times, she upped it to twenty percent! Uh, hello? It didn't sound right. I made some calls to some very connected friends. Nobody had heard of her. Plus, she refused to stop badgering me. Finally I told her: 'Nadia? Are you listening this time? ADIEU.' "

Martin smacked himself on the forehead. "Argh. Sorry. If I'd known…"

"No worries. I enjoyed her schtick, up to a point. I didn't mind buying all the drinks…"

"Oh, she did that with you, too?"

"Never offered to pay for so much as a cracker."

"Now I understand why she's always meeting new people."

"Doesn't take her long to burn through the old ones."

Chapter Twenty-One

It must've been a week, Swanson figured, since he'd left Portugal for the Low Countries. But what did the calendar matter when you were snug in the train's womb-like stasis, gliding through the bucolic landscape, where the only proof they were actually moving was the different configurations of cows and crops? Bruges, Ghent... he'd ticked those boxes on the itinerary. Yet instead of being inspired by all the Memlings and Van Eycks, he found his itch to draw had left as suddenly as it'd come. Temporary burnout, probably. When Lars and the guys from the beach in Lagos invited him up to Stockholm, he'd accepted with relief, as if getting off the hook. Prague would follow, then the fleshpots of Amsterdam. And after that, who knew what. In the meantime, he hadn't disclosed his location to anybody, even to Cardwell, who'd phoned that morning. Paris was going well, apart from the fact that Judith had taken over his room at headquarters. And that Martin's business idea had not panned out.

"Nadia's place?" Martin had sighed. "Ugh. A few people rented from her, but then she'd do stuff like go into the apartment while they were still there, saying she 'forgot something' — obviously checking on them. Even yelled at one couple for moving a couple tables around."

"Ouch."

"We've already gotten a shite review because of it, so I booted her off the website. Then Jerome told me..."

None of it came as a surprise. Nadia had emanated waves of bullshit from the beginning. Martin went on for a while about his new job — some academic nonsense. How could such an intelligent person put time into such lame people and pursuits? Then again, he thought afterwards, he was doing the same sort of thing with Duncan, who had just sent his first email since the deposition.

> *From: slam@dunc.com*
> *To: swan@geach.com*
> *Subject: Backing*
>
> *Hey - sorry to be asking you, especially after what happened, but if you could front me some cash, it would be a huge help right now. I got cleaned out last week by a couple assholes who were colluding. They got caught the next day, not that it did me any good. Anyway, if you can back me, I will pay it back with interest. Hope you're doing well.*

The response hadn't taken two seconds. Help Duncan get a job, yes; flush money down the toilet to feed his demons, no. Even his "hope you're doing well" somehow rang false. If he really hoped so, why not ask for specifics? Maybe the right thing would've been to craft a strongly-worded phrase, cajole Duncan into changing course. But no, he'd have found it patronizing, or used it as more ammo against himself. And how much more could be put into Duncan, given what it had already cost — company ratfucked, house robbed, career in the toilet? Cliff had been right: trying to fix matters would only make them worse. In the end no one but Duncan could wake up Duncan. Swanson stared out the window. Friends… screw 'em! He unfolded his seat table and brought out one of his father's dossiers. The dense pages, packed with spidery handwriting, were in no apparent order. No wonder his study of them had stalled. Then a paragraph jumped out at him.

Swanson softly whistled: so he'd written on the right-left split after all. But which painting was he referring to? It could be the Louvre self-portrait or any number of others. Or, indeed, all of them.

"Now arriving in Stockholm," announced a spookily neutral voice.

After checking into his hostel, on a boat on Lake Mälaren, he headed straight for the National Museum. The R thing was now back on his mind. Not just R as an artist, but the fact that he kept going, no matter what. It felt important to see that right now, before the social distractions. Who knew when he'd be back this way. The museum, though, had just a couple of the self-portraits: the comical etching of the artist with his mouth forming a surprised 'o,' and an early painting from 1630 that had been stolen. The reproduction hanging in its place showed the familiar crease between the eyebrows, the beginnings of pain in the right eye, the left eye that cooly registered everything: telltale signs, at age 24, of what would come later.

In what they called their real life, Lars and his friends occupied normal, non-beach-dude positions. One taught literature, another sold cell phones, Lars managed an IT department, and had even heard of one of Swanson's defunct startups. Professionals or not, they had chosen quite an upscale bar.

"My God," said Swanson, looking at the drink menu. "I thought New York was expensive."

Lars laughed. "Sorry. Our alcohol taxes are ridiculous."

"No wonder you guys vacation in other countries."

"We have our tricks to get around it," said Lars, turning to his friends. "Tomorrow is Saturday; shall we show him the ferry to Helsinki?"

Swanson balked. "Uh, sounds like fun, but..."

"No, really — it's a huge party."

"In Helsinki?"

"You don't understand. Alcohol isn't taxed on board, so the party happens on the way. Usually we come back to Stockholm the next day without ever getting off the boat!"

Swanson laughed. "You guys take a tugboat to Finland just to avoid alcohol taxes?"

"This particular tugboat is seven stories high, has three discos and probably ten restaurants. Don't worry, you'll like it."

The next afternoon, they all met at the ticket office alongside the gargantuan boat. After paying, they followed a covered gangway that led to a huge atrium, extending to the full height of the vessel. Their shared cabin was at the extreme low end of the scale: four bunk-beds, a sink, no window. No sense paying for a nice room, Lars pointed out, when you'd only use it for sleeping on the return trip, if you got lucky. The Swedes went straight to sleep and advised Swanson to do the same: nothing would happen until evening. When he awoke, his friends were in dress clothes. Swanson squinted, then sat up.

"Hey! You guys didn't tell me this was formal."

"It's okay — you can go as you are. But if you want, there's a shop on the second floor."

By the time he'd made himself presentable and tracked down the others, in a white-linen-tablecloth restaurant, they'd already met some girls, rosy-cheeked, beautiful, and half-drunk. Everybody politely switched to English, but after a couple drinks, and who could blame them, they lapsed back into Swedish. For many months, his thoughts had not been on women at all. But across from them a cute blonde, American, shouted over the music to a tall guy in a white suit. When the suit got up, Swanson moved in. He began by miming, not saying a word so as to draw her in closer, then talking into her ear, pretty soon nibbling it. All he caught was that she was from Wisconsin. Grinding against each other, they slow danced to even the fastest music, ignoring whoever bumped into them. Later, up on deck, far from the crowd, the Baltic sun had risen, if it had ever set, and they staggered to the front of the boat. She insisted that they not 'go there' — anybody could walk in on them — so for hours they kissed and groped. During short breaks, they watched the primal drama of the ship, alone on the waters with no land in sight, plowing on toward the horizon.

He awoke in his bunk, still dressed, alone. The boat seemed to have docked. Lars and the others had apparently gone ashore after all, or found companions of their own. On top of his pack, a note read: "I'm in cabin 43-A — Patti."

Though hung over, his body, as pent-up as he'd ever felt in his life, wanted not food or sleep, but sex. It was almost noon; hopefully she was still there. He knocked, waited, then knocked again. She opened, wearing only a long, transparent t-shirt. "My mother went on a tour. I told her I'd catch up with her later." She demurely locked the cabin door behind him. Sexy as she looked, her nighttime enthusiasm, in the act, turned puritanical. She lay absolutely still, looking at the ceiling. He didn't care, almost didn't notice. All those hours of unfulfilled lust trumped the tiredness, the headache, the narrow, rickety bed. As he felt himself getting close, she began to snore. He kept at it, between laughter and a kind of desperation, fucking away, wanting to finish but in need of a psychological push. Pornographic images refused to arrive. He tried rockets launching, oil derricks, geysers… He pictured her room at home. There would be the huge TV, a bookshelf for decorative plates and ceramic animals, a sofa, covered in protective plastic. It would all be pink, with rock star posters from a few years ago, maybe an Impressionist print. The image of her nude except for a pair of long socks, holding a teddy bear in one hand and a whip in the other, finally put him over the edge.

She was gently shaking him. It was afternoon; soon she'd go meet her mother. While he'd lain there naked, asleep, maybe even snoring, she had dressed, and now looked ready for communion in her sky-blue sweater and gold necklace. Ashore, the day was cold and dreary. She said she still had time to kill. It being Sunday, nothing in Helsinki was open. They began to wander aimlessly through the deserted city center. So they'd make small talk, trade numbers, promise to stay in touch — then forget the whole thing ever happened. The epitome of his pointless trip up here. Sure, let another hour tick away, add to the time he'd wasted like a goddamn fool. Swanson stopped short, abruptly eager to cut through the BS, to have that acrid truth-telling taste in his mouth, the way a vampire needed blood.

"I'm going back now," he announced. "Enjoy the rest of your trip."

She looked startled. "Well, bye. I had a great time. I hope we can stay in t—"

"No, we won't be doing that," he broke in, the empty street making the words sound louder. "We have nothing in common and never will. You know it as well as I do."

She stood there, open-mouthed. He turned and walked off, feeling clean, a little exhilarated, as always after such a burst. Not at all cold, either. Same as with Caitlin, even if nobody else saw it like that. What she felt in this moment didn't matter. If she had a brain she'd recognize he was right, whether it took minutes or years. The sharper the hurt now, the better she'd remember it later. Maybe she'd even tell the truth herself sometime, though it was all the same to him.

After a few blocks he stopped. Return tonight, with Lars and the others? No, that acquaintance was over, too. He checked into a hotel and spent the evening watching soccer on the restaurant's television, listening to the vowel-laden speech of the Finns at the next table, which sounded like bubbles being blown. The next day he sailed back to Stockholm, again stationing himself at the bow, as the vast open sea rolled out in front of him.

Part Four

Chapter Twenty-Two

Toy robots, a lava lamp, wind-up chattering teeth, prints of old sci-fi book covers — enough of his Silicon Valley office décor for Martin to feel at home, to uphold his image as Mister Technology. And a private joke on the way people in the office seemed to view him: a benign visitor from another planet, a possessor of esoteric powers. He twirled the propeller on his old Panoptical baseball cap. No, he wanted to say as he performed the customary French handshake with the entire office, every morning: my skills are ho-hum; what you know is strange and special. The intellectual foundations of the Centre seemed as far away as ever, not to mention the nature of Simone's gentle but uncanny insight.

He pushed away from his desk, late for the least favorite part of his week, Lacroix's status meeting. After André finished explaining the latest revisions to his book, Martin launched into his piece, then suddenly stopped short. Inches away from his face was an outstretched palm. A palm, connected to a central nervous system, muscles, blood, afferent and efferent pathways: a physical unity that in human society wore clothes, produced memos, answered to the syllables La-croix, and was now speaking into his cellphone.

"It really is a bit absurd," Lacroix said loudly, his hand still extended, as if Martin might interrupt at any moment, "that you can somehow find time for that, but not for your homework, *n'est pas?*" His eyebrows formed a triangle of hurt, bewildered surprise. "I am going to let you handle this predicament yourself. You can tell me tonight how you managed."

Lacroix put away his phone, lowered his palm, and turned again to Martin. "Sorry. Sometimes you have to remind them who is the parent."

Martin took a deep breath, but before he could continue, Lacroix added, cuttingly: "Anything at all to report on the software?"

Martin did have a working prototype, but had told only André, knowing better than to mention such progress within earshot of an ambitious manager. So he was doubly confounded to hear himself blurt out his secret, as if the words "anything at all," implying laziness or worse on his part, had provoked a pavlovian release of the trapdoor of his mouth. He immediately tried to backtrack.

"It does sort of work, but it's not ready to show yet."

But Lacroix, apparently only hearing the words "does" and "work," left the conference room, returning minutes later with Simone. Sheesh, thought Martin, this guy really is a dick.

"It's still very primitive," he announced. "Please don't expect much."

He reluctantly fired up his laptop to launch the demo. A sentence appeared against a grey background: "The cat is on the mat." To its right, another: "*Le chat est sur le tapis*", a yellow bubble highlighting the verb. Under the gaze of an audience, everything about the program looked painfully cheesy and amateurish. Martin grimly clicked on a red button that flashed the message "Generate all verb tenses." Beneath, two columns of sentences appeared: an English one with verbs highlighted, a blank one to be filled in with French.

"The student puts answers here." He moved the cursor into an open bubble and began to type. Suddenly the program froze, the screen turning a familiar azure shade.

"Oh, la, la, la," tsked Lacroix. Even he recognized the Blue Screen of Death.

"We will now have a brief intermission," Martin joked as he rebooted the machine, badly wanting to reach across the table and throttle his boss. The second time everything worked: typing a wrong conjugation turned the bubble red, which generated a new set of questions, based on the mistake. He closed the window. "For the moment that's all there is."

Simone smiled. "This reminds me of the first exercise I was taught by my childhood piano teacher. A simple one, all on the white keys. Then he had me play it again, but one half-step higher, in C-sharp. Not so easy! Then a half-step lower, backwards, in different rhythms, and so on. If I made the same mistake twice, he created a special drill for it. We spent months just on that one sequence."

Martin nodded, the ideas bubbling up in him. A pattern to manipulate patterns, an exercise that generated exercises — which could be applied, with appropriate changes, to music, languages, or anything. He suddenly felt sure she had seen the implications of his whole idea long before, maybe from the very beginning, and had now dropped a hint to see if he'd pick it up. Who was this person?

Back at his desk, he teased out the possibilities. You could vary different parts of the sentence, for example the nouns: *The rabbit is on the grass.* Or pronouns: *She* is on the mat. Invert the sentence's meaning: The cat is *not* on the mat. And so on. What else? Let the user's mistakes guide the drills the program would create, as per André's idea. Introduce a time limit, since the whole point was for the responses to be rapid, automatic. Limit a session to specific categories — household objects, sports, nature. Include the usual dog-training rewards: new levels to climb to, smileys, competitive scores... The programming wasn't difficult, but the short deadline added excitement. Enjoying himself too much to stop, just like in the old days, he ordered in some dinner and 'wrapped around,' working all night, into the next day.

❂

Ting.

That silvery note chimed at odd moments, day or night, whenever Simone was working nearby. Martin had known many busy, methodical people, but none who put timers on themselves day in, day out, sometimes for intervals as short as five minutes. One morning in the break room he asked her about it.

"A timer keeps me focused," she said. "The closer our September deadline, the more I rely on it."

"Isn't it hard to accomplish something in such short bursts?"

"Not at all. When I pay complete attention to just one thing, five minutes can seem quite long. It also leaves me refreshed for the next task. Working uninterrupted for long periods is in any case impossible here, given my position."

She turned fully toward him and lowered her voice slightly. "And everything goes, Martin: teeth, hair, vision. Once it's gone, it never comes back. We have to steal the minutes, fill them with what we want."

He thought of what happened that day in the Jardin du Luxembourg, the way time had seemed so unreal, even as his surroundings moved and changed. To speak about it demanded a vocabulary he still didn't have — if one even existed. He tried anyway, a little self-consciously, worried it might sound too mystical. When he finished, she wore a sympathetic smile.

"You wanted to hold onto it, I'm sure."

"Yes. That's just when it started to disappear."

214

"All you can do is prepare yourself for the next time, although if there is one, it won't be the same.""It won't?"

"Not quite. For one thing, you won't be the same person as you were."

"It's happened to you, then?" He almost felt he shouldn't be asking questions, but here was someone who knew, and he needed an answer badly.

"Yes, but each time a little differently. I try not to underestimate or overestimate those moments. It's more important to prepare, to live in such a way that you're ready for them."

She'd said it again. This time he actually heard. "Prepare how?"

Just then her phone rang. She looked at the number. "I'm sorry, I have to take this call." Then walked to her office and closed the door.

He went back to his desk, wanting to kick himself for being so slow and missing out on an explanation that felt more important than anything else he could think of. André stood at the whiteboard, revising the outline of his argument. Martin watched a minute, then said: "I have never met a boss quite like Simone."

"She is the first real one I've had, but from what I've seen, they are usually more like Lacroix. What was she saying?"

While Martin summarized the conversation, André sat at his desk, tilting his chair back to look at the ceiling. "If anyone would have the answer, it would be her. She's farther along than anyone else I've ever met. Even the way she walks around the office: you don't see her make restless gestures or use typical expressions."

"I hadn't noticed that, but you're right. She's relaxed but never idle."

"A writer of ours had an expression for that," André said. "*Tuer la marionette.*"

Martin laughed. "Kill the puppet?"

"You know, the way most people make gestures and say things automatically, without thinking."

"So you've studied her, too."

"Since I started here. Between her and Henri, one is never bored. She rarely says or does what I expect."

Martin felt favored by her words, somehow special. But one morning, having left home without a jacket or umbrella, he got caught in a rainstorm. As he walked into the office soaking wet, Simone happened to be standing there.

"What on earth…?" She looked at him incredulously.

He tried to laugh it off. "It's just a little water —"

That only seemed to make her more indignant. "Would you accept that from a five year-old? It's to behave like an imbecile when you are not an imbecile at all. If you don't treat your own body like a friend, how can you be anybody else's friend?"

The word 'imbecile' stung like a slap in the face. Sure, he should've prepared for rain, but adults — assuming she saw him as an adult — didn't talk to each other that way, let alone at work. André, who'd heard it all, was smiling when Martin entered their office.

"Very funny," said Martin. "I can't believe she chewed me out for that, like I was a baby."

"You should be happy," André replied, munching on a croissant. "She doesn't waste two seconds on most people."

"Why such a big deal over such a tiny mistake?"

André didn't commiserate as expected. "Small things are big."

"But why lean so hard?"

"She sees the way people take care of themselves as a kind of symptom for how their minds work in general. It comes out harsh so you'll remember. If it's a really stupid blunder, trust me, she'll remind you of it again and again, even once you're sure you know better. It's like being branded with a hot iron: you never make that mistake again. Or if you do, you can't plead ignorance. It doesn't feel like kindness or generosity, but it is."

"Sounds like you've been on the receiving end, too."

"Oh, yes. She gives me tremendous grief for smoking. And I've received the raincoat lecture myself — among others. When I first started here, I showed her an essay I was extremely proud of. She read it and told me: 'Anybody could have written this. You can do much better.' As soon as she said it, I knew she was right. Which meant some part of me knew beforehand. It hurt, but at the same time I was glad. How many people will respect you enough to be honest? And manage to say it so you are more motivated, not less?"

"I suppose…"

"Plus, it forces you to ask yourself: how much do I want to be working here? Am I going to be like a pot that complains when it gets scrubbed — just because my pride hurts a little? What matters is whether she was right."

Martin shrugged. "Oh, I can't argue with anything she said."

"Then what are you protecting?"

"You'll have to do better," snapped Lacroix into his cellphone, as he paced up and down the hall. "I can't have teachers calling me about your discipline problems. It's unacceptable. While you're living in my house, you need to obey my rules."

Martin and André both held their breath. Lacroix passed their door again, oblivious. "Have you thought of how all this is affecting your mother? She expects so much better from you. I don't understand it. We give you everything necessary to succeed, and you do nothing but hurt us." His voice faded away down the hall.

André, eyes still on his monitor, said: "I feel sorry for his kid. If we could just get rid of that clown…"

Martin cleared his throat. André turned around to see Simone standing in the doorway, smiling.

"Go on," she said. "I want to hear how you'd manage."

"Er…" *Damn it! All that effort pretending everything's fine, up in smoke.*

"Have you ever met Lacroix's son?" she pursued.

"No," André admitted.

"Then how can you judge? Maybe you could try to get to know Lacroix a little better," she said casually.

André bit his lip. *I'd rather eat my laptop.* "What an interesting idea," he croaked.

"You might get the chance to see his side."

His side? Should I try to see Attila the Hun's side, too? "I'll do my best."

After Simone left, he remembered a phrase of Dominic's: "when you have the right attitude, everything is fascinating." A walk down the street came alive when you observed the facial expressions of passersby, guessed where this or that stranger would be in twenty minutes… The key was to limit one's focus, look actively; then the world began to dance. That's how he'd relate to Lacroix, too, but a less evolved part of him wanted a little commiseration first. "*Merde*," he said after Simone had left. "How am I going to survive playing patty-cake with that bastard?"

Martin laughed. "What were you saying about not being a slave to automatic reactions?"

"Yes, you're absolutely right," André sighed. "Now please shut up."

Chapter Twenty-Three

Swanson put on his shoes and socks, still thinking of last night's dream.

"Sorry about those Koons and Hirst posters," he'd been saying to his father.

"Oh, that." His father, snow-white hospital bedcovers up to his chin, waved his hand, then let it drop. "Don't worry, I expected you to rebel at some point. Would've been disappointed if you hadn't, in a way. Now, if you tell me you still possess those monstrosities…"

"No, no. Long gone."

"Good. Otherwise I really would croak."

Swanson generally ignored his dreams, but this one struck him, being the first he'd had in Prague. It was the one place in all Europe his father had insisted they visit, based on his own first time there, decades before the American influx, before the fancy hotels and fast food, before Swanson was born. The city itself was the real treasure, he'd said, more than any museum. Swanson remembered only fragments of that trip: wandering alone through the side streets, accompanied by a low melody from an unseen cello that pursued him for blocks and blocks. Crossing the fogged-over Charles Bridge, where a busker had adorned his kneecaps with sock-puppets whose eyes rolled as the man sang and danced to keep warm. The clock in the Old Town Square, its figures of saints gliding by in the upper window until a skeleton rang the bell to mark the hour. He'd tried afterwards to capture those memories in art, but the atmosphere, which was everything, never came out right. Nobody else had gotten what he was looking for, either. Kubin or Rops sometimes came close, Goya's etchings, a detail or two in Dalí, but none hit the bullseye.

He grabbed his laptop, then sat down again on the narrow bed, inhaling its fusty, mothballish odor. In the days since he'd arrived, he'd felt the purpose of his trip subtly evaporating. Prague seemed flatter, smaller than before. Full of Americans now. From all the castles, churches, cemeteries, and museums he'd seen this time, only one piece of art had stayed with him, a *capriccio* by Guardi where an elegant couple tried to outrun the wind that chased them through the Venetian ruins… Obviously he was the one who'd changed, and couldn't in any case expect the magic of a first-time experience. The fantasy of creating a book from his dad's notes was also not panning out. The further into them he went, the deeper the morass of obscure references and allusions. It would take months if not years to track down and decipher it all.

Maybe, out of need, he was trying to squeeze more significance from this trip than it was ready to give. Silverware clattered in the kitchen. The aroma of toast tickled his appetite. His elderly landlady, Madame Daskalova, would soon offer him breakfast in her accented but accomplished English, a lilting, old-school music full of words like 'bountiful' and 'utterly' — the archaic vocabulary of old novels. First, though, email. The internet connection existed, but only as — what was the new cliché? — a known unknown. Eventually he managed to piggyback on somebody's unprotected wifi signal and began going through his messages. His brother and sister had a long complaint regarding their father's estate — they, who until now had always disdained vulgar economic matters. A note from Martin went on about his new pursuits that sounded to Swanson like the alien academic interests of his siblings. Martin also wanted more help with the Paris apartment. Forgetting, damn it, whose expertise had made the whole venture happen! Meanwhile Cliff was back in New York: *I hope you are still considering my offer. You are a natural, and after a little training would be your own boss.*

His cellphone rang.

"Hey Swanson, it's Duncan. Look, I'll come right to the point. I am in dire straits and I need a loan."

"I already told you: clean up your act and no problem."

"That's the thing. I need the money to get out of here and clean up my act."

"You're still in Vegas? Gimme a call once you're back in the Valley."

"You don't understand. I can't leave."

Swanson grimaced. These mysterious self-inflicted calamities were beyond irritating. Duncan went on, in a pleading tone Swanson hadn't ever heard from him before.

"C'mon, dude. Remember how I helped you when you needed it? I didn't let you down. That's called being a friend."

The real Duncan would never have called in a favor like that, by turning on the guilt. To barter his original generous action, in order to buy his way out of whatever sorry mess he was in now, was to negate it. The transformation of his character was sadly complete. Swanson walked in circles around the small room. He thought of what Cliff had said: anger at Duncan — his own worst victim — made no sense; demanding that he change would only backfire. Perhaps only a shock would get through to him.

Swanson took a deep breath. "You're right, I do owe you," he continued evenly, "that's why I can't go along anymore with what you're doing to your life. How am I supposed to help you out of the hole when you keep digging? Get straight, if you want. Until then, don't call, write, or get in touch. If that means never, then it's never. Your choice." He hung up.

For a long time he stood looking out the window, onto a narrow courtyard where children were playing on a patch of asphalt bordered by scrubby trees. That scene, which he barely registered in the moment and had no relevance for him whatsoever, later became, in a kind of bank-shot of the mind, the one sight from Prague he never forgot. He'd done the right thing, without a doubt, but was in no mood for breakfast anymore. He needed to get outside, to clear his head. He circled his own familiar few blocks, then headed away from the city center.

It seemed his few real friends were growing more distant, as if betraying what had made them friends in the first place. Bah. Career, friends, romance — *aux chiottes* with it all. Art, too: he'd done almost no sketching since the Low Countries. Being a lone wolf these last few months hadn't worked. His competitive, hypercritical energy, lacking an outlet, could easily turn against himself. Dangerous. Maybe the best place after all was with other wolves — at least you knew their agenda.

After walking for hours, he became aware that he'd wandered into a dodgy locale of squalid vacant lots and graffiti-covered storefronts. No landmarks in sight. A stocky man wearing a porkpie hat was walking alongside him.

"Hello, my friend," the man said, in English.

Swanson didn't stop. "Sorry, I'm not interested." *Damn, should've said it in French. Bastards always assume you're American.*

"Hello, my friend."

"Look, I'm not your friend. Goodbye."

"My friend, hello. Please you to visit the tavern of cousin of me." He held out a flyer for a bar, pointed to it, on the far corner across the street. "Come, I show you."

At the intersection, Swanson hesitated. He'd eaten nothing all day and was even thirstier than hungry. Out here in the sticks it might take an hour to find another place to sit down. It wasn't in a basement, but right there, in broad daylight. Besides, shouldn't the complete person experience everything, including — especially — visits to dubious joints in faraway lands? He could already imagine telling people: "Then, in this dive in Prague..." What decided him, he realized much later, was the novel feeling of not giving a damn what happened. Jumping into the unknown seemed no better or worse than anything else. He followed the annoying lunk across the street.

The place was deserted, except for a huge, thuggish guy, his leather jacket collar turned up, with his arm around a big blonde. While he talked in a low snarl, she stared straight ahead, even when bringing a cigarette to her lips. Past the bar was a dance floor, with seats and tables on the far side. Mirrors and red velour everywhere. The faint smell of ammonia. A disco ball gazed onto the parquet like a lonely Cyclops. Swanson ordered a whisky. Music came on: K.C. and the Sunshine Band. He thought of his first transistor radio in fourth grade, the long afternoons in front of his bedroom mirror, learning the Hustle to impress Jenna McCoy. He'd finished about half of his watered-down drink when the bartender slid the bill under his coaster. The number didn't compute. He did a quick koruna-to-dollar calculation.

"Er, excuse me, there's been a mistake. I only had one drink."

"No, friend, this is correct — fifteen hundred koruna, please."

"You've got to be kidding! That's the price of twenty drinks."

A group of sullen, feral men appeared around his barstool. The lightbulb finally went on. No need for them to speak. At least he didn't have much money on him. He took out his wallet. One of them laid out the bills on the bar — about fifty dollars worth. They started arguing amongst themselves. The waiter picked up Swanson's glass as if this happened every day, and poured his unfinished whisky back into the bottle, which he set carefully into the display case above the bar. A couple of the goons pulled Swanson off his stool and started patting him down.

"But you already got —" He stopped himself. Just shut up.

Someone shoved him from behind. This was escalating beyond ugly, straight to emergency. His existence, more fragile than he'd ever realized, could be ripped away for no reason, against his will. These troglodytes looked more than ready to drag him to some vacant lot, dismantle him, then walk away laughing. Instead they went silent. A stocky man in a suit had pushed to the front. At a sign from him they stood back, then melted away. Beneath the buzz-cut hair, his florid, freshly shaved face wore an impassive, unreadable expression, at odds with the bright pink carnation in his lapel. He motioned for Swanson to sit down again, then plumped himself on the neighboring stool.

"Please excuse my friends. They really have no manners."

Swanson said nothing. This was all too James Bond.

"I hate doing this," the man gestured around him, "but it's the only way I can make a living here."

Swanson had no idea what to say. "You're mafia, I guess?"

"Sort of. It doesn't matter. You're American."

"Yes."

"I have cousins in New York. Their half of the family left thirty years ago; our half stayed."

Was that supposed to be good or bad? Now that his adrenaline level was subsiding, Swanson just wanted to get the hell out before anything else happened. But the man went on, confessing, joking, recounting his life as if giving a testimonial. Then he signaled for food and gestured towards a booth.

"You are my guest." It was not a question.

Well, they had his money; what else could they do? Chop him up and feed him to the pigeons? In that case they wouldn't be wasting a meal on him. Still, he made sure not to be the first to sample any of the dishes. As the courses kept coming, his amigo in the porkpie hat ushered new patrons into the now busy club. Each received the same treatment: an unfinished drink, sticker shock, a visit from the no-necks.

The owner polished off the last of his baklava and pushed back from the table.

"I need to get back to work. But you're okay — stay as long as you like. You can go upstairs to the hospitality suite, if you want. It's on me. Come back whenever you like." He tossed some brightly-colored pills and a fresh pack of cigarettes on the table, then vanished.

Ignoring the stuff, Swanson tended to his full-strength whiskey and the tingling sense of vertigo that came from looking at the mirrored walls, whose reflections overlapped and receded into infinity.

Not long after daybreak, Swanson awoke, cold and damp, on a park bench. Light was peeking through the tree-tops. He had no idea where he was. He turned over. On the ground beneath him a pool of vomit spread out, the taste in his mouth confirming that it was his own. A dog was lapping at it greedily — which made him puke some more. He groaned and rolled onto his back again. The last thing he remembered was the club emptying out and everyone drinking Campari and absinthe on the sidewalk, some even mixing the two "for the colors"… He rinsed his mouth at a water fountain, smoothed his hair, and began to walk, stiffly at first, then more resolutely. Okay, that's it, he thought, this phase is over. Before the new one could begin, though, the crap from the past weighing him down would have to be cleared away. After hours finding his way back to his room, he went through everything from the trip so far: brochures, maps, messages, phone numbers on napkins or beer coasters. Except for one business card, it all went in the trash.

His drawings were next. He ceremoniously washed his hands, so as to conduct the examination in all dignity and fairness. He spread out his works on the table, the bed, then on the floor against one wall. Walking back and forth like a general reviewing his troops, he tried to take them in as if they'd been done by someone else. They showed technique, enough to impress almost anyone. Far beyond competent; far more realized and expressive than the shit one saw in Chelsea or Charlottenburg or the Place des Vosges. Each had its reason for being, somehow represented his best. Which made it all the worse. None had that spark of the art he admired, let alone the ideal art that existed only in his head. He made another complete pass, then another, looking for just one that went beyond, took on a life of its own. But none did. There was no way around it: they had no genius.

He'd suspected it, perhaps for longer than he knew. This must've been the test he'd avoided when dropping art the first time. Having some talent was worse than none, even if nobody else caught on. Oh, maybe he could've made a career of it, developed a marketable style, hung out with the right people, said and done the jive bullshit that attracts attention. But he'd know. And his dad, the one inside him who wasn't dead at all, would know, too. He picked up a sketch of the kitchen at headquarters back in Paris and tore it in pieces, feeling, with a thrill, that something inside him was tearing, too. Eyes glittering, he shredded them all one by one, slowly at first, then faster, chucking them in the air like confetti. The last, best drawing was of a girl in a café, talking to a friend. Just a few strokes had captured her droll, sarcastic expression. This deserved special treatment. In the kitchen was a box of matches; he lit one and held it to the page, which browned, curled, and was consumed.

Exhausted, Swanson returned to his room, kicking the colorful bits of paper scattered on the floor by his orgy of disappointment. A profoundly uncreative act, lacking any positivity. Well, a vain, selfish bastard he might be — but not a fraud. His choice as a kid had been the right one after all. He'd given art another shot, his best, and now was free from it, instead of torturing himself trying to climb a peak that in the end would have been inaccessible. On the table was the big box of his father's notes… But no, he wasn't so far gone as to destroy those. He picked up a dossier, paged through it. Any number of reasons might explain why his dad had suggested this trip, willed these notes: to reconnect Swanson with that early talent, to see whether he had a vocation in him, to spare him the pain of always wondering what might have been. Or just to remind him that art was part of his life, a counterpoint to pursuits where he really did have a gift. Whichever it was, that connection still mattered, unlike all the others. Apart from his dad, who else had taught him — using actions, not just words — something about how to *be*? Duncan had, but he only served as a negative example now. Martin had also been crucial: his openness, curiosity, unconcern for what anybody thought. Lately though, he was starting to seem like a stranger. Openness to what, curiosity that led to what? What Swanson had heard from him was a bunch of academic ideas that'd make no material difference to anybody. Proof once again that people's strong points, when poorly used, became weak points. Instead of always seeking, shouldn't Martin be finding by now? How, after thirty-five years, could he still be discovering himself? More important, what, here and now, was the basis of their friendship?

Swanson sat down again. At one point he'd read a lot about the vocation of artists, how they had to prune their lives of what didn't serve their calling. His own vocation was different, but it seemed he'd arrived at that same point. If so, it was no time to shrink from what had always been true: once he no longer needed people, it was over the side with them. And right now he felt nothing for anybody, including himself. Empty or not, though, he had to either keep going or blow his brains out. Picking up his phone, he read the number off the one business card he'd saved and began to text.

Chapter Twenty-Four

His name: Angus. His game: guide the user, via question and answer, through the various ways of combining the elements of a sentence. The idea was for him to eventually be an animated character, but for now he was just text on a screen. To liven things up in the meantime, Martin gave Angus a snarky, rude-boy attitude. Lacroix, getting testier as the weeks went past, vaguely understood and discouraged it.

"Remember, just the basics for now. We do have a deadline. Also, please give him a French name. 'Angus' sounds like an English *footballeur*."

"Let me know if you have any preferences," Martin replied coolly.

"Something kids will enjoy — perhaps Félix, like the cat," said Lacroix.

Lacroix was of course right about sticking to basics, but adorning Angus' rudimentary personality with moods, tics, and complexes became hard to resist. Martin duly renamed him Félix, but inserted a hidden 'Easter egg' option for his own amusement: with a keystroke, the program flipped back to foul-mouthed, nutcase Angus mode. Angus appeared in the evenings, after Lacroix had gone home. For weeks now, Martin and André had both been coming in to work around noon, then leaving very late. Though it bugged Lacroix no end, he couldn't complain, with the team meeting all its milestones. André in particular had hit his stride, producing a detailed outline and the first five chapters in one concentrated burst.

Apart from André and Henri, only Judith was in on the joke. "I hope Angus doesn't mean I'm infecting you with my procrastination cooties," she said one night.

"Nah, he's just an outlet."

"Good. I was getting worried the two of you were going to run away together."

"What's with the procrastinating? You seem like you're working pretty hard."

"I am, but I'm less sure now that I understand the root cause of the pornification."

"There's always the existential void."

"Ah, the void," said Judith, waving an imaginary cigarette. "Dahlink, the void is so out of date! It's simply lost *all* prestige."

"What, then?"

"Maybe it's cities themselves," she replied. "The way crowding people together physically can isolate them emotionally. Everyone plays their part in the machine, specializes in some function and is reduced to that. They start treating each other like objects, which is the essence of porn. But if I try to incorporate all that, it would take the thesis in a whole different direction, and probably push it back a year. Plus, my advisor in the States hasn't gotten back to me in ages. I have no clue what she thinks of my critique as it stands, whether it's good, or too radical, too tame, or what."

"Hey, don't worry. You'll pull it together."

She went quiet.

He wiped his glasses. "Anything wrong?"

"As of today I have one month before I go back to L.A.."

He pushed his laptop away, though he really wanted to finish that piece of code. They'd danced around The Conversation for some time — no avoiding it now. "Are you upset?"

"What kind of question is that? Of course I am! Aren't you?"

"Sure," he said. "I wish you weren't leaving, but we knew from the beginning you'd have to, for a while. You're coming back, right?"

She didn't answer.

"What's the alternative?" he asked, alarmed. "I can't just pick up and go. I've got the apartment to deal with, the work at the Centre. But I can visit you out there. And you can come back. You should. Europe is the place for both of us — I'm sure that's why we met here." It would test her feelings for him, too. If she couldn't handle a period of separation, maybe he wasn't that important to her.

"I'm still a year away from finishing the damn thesis. Do you have any idea how *long* that is?"

Her sour tone caught him off guard. You've always been this way, he thought to himself. Once you finally let down your barriers and trust someone, time loses all reality — the relationship becomes fixed, sealed off from whatever else might happen. Because you love. If you and she have to part, you'll reunite seamlessly, no matter how long it takes. You don't change, so she won't, either. The physical ways a woman is bound to the calendar — is so much more aware of her position within its cycles, of physical deadlines and limits — are facts you, living as if time had no stop, have managed to ignore. The loyalty you give and want in return only takes into account your half of the equation, which comes more cheaply. All that flashed on him and was gone, in the urgent need to find words. For such questions, he was never prepared.

She clicked her tongue. "Aren't you going to say anything? You are so passive sometimes, it drives me crazy!"

"I see," he tried to joke his way into the clear, "I'm the martini, but you're the one who has to be shaken and stirred." Silence again. "Look, what do you want me to do?" he said, his voice rising. "Drop everything and move back to the States?"

"At least have the savoir-faire to pretend you want to," she said acidly.

"When have we ever played games like that? I mean, you know how much I care —"

"Oh, let's drop it." She went into her room and shut the door.

They'd squabbled a few times since she'd moved in, but breaking off discussion was new; it seemed so not Judith. Maybe it really was his fault; he'd heard the passive accusation often enough; there must be something to it. He stood at her door, raised his hand to knock, then stopped. No, he wasn't going to apologize; what he'd said still felt right. Now wasn't the time to prolong the discussion anyway. Things could go in the wrong ear, feelings might get hurt, or stuff blurted out with no sense of the big picture, stupidities that could never be unsaid. A few hours later, she came into his room and lay down beside him, molding herself to the curve of his spine, the way that always brought him such well-being. The next morning they seemed on track again, especially after a long pre-dawn love-making session.

"Do you want to stop by the Centre tonight?" Martin asked as he ground the coffee. "Henri's giving a talk. Maybe you could even…" He almost said: "consider working there." What a bad improvisation that would be! She couldn't do that for another year, minimum, and it was exactly the wrong moment to emphasize that fact. Working together might not be such a hot idea anyway. Pleased at having mindfully dodged a needless, self-created pitfall, he continued: "….visit André. He's been glued to his desk for the last month."

Friday afternoon conferences at the Centre were rare, so most people stayed on to talk afterwards. Martin enjoyed seeing Judith with her friends — their friends. It brought out a different aspect of her crackling, shiny energy from what he saw when they were alone.

Henri, almost a head taller than the others, saw over the crowd as Simone arrived unexpectedly. "Ah! I assume this means the grant applications are all done."

Simone joined them with a tired smile. "Yes, no more for this year."

"You might be surprised," Henri said to Martin, "how much diplomacy and public relations work is involved in keeping the lights on here."

Simone sighed. "Before the Centre, I barely knew who the president of the Republic was. Now I need to know the name of every politician in the whole educational sector, including their family and pets."

André asked: "Will you have some time for the piano, now?"

She nodded.

Martin remembered all those scores in her office. "Were you a professional musician?"

"No, although I trained to be one. I started with the piano very young, before my feet could reach the pedals. Growing up, the only thing I wanted was to become a concert pianist. Then I had an experience that put me off the idea."

This was new information even for Henri. "What happened?"

"In my late teens I attended a conservatory; let's just say it was somewhere in greater Europe. For my second-year final exam, I played the Chopin Polonaise in F# minor, Op.44. It is a martial piece: you are on horseback, about to ride into battle. In the first few bars, you hesitate — you will probably be dead within minutes — then you launch yourself into battle, one-hundred-ten percent. I still have the tape — I'd achieved what I'd hoped for. But walking past the examiner's office the next day, I heard my name, then: "No, two is enough." Two what? In the hall outside the honors program office, I looked down the list of names of those in program. Some women, a man from Nigeria, another from Asia… then two names, Cohen and Rosenberg, jumped out at me."

"Oh, la la," said André.

"So I wasn't surprised when two of the judges gave me a very low grade, barely passing. They said I had not showed 'the proper decorum or attention to the score.' But I knew that piece well enough to play it backwards. In fact, that is how I practiced the most difficult parts."

Martin's eyebrows shot up. "Backwards?"

"Yes; once you can do that, even slowly, with lots of mistakes, playing it normally is simple. It's something my first teacher showed me: when you have to jump three feet, imagine you need to jump ten."

Martin felt a new surge of admiration for Simone.

"Racism isn't just perverse," she went on, "it's idiotic. It corrupts a person, pulls him much lower than the animals. In theory, a racist might wake up after two seconds of thinking. Is an Arab headache different from a Jewish one? If it rains, won't a young black man and an old Chinese woman both get wet? Doesn't every human on the planet descend from Africa, if you go back far enough?"

It was clearly still fresh for her, decades later.

"Did you stay at the conservatory?" asked Martin.

"I left that day and never went back."

"But why stop making music," asked Judith. "because of a couple monsters?"

"Oh, I didn't quit music. I could never do that. But what of real value was I going to learn from those people, who had created nothing themselves? To stay there, and even more so to have a career, I would have needed to become a kind of soldier. I realized I wasn't made for it — they did teach me that, anyway. The most important thing is to play, even if no one else ever hears."

The flight from Prague arrived at Charles De Gaulle in ugly weather. On the train into town, Swanson reviewed his texts with Cliff over the last couple days. It hadn't taken long to come to terms on salary and a signing bonus. Moving costs would be more than covered. But the starting date was tight, only six weeks away. He'd need to find an apartment, quick. As he pulled into the Gare du Nord, he called Martin, giving him a quick, air-brushed version of his trip. Then he cut to the chase.

"I might as well just blurt it: I need to sell my half of the business."

"Whoa," said Martin. "Everything all right?"

"Yep, everything's great. I got offered a VP position at a hedge fund, so I'm moving to New York."

"No shit. Wall Street?! You always said it was a joke."

"I'll just have to un-joke it."

"Why does that mean you have to sell?"

"Ever looked at Manhattan real estate prices? I gotta unload everything liquid, including the Sunnyvale place, just to cover the down payment. Otherwise I'd have to raid my portfolio and take a huge tax hit."

"All right. We agreed either of us could bail out whenever…"

"Don't get me wrong, doing this business was big fun. We had some good times, learned a lot, made some money. But this offer is too good to turn down, especially since the Valley is a closed door for now. So, what about the rental? Do you want to buy me out or sell?"

"Probably sell," Martin replied, after thinking a bit. "I don't have enough to buy you out, even if I turned everything upside down."

"Whatever you want to do is fine by me."

"There goes your good buddy again," said Judith when he told her the news, "throwing you for another loop. I still can't figure out why you put up with it."

Martin shrugged. "It's not like he planned things this way. You should see how far he goes to protect his friends." This time he told her the Duncan story. "We agreed at the beginning," he added, "that either of us could sell our part whenever. He had an opportunity, so he took it. What was he supposed to do?"

She went to the sink to peel some carrots. "And what are *you* going to do?"

"The Centre doesn't pay that much, but as long as the consulting jobs keep rolling in, I guess I'll get a smaller place and rent it out the way I have been."

"So you're happy with the way things are."

"Can't complain."

She peeled faster. This would have been the perfect moment to free himself from this business if he'd wanted to. But he wasn't even going to try to keep her. Just sit there at the kitchen table. How frivolous they were, these micro-improvements he spent his time on, adding features to little pieces of code while the planet fried, society imploded, injustice ran rampant… She turned fully toward him. "You are so frustrating sometimes!" Her raspy voice went up the scale, ending with a squeak.

"Wha…?" He started.

"You just… let stuff roll along however it wants to. Even everyday things. You never take the initiative. I always have to decide where we go or what we're going to do or see. You never even cook."

Martin put out both hands in a calming gesture. "Trust me, you don't want that. I only cook for my enemies. If I have an inner chef, he is locked away somewhere deep inside."

"How convenient for him." She saw it clearly now. Underneath all his hard work was a profound laziness. It lived in a blind spot in him. Only if he saw it could he fight it and win. The way to help him was to press on — who else would? — as an act of love.

"You're not that way just with me," she continued. "Take where we're sitting — in an apartment a friend arranged. Because you'd gone in on a business created by another friend. You said your career started by chance — the video game company was another thing you probably wouldn't have started on your own. You've told me as much yourself: you're not doing those things; they happen to you. It's like you're a ghost who happens to occupy your own life."

"Hey! Enough already!"

He walked out before anything else got said. In the event of a full-scale yelling match, her feelings would bounce back afterwards. His might not. Until now, he'd never been seriously pissed at Judith. Maybe he'd idealized her, had glossed over certain objections, retouched what bugged him or rotated it in his mind until it reached a flattering angle. Her sharp tongue became tartness; her whims, a charming capriciousness; the sometimes stiff-necked political views, intellectual autonomy. Which was it really? Both. She probably did have a point — did he ever set the agenda, saving her the job of making the final choice? Until now, he'd pictured his role as rather gallant, offering alternatives, then nobly agreeing to whichever she chose. But did he even generate the alternatives, half the time? Find something new and different to do? Make anything move from A to B by his own volition? They both had a lot to work on, and the better a relationship, the more vulnerable to the ordinary mind, the part always ready for destruction. One misunderstanding could sow underground resentments, stubborn misreadings of the other… If you let it fester, you could lose everything without even knowing what happened. As if Nature, as soon as it put two people together, began working to break them apart. It was in those moments that they needed to be more conscious, not less. When he returned home, she was still up, red-eyed.

"It wasn't true, what I said. I wanted to get a reaction out of you, but I went too far. I'm really sorry."

Relieved, tired, eager to bury the hatchet, he forgot all his insights and resolutions. "Don't worry about it. C'mon, let's go to sleep."

Chapter Twenty-Five

A week later, Swanson called from California. "Real estate seems to be the only thing out here that's still hot. I already have five offers on the Sunnyvale house, just by word of mouth. Tomorrow I'm flying to New York to look for places. You sure about the apartment?"

"No way I can buy you out," Martin said, "but I want to stick with the business. I'm gonna look for a smaller place, and time it so I can move the furniture straight there from Sébastopol. For the sale, let's just give it to Monique — she did a good job of selling it to us."

"Nah. As the sellers, we have to pay that cost, which is four or five percent — like, twenty thousand euros."

Martin clicked his tongue. "What do you care? You're gonna be rolling in it! And I'll still have enough left over to get a mortgage on a smaller place."

"Going to Wall Street doesn't mean huge bucks in the short run; most of the compensation is in options and bonuses. Hell, I had a bigger salary at Dendroid. For now I'm kinda squeezed, in fact. Plus there is the principal of the thing. Paying an agent to sell the place is giving away money."

"Okay, what, then?"

"We can do a for-sale-by-owner and hire someone to show the place and pass us the offers."

"Who is 'someone' and how do we find him slash her?"

"Post ads, look around on the 'net. Shouldn't be too hard."

"You're expecting me to do that? Interview all those people?"

"Well, you are the man on the ground there."

"Dammit, Swan, why can't you take care of this part of it, since you're bailing? I'm maxed out here. *You* sell the places. You're the sales guy."

"First, I know it's all the same to you engineers, but I'm in marketing, not sales. Second, believe me, I wish I could come back and sell the thing; I love the game of it. But this job offer won't wait. I have until the end of next month to get out of the Sunnyvale place and into the New York one, once I find it. This is a huge opportunity for me; I have got to make it work."

Martin said nothing.

Swanson went on. "Maybe Sébastien knows somebody who needs a little dough. Really, selling an apartment is a job pretty much anybody can handle. We could get some college student to do it."

"Yeah, that worked so well for taking care of the apartments."

The same bells on the door tinkled as Martin entered Monique's agency. She stood and extended her hand, looking just the same — but how different he was! Now he spoke in French, made his own choices, ran his own show. By the time Judith came back, he'd practically be a native.

"Bonjour, Monsieur Cardwell. Nice to see you. Where is your friend?"

Right. She had never seen him without Swanson.

"I'm here because we're dissolving the partnership," he said. "I need to sell the place we bought through you, and find another, smaller one."

"So I will put the existing one on the market and —"

"Unfortunately, my *associé* insists we sell it ourselves. But if you have a small one-bedroom or a studio for sale…"

He handed her a list of requirements: thirty square meters loi carrez maximum, around half the price of the first place, in a quieter, more tourist-oriented neighborhood.

"*Je m'en occupe.* I will be in touch soon."

The only qualified person Sébastien could recommend was an ex-boyfriend, who offered to do the job for fifteen thousand euros.

"We shouldn't pay any more than a couple thousand," said Swanson flatly.

"But we need somebody trustworthy, who knows the apartment and how to present it," Martin insisted. "There's got to be some reason agents get paid for their work."

"I know from experience, 'cause I did it for a while — they do fuck-all! They feed the same line to everybody, stand around, then collect your dough at the end. Here's what we should do: start an all-out campaign to find a salesperson. Post notices in newspapers and magazines, put up flyers around the neighborhood."

"Goddamn it, Swanson, that means interviewing dozens of people, which is already way more work than I intend to put into it. It's a huge amount of effort, all to avoid hiring a professional."

"Like I said before, anybody can do it. Contact all the tenants in the building. Maybe one of 'em would be interested. Hell, ask Paula."

Martin laughed derisively. "Some random neighbor? Our concierge? Are you out of your mind?"

"Headquarters is not that far from Sébastopol. She could handle visitors on her lunch hour. I'm sure earning a little extra change wouldn't bother her."

"That is the dipshittiest idea I've ever heard. She has her own job! Furthermore, we have no idea what kind of response we're going to get.

If it's too much work, she might bail on us and we'd have to find somebody new, at the worst possible moment."

"Maybe so. Look, if you don't want to find someone to sell it, why don't you sell it?" said Swanson, with the voice of a man who's just found the one path to daylight. "Two thousand euros is good money. To sweeten the deal, you can take sixty percent of anything we get above the going rate. Based on the prices last time I looked, the average is six thousand a square meter."

"Me? I hate even the idea of selling stuff."

"You can do it in your sleep! The place is ready to show as-is. Think of the cash — we'll split what we didn't waste on Sébastien's friend, and you'll pocket two thousand euros for doing practically nothing. That's thousands of euros, right there. Plus you get sixty-forty of whatever we receive over the base price. That will make it more than worth your while."

Martin gave a sigh. "Okay, the hell with it. I'll do the thing myself. I'm gonna suck at it, and I've got a deadline at the Centre. But hiring somebody else sounds like even more time and work."

"You mean it? That would solve everything."

"I ought to have my head examined, but yes. I'll leave it to you to tell our upcoming clients that we're selling the place and they need to find another apartment."

"Sure. And really, the sale will go fine; based on my experience, it'll take an hour or two a day, max."

When he told her about the deal, Judith pursed her lips. "You already know what I think. It's good he'll be far away and not able to pull stuff as easily."

Martin shrugged. "By now, I'm not sure what's left to pull. The ads are placed. In another couple days, the place will be on the market. We sell it, divvy up the proceeds — boom, done."

"It's more time, but if you do the selling you have more control."

"I wouldn't want to be negotiating against him, but we're on the same side in this thing, and he's motivated to do as well for himself as possible. He's been pretty agreeable so far. When I told him he had to write the ad and post it on all the right websites and real estate rags, he shut up and did it," said Martin, with a touch of pride.

His phone buzzed. "Ah, speak of the devil."

Swanson, as always, started right in. "You know, I've been checking the latest Paris property values. I gave you way too good a deal."

"How's that?"

"After I posted the ad, I noticed some places are going for seven thousand per square meter."

"We agreed on the price *you* suggested. Are you saying you want to change it? We already submitted the ad, broham."

"The market has moved since the last time I checked. If there's a bidding war, and it goes way over six thousand, I get screwed."

"I wish we had put all this in writing," said Martin, half to himself. His stomach had gone sour. He took a deep breath, tried to relax his face and shoulders. "What would you say if prices had gone down and I tried to renegotiate everything midway through the deal?"

"A closing date is as essential as the price, especially when the market is appreciating," Swanson went on. "The agreement was lopsided in your favor, because you locked in a price based on the market of then, but the actual sale would take place sometime in the indefinite future."

"You make it sound like I somehow planned this, and exercise mysterious control over the value of Parisian real estate."

"But now that I want to raise the price to reflect a more realistic value, you imply I'm trying to pull something. To be quite honest, I feel bullied by you in this. We're partners and ought to do what's fair. You are not acting like a man of your word."

"I think you have me confused with somebody who's not on your team," said Martin curtly. "The main motivation for me to sell it was that someone might offer a little over the price. Seven thousand a square meter raises the bar for me and the place will take longer to sell. Instead of guessing, why don't we ask a third party, like Monique, and accept whatever she says? I'm already seeing her this afternoon."

"I can live with that."

Martin leafed through the apartment listings spread across Monique's desk. He lingered over the last one for several minutes.

"That is the best of them," said Monique. "It's on rue Rambuteau, quite near yours. It's unoccupied, if you'd like to see it now."

"Yes, but before we go, I have a question." It was a little awkward, asking her to price an apartment she wouldn't be selling. But she knew the place very well, and was about to make money off whatever he now bought — that ought to take away any bad taste.

If she was put out by his request, she didn't show it. "I would ask six thousand per square meter," she said firmly. "If you try for more, it might be a very long wait to find a buyer."

"Aren't some places getting seven thousand?"

"Only in the most expensive neighborhoods, like the sixth or the Île St. Louis."

That evening, Martin relayed her judgment to Swanson. Instead of generating more flak, his associé replied in an even tone: "Okay, then. Now we know." After a slight pause, he added: "By the way, I decided on a little insurance and called up a handful of agencies."

Martin started. "What the…? I thought you didn't like agencies. And that we both had to agree how to do the sale."

"Don't worry, I stipulated that their fee will go on top of our asking price. It doesn't change any of the fundamentals, just increases our odds of getting a strong response."

"I'm glad, I guess. I found a new apartment today — empty, so I can move right in. Now I'm double-motivated to sell this one pronto."

❈

Martin woke vaguely excited, never having sold anything, let alone an apartment. It might even be fun. After a long shower, he ate his usual monster bowl of oatmeal in front of the computer, double-checking the ad for the apartment. From the other room came the soft clicks of Judith's keyboard. She had been pushing hard these days, hitting the desk early. He went in to her, kissed the top of her head, deeply inhaled the scent of freshly washed hair.

"I'd better mosey," he finally sighed. "Today's the day; maybe we'll get a couple looks."

The morning being cool but sunny, he skipped the métro and strolled along the boulevard de Sébastopol. A block from the apartment he noticed a line of people snaking out the building door onto the sidewalk. He squeezed past them into the lobby.

"Monsieur Cardwell!" cried the concierge, "Thank goodness!"

"Is something wrong?"

"These people say they are here to see your apartment."

"*All* of them?"

"They started to arrive an hour ago."

As Martin escorted the first half-dozen up to the apartment, his cell phone rang.

"Bonjour," said an unfamiliar voice. "I represent the Central Paris Apartment Group, and would like to arrange for our client to see the apartment."

Martin gave her a time, writing it on the back of his hand. Before they'd even reached the apartment, door, another agent called. Then Swanson.

"Anybody come by yet?"

"Are you kidding? We're being mobbed!"

"Great. Call me when we get an offer."

Martin gave the first group twenty minutes, then ushered them out and had the concierge send up the next bunch. By noon, he had a page full of appointments and interested parties. Swanson called again.

"Anything going on?"

"Hey, we said I'd call if something happened. Now will you let me get on with it?"

"Okay, okay. Just wanna stay current."

"Trust me, if we get an offer, you'll be the first to know."

That night, he looked over his schedule at the Centre. He'd probably be keeping irregular hours until the apartment sold, and Lacroix would complain. Well, let him: there was no choice now. Judith was also in crunch mode since her thesis advisor had finally provided some guidance. It would be pathetic if they both spent what was left of her stay flopping into bed at night, exhausted. The next morning, she left early for the library, while he went straight to Sébastopol for his first appointment. No sooner had he arrived than his phone rang.

"Monsieur Cardwell!" Paula, the concierge back at headquarters. "You must come immediately!"

"That is impossible, absolutely impossible."

"Your apartment is leaking water into the apartment below you. It's very serious!"

"How can that be? I just left there, and nothing was wrong."

"The building superintendent is very upset. Especially because the lock has been changed, and he doesn't have the key. He says if you don't come right away, he will call the fire department and have them break your door down!"

"Okay, okay. Tell him… tell him *j'arrive*."

He tried Judith — straight to voicemail. Of course: she was already in the library, cell phone off. No choice but to cancel the next few appointments and go straight back to headquarters. Halfway to the Place du Chatêlet, there was a familiar buzz in his back pocket. Sheesh. It was the middle of the night in the U.S. — didn't Swanson ever sleep?

"What's happening today?"

"Can't talk now," Martin barked, deliberately sounding even more harried and out of breath than he was. "I had to take off. There's a big plumbing problem at the other place."

"What other place?"

"Headquarters."

"That can wait. We don't want to miss potential buyers."

"You don't under—"

"Martin, do NOT leave!" Swanson bellowed.

Martin hung up. "Fuckingassholesonofabitch…"

Outside his door, the downstairs neighbor and building supervisor stood talking to the plumber, a short, burly man with droopy, bassett-hound eyes. It took half a minute to discover the problem. "*C'est le robinet. Voilà tout.*" After all that, a ten-cent valve washer on the toilet. Martin apologized, then excused himself to hurry back to the other apartment. As soon as he hit the sidewalk, his pocket buzzed again.

"How could you hang up on me like that?" Swanson started in. "And leave the place while we're selling it? I need to know I can trust you to keep me updated and do the right thing. Right now I don't feel like I can."

"I had to get back to headquarters — they were going to break down the door! The toilet was leaking water downstairs like crazy."

"Why didn't anybody — why didn't you notice?"

"In headquarters you couldn't see anything. We lucked out that the guy below us is doing renovations and saw the damage early."

"Couldn't you have said so instead of hanging up on me?"

"If you'd given me the chance instead of constantly interrupting, I would have. I wish you'd put as many hours into selling this place as you are into back-seat driving."

"You know I can't do that."

After they hung up, Martin wished he could talk over Swanson's bizarre attitude with Judith. But he knew how she felt; no good would come of it. He called Sébastien who seemed to know more than he wanted to tell: "What you describe doesn't surprise me." When pressed, he coughed up a few incidents from Swanson's tenure in Paris: cutthroat dealings, intrigues… None of it explained him trying to browbeat a lifelong friend, but maybe that was thinking about it wrongly.

Swanson crossed the chilly air-conditioned bank lobby and went out its enormous revolving door, immediately receiving a blast of muggy heat to the face. He loosened his tie and walked down Fifth avenue. The day's meetings — the coop board for his prospective apartment and now the bank — had gone as well as he could've hoped. His ducks were all in a row, except for the Paris apartment.

For weeks he'd watched the changes inside him with the cold eye of a chemist mixing unfamiliar, combustible elements. He was in a hurry to unload the apartment and start his new life. And yet… he couldn't help himself from rabidly seizing on every aspect of a deal that might lead to his advantage, even with friends: one of the few sides of his personality he'd never been able to control. It didn't matter much anymore which side won. As a student of human behavior, he was curious how Cardwell might react to finally getting pulled down into reality, where determined pressure usually revealed people as they were, beneath all the bullshit. Expediency, though, meant moving the sale along. He pulled out his phone and speed-dialed Martin.

"We're two weeks into this, with no solid offer. I'm getting nervous." Martin sounded tired. "You said it might take months, remember?"

"Neither of us want to wait that long, am I right? Unless there's an offer soon, we oughta reduce the price. We're now at four-ninety. Let's say if we don't get a serious nibble by Friday, we lower it to four sixty."

"Fine by me. I am sick of this job." A doorbell rang on the other end. "Gotta go," Martin said. "The last appointment of the day just showed up."

On the threshold were an avuncular, middle-aged man and a stout, somewhat younger woman with a sharp voice. Two more like so many others. Martin listlessly gave them his rap then let them wander around. They went through the entire apartment several times; each time the man's smile was wider. He introduced himself as M. Nodier, an inspector of public schools. The woman was his niece. As the two made one more circuit, Martin heard her say: "Are you sure?"

His raised hopes were exceeded when Nodier approached him again and said simply: "This apartment is just what I'm looking for."

Sheesh, thought Martin, this guy bargains the way I do.

"I'm prepared to offer you four hundred eighty-five," Nodier added.

Martin pretended to mull it over, trying to hide his excitement. He leafed through his appointment calendar as if it held various competing offers. Try to get full price out of him? For five thousand euros, it wasn't worth the risk. After a bit more playacting, he almost reluctantly said: "I don't have any official forms, but yes, that amount would be acceptable."

"Then we have a deal," Nodier said, smiling. "My only condition is that I want to move in as soon as possible, since I have sold my current apartment."

"Really? Before finding another?"

"I had an agreement on one, but the seller backed out; he even had to forfeit the money from the *promesse*. Perhaps we can come to an arrangement ourselves, so that I can move in earlier."

"I'm sure we can work something out," said Martin, desperate not to let him off the hook.

"But first," said the niece, "there should be a signed agreement to make it official."

Nodier wrote out an improvised agreement and made a copy. The niece read it over, nodded. Once both copies were signed and hands shaken, Martin let them out, locked the door, and strutted around the living room, brandishing the signed document like a bandleader with a baton. He pulled out his phone to share the good news.

"You did *what?*" Swanson exploded, "How could you accept an offer without consulting me?"

"The guy's giving us almost full price!" Martin sputtered. "You told me a few minutes ago you'd consider four-sixty. Now you harsh on me when we get four-eighty-five?"

"Can't you understand? You do not accept a bid before talking to your partner. I don't care if the guy offered you five hundred and a blowjob. What is *wrong* with you?"

"We get this great offer, and the only thing you bring up doesn't even matter on the bottom line?"

"It's ethics, Martin. How can you talk so much about philosophy and not even apply it to your own life? If you were working for me, you would be so fired right now."

That was too much. "*Fired?* Oh, really? Why didn't you delay things in New York and do the damn job yourself, then, if you were so concerned? I never knew ethics meant so much to you."

"In a partnership, there has to be trust. Unless your partner agrees, you cannot go around agreeing to stuff, especially accepting an offer. You know it's wrong."

Those last words stopped Martin. Years ago he'd been involved in an argument over a parking space. The other guy, some slick in a Mercedes, said of Martin's unwillingness to back up: "It's wrong; you know it's wrong." Martin, not wanting to sit there all day over it, and so easily convinced that he was, a priori, wrong, backed up, furious — to the point where he seriously considered dragging his keys across that beautiful blue Mercedes. For days afterward he'd been ashamed to have even considered such a cowardly, sneaky move. But to have backed down was bad in a different way. What to do? Society demanded a man be both reasonable and a caveman, without providing any rules on how, when, or why to be one or the other. And now he needed a reply. Tell Swanson to go fuck himself? That would mean instant war. Besides, what if he had a point? Or had no point, but was under too much stress? Then Martin would regret saying what was coming to mind. It probably was wrong to have accepted the offer. To call would have taken just a minute, if he'd thought of it. And yet… Swanson had started this business, then basically dropped it. He'd only made an effort when he didn't want someone to get the better of him. Then there was this latest thing of trying to change his commission… after having boxed Martin in, leaving him no alternative but to sell the place himself. No way could Swanson have been serious about having some college student or the concierge do it, or posting thousands of notices. The right response was too complicated to figure out on the spot. Bottom line, they had an agreement; without that, there was chaos.

"Maybe I shouldn't have accepted," Martin finally replied, cutting in on whatever Swanson had been saying, "but what can we do now? And what do I tell the guy who thinks he just bought the apartment?"

"Tell him it's your evil associate's fault. We can continue to see people the next few days, until the ad runs out. If we're lucky, another buyer or two will show up and they'll get in a bidding war. So you should get on the phone and call all the prospective buyers who gave you their number and tell them that you've received an offer and ask if they'd like to make a counter-offer."

"If you want this so bad, you call half the numbers, and I'll call the other half," Martin said lamely.

"Okay."

The next day, an agent called. "We have a serious prospective buyer. Can he come by at three-thirty?"

"Yes," Martin said. Then blurted: "I should tell you that we've already received a solid offer."

"Is it for the full price?"

"No."

She exchanged a few muffled words with someone on her end. "He would like to have a look anyway."

Two hours later the agent, a compact woman with a sharp, birdlike expression, and her client, a foppish young man in a shiny black suit, met Martin at the apartment. He hoped they'd take one look and leave. But no — the man did a slow walk-through, measured the dimensions of each room and sketched their layout — the opposite of the romantic, impulsive Nodier approach — then pronounced that the place met his requirements to perfection. After they left, Martin phoned Swanson.

"The new guy sounds ready to offer the full price."

"Awesome!"

"No, un-awesome, anti-awesome. I committed personally to Nodier. How can I go back to him and say he won't have an apartment to live in after all? He already sold his own place."

"You have to get over thinking that that is your — our — problem. He is responsible for his own irrational exuberance. Just tell him your hardass *associé* is demanding more money because he was not consulted on the deal, which you had no legal right to offer in the first place. He might threaten to sue us, so make it clear that whatever you and he signed is worthless, legally speaking. If he wants the place so badly, let him cough up the extra five thousand euros."

"Are you sure that's even legal?" Martin asked. "Have you checked the laws here, or are you just making it up?"

"No, I asked a lawyer friend of mine. Look, this is no time to get sentimental. We're in this fifty-fifty. The fact of the matter is that you're working for both of us, not just yourself. You may want to throw away five thousand euros, but I don't."

"But we promised the place to him."

"*You* promised it to him. Now you are going to have to explain the new context. You don't know this guy at all — why do you want to hand him all that money?"

"I don't care about that. I care about not being a scumbag."

"Like I said at the beginning, people are animals! Especially when big money is involved. As soon as it's in their interest, they turn on you. Whether they know it or not, they expect you to do the same. So don't feel bad. Look, if you can't stomach this, I got my loan okayed for the New York place today — I could fly out over the weekend and finish things myself."

"No, forget it. I'll handle it," Martin snapped. He didn't want Swanson ragging on his lack of testicular fortitude for the rest of his life. "I can talk to Nodier tonight. He's coming over to Sébastopol to maybe buy some of the furniture."

Nodier arrived alone, fortunately. Martin offered him a seat at the table and went straight to it: "I neglected to tell you the other day that I own the apartment with a business associate. He is very upset that I accepted your offer before consulting him. He insists that we leave the bidding open, especially since we have someone else who has offered full price."

Nodier's face fell. "But we made an agreement! We both signed it."

"I understand your position." The weasel words vibrated in the air. "I would feel the same way. Believe me, I want you to have this place. But my partner is half owner, and insists on this."

After an excruciating silence, Nodier said: "What am I supposed to do? I already sold my apartment, because I had bought another one. At the last minute the seller was unable to sell. Now this — what a horrible surprise!" He looked more bewildered than angry.

He's not made for this any more than I am, thought Martin. Suddenly he made a decision: "The place is yours if you can meet the full purchase price."

"I see. I will discuss this with my niece," he said wanly, then left.

When he heard the news, Swanson was confident. "Nodier won't back out now. It's only five thousand euros. And if he does, we go back to the other guy. Hopefully they'll try to outbid each other."

Oh God no, thought Martin, anything but that. "Sure, if one of them doesn't kill me first."

Part Five

Chapter Twenty-Six

Martin arrived at the agent's office at half past seven. The buyer was playing solitaire on his phone. The agent, her sludge-colored hair pulled into a tight bun, donned a smile and began briskly: "My client is prepared to pay you the full asking price. As per your agreement with our agency, that should be enough to seal the deal."

Tensing, as if he were about to enter a long, dark tunnel, Martin recited what he'd prepared: "Ah, unfortunately, this afternoon, we received an offer from the original buyer, for the full asking price." He pushed on, ignoring the two death-ray stares now focused on him. "However, my business associate," he forced the words up his throat and out of his mouth, "said he would consider a higher offer." *It's not my idea, not my idea, not...* The buyer glared at him the way one might a nazi child molester. The agent rocked back in her chair. The meeting's scripted politeness shattered, she leaned forward again, eyes narrowed.

"How dare you! That is against the law! I don't know or care what happens in the United States, but we do not do bidding here. The contract you signed states that any full-price offer must be accepted. You cannot turn it down in favor of a higher one."

"But I already have a signed offer for the full price."

"You signed? Why didn't you tell us that before the meeting? Is it official?"

"Yes, completely official," he said, though unsure what that entailed.

"Then there is nothing to discuss," she spat out the words, "You have to sell to the other buyer."

"Again, an offer made outside the boundaries of the original agreement might be possible…"

"*Pas de question*," she said, standing up and mechanically straightening her dossier. "What you are proposing is illegal in this country. Goodbye."

After spending the better part of a Saturday afternoon, Martin could see the surface of his desk again. The now-irrelevant lists of appointments and potential apartment buyers had gone in the trash, leaving only paperwork for the new apartment and sale documents for the old one. Nodier had ponied up. Not happily — any warmth in his attitude was long gone — but he'd paid the extra five thousand, then immediately mobilized his notaire. He and Martin, for their own reasons, had in retrospect been comically eager to sign and get it over with, before lightning struck again.

The phone buzzed. Martin answered, surprised. André rarely called, let alone on a weekend.

"Hi, what's up?"

"I wanted to let you know that it would be a good idea to make a physical appearance soon. Lacroix has kind of lost patience; he's even got Simone wondering where you are all the time."

"Understood. I'll be in on Monday for sure. I've basically finished the apartment crap."

"Good. Lacroix wants to start demos the week after next."

"Hope he hasn't been riding you too hard."

"No. Well, yes, but I've learned to ignore him. The draft of the book is ready to show to people, so the pressure's more on you, *Monsieur le programmeur.*"

"I've been working on the software at odd moments; it's pretty solid now." The documentation was sketchy; the number of translated sentences and variations was pitifully small. Still, it could be demoed without embarrassment, and he had time to fill in the blanks now.

"Besides," he went on, "what can he say? We're gonna kick butt!" In saying the words, Martin realized that despite its rough edges, the first iteration of their idea, of a different way to study and teach, really had come together. "I mean, this stuff works. Isn't my French better since we started?"

"Oh, yes."

"That's all from working out with Angus, er, Félix. Nobody can say we don't eat our own dog food."

"What?" said André.

"Sorry. Silicon Valley talk. We use our own product."

"It must be an interesting place, your home planet — sausage machines, dog food... And how is Judith?"

"She's fine. Getting ready to go back to the States for a while."

Actually, she hadn't been fine — or maybe it was he who hadn't — since her outburst. Things had sort of returned to normal, but behind what they said or did together, the impending separation always hovered. Which might be why she was working all the time lately: to close herself off in advance. After hanging up with André, he went to her room.

She looked up wanly from her laptop. "Hi there."

Hugging her from behind, he felt her sobbing. He'd never seen Judith so vulnerable, and when she stood and turned to him, crying for real now, he started to cry, too. They rocked back and forth, saying nothing, for a long time. The refrigerator began its lonely, indifferent drone, a background not just for their solitude, but that of the other occupants of the building, the city, the whole planet. Everyone ultimately alone, yet together in the sense of all playing the same rigged game, where the present was inscrutable, where at best you could know what the right choices were only after the present had become the distant past.

"I have a hypothetical question," said Martin, handing back the last of the preliminary Rambuteau paperwork to Monique. "Suppose someone else bids on the apartment before I sign the *promesse de vente.* What happens then?"

"Oh, it's too late for that. You met the asking price."

"But another buyer might come in and offer more," he said casually.

"*Mais non.* The price cannot be changed after it has been met."

"If the seller had a partner who felt the price was too low, couldn't he force a renegotiation?"

"No, they have to hold to the agreement. When either one signs, it commits both." She smiled, perhaps guessing what lay behind the questions. "You — the partners, that is — can settle the differences between them, but cannot go back to the buyer and ask for more. Otherwise there would be no trust between parties; the whole system would break down."

He left her office, satisfied on all counts. The other agent had spoken truth, Swanson had been full of it, and steering the place to Nodier had been the best course. Or felt like it, anyway. At the St. Paul station, he paused by the carousel. Often dark and empty, today it was full of children. Their parents looked on, taking pictures or waving each time their offspring went past. Funny how some children waved back, while others looked straight ahead, absorbed. Wondering which kind he had been, Martin started down the steps into the Métro. Coming the other way was a familiar face — Nadia. The stairway was too narrow to avoid her. She looked up and, perhaps making the same calculation, widened her eyes in faux happiness.

"Martin!"

Out of habit, he slowed down. Then Jerome's words came back to him. Behind this smiling face was someone who'd done nothing but waste his time, a sponge who'd repaid his help by trying to snatch away his best customer.

His expression hardened. "Excuse me, I'm running late."

A jet of ice went to his stomach as he continued down the steps. He had never failed to oblige somebody who pretended to make nice. However much she deserved it, he'd violated a rule he had always carried inside but never articulated: give people every possible chance, never give up on them regardless of what they do. Shunning them meant *he* had failed. Human beings, all of them, were good by default. If they strayed, it was due to accident or environmental factors that could be debugged; or they'd right themselves once they saw sweet reason... How had he evolved such an absurd doctrine? How many disappointments would it take before he stopped trusting people who were essentially strangers? On that point, Nadia herself had nailed him — he'd been *gamin* all right, *tout à fait gamin*.

Judith's suitcases had been on the floor of her room for a week now, opened so she could drop things in them as she passed. A visible reminder that her time in Paris was running down. Now, on the morning of her last full day there, they stood in the main room, zipped up and ready — enemy symbols, not just of her leaving, but of how she'd pulled away recently, spending more time, it seemed to him, in preparing to leave than in enjoying the hours they still had. It was her way, he was sure now, of making the separation less painful. He'd done the same: the fact that he'd soon be sleeping and waking alone had been the last thing he wanted to contemplate. As he browsed online for a restaurant worthy of their last dinner, already feeling sorry for himself, his phone chirped the Swanson-specific ringtone. Martin weighed not answering. Maybe his friend had come to his senses, though, or even wanted to apologize for his behavior during the sale. In that case, it would be better to forgive and forget. It had been stressful, ugly, even, but it was over now. They'd gotten full price, the place had gone to the right person, he hadn't done anything wrong or illegal.

Swanson went straight to the point. "Now that the sale is finally over, I've been rethinking how we ought to divide the proceeds."

"What do you mean? We split fifty-fifty like we've said from the beginning."

"In principle, but there are certain extenuating circumstances. First, this whole operation was my idea. The Euro has gone way up; so has the Paris real estate market — the way I said it would. That was the key idea of the whole venture. Think: how much of that is the result of you and how much the result of me?"

Martin tried to stay cool. "You're joking, right? I bootstrapped the goddamn business, not you. I supervised the renovation, built the team, and fixed all the problems. You were in California or on the road almost the entire time."

"The project was my idea," Swanson went on, as if talking to himself. "I did all the work that counted. We found the place because I studied the Paris real estate market. We got a loan and completed the transaction because I knew French. After that, it was a matter of inertia."

Martin laughed sourly. "Inertia? After you dropped it on me and split, mister brains-of-the-operation, you did pretty much fuck-all except for talking to the architect."

"I think I deserve extra consideration for that as well. It involved a very technical transaction that added a lot to the value of the apartment."

"Putting in the skylight was my idea," Martin shot back. "Like expanding the business."

"Look how well that worked out."

"Hey, it was an idea — which was more than you contributed after the first month or two. Anyway, how can you even think like this? Neither of us has ever been paid by the other for work we do. I can't believe we're having this discussion."

"I spent a huge amount of time on it," Swanson continued, impervious, "Had to get architectural sketches done, outmaneuver some asshole bureaucrat..."

"Poor baby! I did stuff like that all the time."

"It didn't take any special skill to let Donatella do her job. And anybody could meet and greet people, or hire someone else to do it. I figure my contribution is worth an extra fifty thousand. But since you do have a point about my absences, I think a fairer number is ten thousand."

Martin felt pressure building in his chest. The nightmare of the sale had finally ended, but things were careening off again into unknown territory. In a few more seconds, he would lose it and make a reply he couldn't retract. "I'll get back to you," he managed, before hanging up. This should have been in writing from the get-go. Oh yeah: 'we're friends, there's no need' — bullshit! It was because they were friends that they should've spelled out the entire agreement, to prevent any misunderstanding. These phone conversations only made matters worse. Jaw clenched, he closed his laptop, so as not to send the first words that came to mind. He grabbed a blank sheet of paper.

~~Dear asshole~~
~~It seems to me~~

<del>You fucking</del>
<del>Maybe we should step back and</del>

Hold on. Stick to what's important.

I do not accept that your time is valuable and mine is worthless. I didn't tell you half of what I did day to day, because you were in the middle of so many heavy issues. We agreed from the start to split the proceeds down the middle. Now you change the rules after the fact and want ten thousand for your efforts. Fine. I supervised the renovations, got the team together, and sold the place — give me ten thousand and we'll be even. While you're at it, pay me rent for when you crashed at Headquarters.

More thinking would only give a different answer, not a better one. He typed it into an email and sent it. Swanson's response wasn't long in coming.

Martin, I find your request to be paid more, if it isn't some kind of sick joke, to be incredibly inappropriate. You are forgetting all I've done for you. You never would have become involved in this business, which has made you a lot of money, without my expertise. I had the original idea, negotiated the deal — and didn't ask anything for it until now. You say you want the same amount of money I would receive, but you overlook a lot. My labor was skilled, yours wasn't. I knew real estate and spoke French, studied the tax implications, the purchase strategies, and so on. Renovations and client meet-and-greet are minimum-wage jobs. To sell the place, all you had to do was open the door and show the apartment. But you didn't even do that right!

This, after he'd pushed Martin to sell the place, knowing full well he didn't want to, then constantly interfered, micromanaged the whole process. And now that the sale was safely over, an all-out attack. Martin's stomach churned as he read on in disbelief.

> *How can you compare our efforts? You accepted a bid without consulting me, your friend and partner. You bitched and complained when I insisted that you bargain— which made you even more money. You never even gave me a word of thanks for all that cash I put in your pocket. This venture I started has made you wealthier from start to finish. Now you, who should have been fired and paid zero for the way you sold the place, want ten thousand euros. Fine. In that case, I will charge you full price for my work. My advice left you a hundred thousand euros richer, although you never even bothered to thank me. If you demand compensation for your badly done work, you are dictating that we operate by the laws of the jungle, and I will have no choice but to do the same.*
>
> *Think about it,*
> *Swanson*

Ah, yes, the jungle, Martin thought bitterly — where friends need each other the most. But his oldest friend in the world had become another person. Or had he always been that other? And was it only one other? Martin stood up and began to circle his desk. Those traits of Swanson's he'd once found charismatic or different — unpredictability, boldness, inventing the rules when it suited him — to what kind of person did they add up? What had he himself gotten out of being around him — compensation for his own shortcomings? Was that why he was worried about saying something he couldn't retract?

The front door rattled. Judith entered, looked at him, put down her bags. "What's wrong?"

He sat her in front of his computer. While she read, he tried again to review the situation. How, why had it come to this? His acceptance of Nodier's offer? No, money wasn't the issue. For Swanson to blow up the friendship over ten thousand bucks meant that blowing up the friendship had been the point.

Judith pushed away from the laptop. "Well, he may be a misogynist frat-boy art snob, but at least he's a total jerk."

Martin laughed ruefully.

"What'll he do if you insist?" she said.

"I have no idea, but it won't be good," said Martin, circling the computer table. "I feel like I'm being carjacked. On the other hand — and I'm not saying he's right — maybe it did take chutzpah to ask for money after my own mistake."

"That came after *his* demand, though." She sighed. "Sweetie, trying to understand both sides is one of your best qualities, but it's also a way to avoid conflict. You need more sand in your Bozo."

"Excuse me?"

"Ever have one of those inflatable Bozos? Unless there's sand in the bottom, they lean whichever way the wind blows. Sometimes you try so hard to see the other person's point of view that your own gets lost, and you hide behind that smooth surface again. It's hard to gauge how you really feel or what your stand is, even when someone's attacking you full force."

He continued pacing, hoping she wouldn't see his hurt. "Look, you're probably right, but can we dissect my foibles some other time? I need to respond here and this is not helping. I'd never have asked for more if he hadn't made all those demands. It's like he won't quit until he's wrecked everything."

"From what you told me, he's acted that way before — only with others."

Martin sat on the couch, lost in thought.

She softened her tone: "You two have known each other forever and been through a lot, but he doesn't seem to remember that. If he's willing to risk the friendship by squeezing every dime, it can't be that important to him. Maybe he's changed for the worse, the way you have for the better. Or maybe he always was a plain old opportunist. You're trying to hold onto the way things were, but it no longer applies. His actions say it all: you're just another obstacle in his way."

Without replying, he petted her hair a little, then went out for some air. Only after he'd returned and they were dressing to go out did he hit on the one correct way to respond to Swanson. But that was for later. He'd wasted enough energy on Swanson for one day — especially this day. Their dinner, at the Corsican place in the Marais Martin had chosen, was leisurely, intimate in a way they hadn't had time for in a while. The contrast made Martin wonder if he might have welcomed all these hassles in some way, to avoid confronting Judith on where she stood. He still had no idea whether she meant to come back to Paris or not, but asking her now would only receive an answer in words. For deeds, it would come down to how she felt once she was back in her California life, which even she, self-aware as she was, couldn't be expected to know. They walked home through the narrow streets, molded to each other. His hand rested on her shoulder, feeling her bra strap bouncing slightly with each step — an incredibly erotic sensation, the more so for her being unaware of it. Like certain facial expressions or moves in bed or phrases she used, to tell her how much they affected or excited him would be to make them conscious, rob them of their juice. Approaching the apartment, they started to walk faster. Maybe she had been on his wavelength after all. When the elevator arrived at their floor, they ran down the hall and Martin, hands shaking, opened up. Off came the clothes. Locked in an embrace and not wanting to let go, they duck-walked as a unit into the bedroom. One upside of all this recent fussing and fighting, Martin thought as he rummaged one-handed through his fuck-drawer for a condom, was that the reconciliation sex afterwards had even more heat and bite. They were back, one last time, to the healthy, uncomplicated intimacy of the beginning; no thoughts or overtones, just sex as sex.

Chapter Twenty-Seven

Martin woke up late, light-headed and feverish. Shit — if there was ever a moment not to get sick, it was now. It didn't help that he'd been sleeping so poorly, obsessively running down his mental list, uncharacteristically doubting whether he'd done something or not. Cancel the old mortgage, open the new one — check. Revamp the website — no, couldn't do that before moving into the new place. The latest round of improvements for Félix? Done last week. Something about M. Nodier... Right, Sébastopol had to be vacant before Nodier moved in, but they'd agreed to the earlier date. But that meant moving out by the tenth: three days from now... And he hadn't even started looking for movers. He slowly got out of bed and began calling every moving service he could find. He needed a team — today. But they all said the same thing, sometimes with a little laugh: "In the next three days? *Desolée, c'est impossible.*"

When he was almost to the end of the advertisements from his mailbox a gruff-voiced man finally said he could do the job. Martin almost giggled from relief. "Am I glad to find you! I need to vacate my apartment in the next three days."

The man put his hand over the phone a moment, held a muffled conversation, then replied. Yes, they could do it on short notice, though of course it would cost extra. "We can come tomorrow morning," he said, "then finish the following day. The price is two thousand euros."

Martin almost retched — double what he'd expected. But if he bargained, they might well hang up on him. He accepted, annoyed at having once more worked against himself. Only an idiot, he could hear Swanson saying, admits how desperate he is before talking price.

The next morning, he greeted them at the apartment, then immediately forgot their names. They were from Morocco. Martin smiled and nodded, hoping the United States had not perpetrated any atrocities there recently. One was stocky, with a shaved head, while the other, medium height and pale, had frizzy hair and a thin face. For him, they would be Larry and Curly. Which left him in the role of Moe — the last person he felt like today. He told them what to do and wandered through the apartment, mulling the unreality of time. Images flew past: Monique showing them the place, Donatella, facing the pile of kitty litter; their first rental, when Jerome had arrived; Moon freaking out over the water-heater. Now the place was almost empty again, as if none of it had ever happened... Unlike their namesakes, Larry and Curly were meticulous, carefully covering everything in padded blankets or bubble wrap. As their work wound down for the day, Larry approached.

"You will pay us now."

Just then André called. "I'm with Lacroix and Simone," he said, sounding frazzled. "We're showing Félix to the biggest textbook company in the country. I started the demo and somehow Angus has got loose. Whatever I do, it insults everyone who asks a question. When I reboot, I get Angus again!"

"Calm down, there's an easy fix. Just press the Alt key when you restart the program. But don't hold it down next time — or ever again."

After hanging up, Martin took out his laptop and obliterated the Angus code from the program. Larry stood patiently waiting as Martin closed the computer and counted out the bills.

"That is one thousand euros. Pay all, please."

"But you've only done half the job."

Larry's voice rose: "Are you saying you don't trust us to come back tomorrow?"

"No, but I'll pay the rest at the end, that's how it's done."

"We do not work that way," Larry said coarsely. "We will be here tomorrow. I swear it. But we want the money now." His friendly attitude from the morning dropped away like molted skin. The three of them were alone in the apartment. Curly happened to be holding the crowbar he'd used to dismantle the desk. Martin felt light-headed to the point of falling over. He could not have found the French words with which to argue, even if he'd wanted.

"Don't worry," said Larry, as he pocketed the full payment, "We'll be here tomorrow."

His head pounding, Martin went straight home to bed. He'd overpaid for the job, then caved on the payment. Who knew if they'd even come back? They probably did this kind of thing all the time, bullying weak-minded Americans who have no clue what money is worth.

The next day he woke up and went straight for his laptop. Still no word from Judith. Her silence had made sense, at first: to unpack, reorient herself, reenter her mother's atmosphere… it must have been a strain. But his notes and calls were going unanswered, and every new email triggered hopes that fell flat: spam, work, more spam, friend, spam, family. He regretted their awkward goodbye at the airport. There'd been so much to say and so much unsaid that one conversation could never have made it right. So they'd talked only of the immediate future, which had seemed for the best at the time. Not anymore. As for today, his inbox had just one genuine email, from Swanson.

Haven't heard from you. Meantime, I've been thinking. Since you've decided to continue the business, we need to address its common assets. I believe I should be compensated for my share, especially as the architect of the whole operation. First, there is the website: for you to get it for free does not seem right. I also created the rental agreement we had clients sign. If you're going to use and profit from things that are half mine, you

This was getting to be like pulling up a wild blackberry bush, that constantly snaked underground to sprout up somewhere new. "I know you think of him as a friend," Judith would've said, "but when was the last time he acted like one?" True. But how to convey to her so many years of good times with Swanson — in school, building Dendroid together, the conversations he couldn't have had with anybody else, the Paris adventure? Could all that have a sell-by date, like a piece of cheese? Apparently it could. To keep excusing or rationalizing Swanson's behavior was naive and pathetic, not to mention the physical toll it took, of lost sleep, a stomach in knots, as if a sludgy, rancid juice were fermenting inside him. He'd even felt his blood pressure climbing these last weeks — he, whose B.P. was usually so low his doctor sometimes measured twice to make sure he wasn't mistaken.

Living behind his bland mask — which others sensed, but had been hidden from him — took a toll, one Judith had tried to help him see. That mask that ran the show, it pushed him into peacemaking at his own expense, into wooden remarks when under fire, into standing for nothing. Did he never fight because he had no core, or did he have no core because he never fought? Nadia, that hustler woman who'd walked into his apartment, those movers... As long as they got what they wanted, they wouldn't have cared if he'd dropped dead in front of them. And now for whatever reason Swanson was trying to steamroll him, too. Martin typed his response, finally ready for it to be the last one.

I am done discussing this or anything else with you. If you want to sue, be my guest.

Ill as he felt, he went over to Sébastopol, ready to hunt down Larry and Curly if they didn't show up. To his surprise they arrived at noon sharp, as if yesterday's conflict never happened. After they'd moved everything over to the new place, Martin went home, feeling dizzy, sick beyond any doubt. There he found a reply from Swanson.

> *I see that money means more to you than friendship. My requests were reasonable and based on who had contributed what. If I had time, I would of course pursue this in court. Instead, I will leave it to your conscience and sense of fair play to make it good once you see the light.*

He deleted the message. And would nuke anything else from Swanson. The idea of tolerating any more was intolerable. Peace at all cost had cost him. Enough. He crawled into bed and stayed there for a week.

Chapter Twenty-Eight

Martin sat in the kitchen, as the sun cast longer and longer blades of hot light across the floor. A month now since he'd heard from Judith. He stared at the formica table's interlocked red and green circles, as if they were a diagram that might explain his life. But now it was time to go. He got up to shave. On the bathroom shelf was a bar of soap Judith had left behind, one of those tokens of her still scattered around the apartment. He held it in both hands, inhaling the aroma deeply, eyes closed. Forgotten moments came back: sexy shower games, her brushing past him in the apartment, trailing this same *sillage* of fresh lavender. He set the bar back on the shelf, behind the shaving kit, where he rarely looked, putting off the day when it would become just a bar of soap again. He went out. His shadow preceded him on the hot sidewalk; he followed it, imagining himself already dead, stuck among the living with their strange concerns. It was feeding time. Diners sat at outside restaurant tables on the rue Montorgueil, their plates piled high with cooked animals, brightly colored vegetables, *pommes frites*. All of it shoveled into gaping mouths. Once chewed and assimilated, the dead flesh and guillotined vegetables would exit the collective poop chute for parts unknown, thanks to urban hygiene and engineering of which one knew nothing — giving the planet its one sure gift from humanity.

If he weren't meeting Sébastien soon, he might have stayed home, sitting in the kitchen like a house plant, as he had for days now. Instead he aimlessly swerved left. On the rue St. Denis, sex-shop displays glittered: what you've always wanted, been forbidden, could only imagine — just step inside. He hadn't been in one of those in a good ten years. Parting the black leatherette curtains, he was hit by an overpowering smell of ammonia. To the right, a series of glass cases contained videos, arranged by category, gender, fetish. Meh. His own hard drive had better filth. Even the novelty items didn't raise a smile. There was something so sad and remote, so nineteen-fifties, about an inflatable sheep or a wind-up hopping penis… A blowup doll stared at him from its package, the gash of its bright red mouth the most lonely, depressing thing he could remember. Further inside, beyond a sea of dildos, was a private-show area. A man with an enormous, droopy mustache stood on a raised platform, microphone in hand, repeating: "*La couple ! Venez voir !*" His sad, glassy eyes stared straight ahead as he gestured mechanically toward the closed booths behind him. Brrr. Back on the street, a forest of signs tried to attract his attention, fixate it, turn it into mercantile action by short-circuiting all second thoughts, by defeating thought altogether. Whether sleaze or ultra-chic, the rue St. Denis or the Place Vendôme, the same mechanism applied — just as in Judith's thesis. For that matter, competition permeated whatever he could think of: memes, flowers growing toward the sun, politicians, spermatozoa, startup companies — everything striving, competing, trying to elbow its way to the pole position.

"We have our logic, they have theirs," Sébastien affirmed, "In other words, don't sacrifice your dignity. If she wants you, she'll find a way."

"But what if there's some misunderstanding?" However solid his decision to stay in Paris was, he couldn't help feeling tortured by the thought of Judith straying. A male opportunist slithering into her bed, replacing him in her heart. A girlfriend determined to set Judith up with some Hollywood cretin. Or Caitlin; it would be just like that little bitch to try and ruin things for the hell of it.

Sébastien leaned forward. "Look, in a serious case like this I will not bullshit you, *un vrai copain* — that would break one of the few rules actually worth following. It seems to me you are in deep water."

"Uh, Sébastien? You're supposed to be helping me out here."

"I wish I could. Unfortunately, this love thing is uncharted territory for me."

"Really? Never?"

"Not once. Naturally, you try your best to make sure things never reach such a point, but if it happens and it's real, what can you do?"

"What?!"

"That's right, *mon grand.*" He clapped Martin on the shoulder. "It's rare, but I've seen it happen: if you really love, there's not much to be done — you might just be... a slave for life."

"You. Are. Useless."

"I can only offer you my sincere condolences. However," — he raised his index finger — "it may not be real. Either way, you have to act before this thing poisons your existence. Either go to California and get her, or find somebody else, quick! Take a vacation. Anything."

"Come on, that is such a cliché."

"So what, if it happens to be true? If you win the lottery, do you worry about where the ticket came from?"

Simone walked into André and Martin's office. In an all-business voice, she announced: "I would like to speak with the two of you, please."

They exchanged a glance, then followed her into her office. She shut the door and sat behind her desk.

"I have just received a call from the Minister of Secondary Education for the Île de France," she said solemnly. "He informs me..." She paused, unable to keep from smiling, "that we will shortly receive a contract to produce a textbook with accompanying software, based on your project. The Centre will receive a guaranteed revenue stream for three years, and the book will be published by one of the larger *maisons d'édition*."

The two sat there, dumbfounded.

"Congratulations!" She said loudly, jolting them. "You may now celebrate!"

Laughing, almost running down the hall, they piled into Henri's office. He listened to them, smiling. Either he faked it well, thought Martin, or Simone had done them the courtesy of letting them be the ones to spread the news. Class.

"It's amazing what you two achieved in such a short time." Henri beamed. "Now for one more very important task: a philosophy-themed open bar."

While André ran out for liquor and Martin set up the conference room, Henri went from office to office gathering everyone. The assembly was boisterous, ready for a good time; it had been a long while since the Centre had had such positive news. Behind the makeshift bar, Martin made a hand-written sign for the drink menu: Brain In A Vat, Spinoza Around The Park, Sextus on the Beach…

Henri ordered a double Socrates, "easy on the hemlock." He raised his cup. "Well, André, here's to immortal fame."

André put up his hands in mock horror. "Anything but that! I just want to publish my little book and see it in the neighborhood bookstore."

"Liar!" said Henri. "You think we don't know you? You won't be happy until it is in the window of every *librairie* in Paris."

"Okay, okay, I admit it!" André laughed, giddy now, "For that matter, why stop there? New York! Tokyo! Moscow!"

"As a freelance author," said Henri, "you'll only starve for five, ten years at the most. But what good is philosophy if it doesn't help you endure poverty?"

"Ah, but to lack money is not the same as to be poor."

"*Touché.* Still, I suggest you stay here a while longer."

Lacroix entered, looking relatively relaxed. He walked over to André, who braced himself for some cutting comment. But Lacroix shook his hand, apparently sincere. "Bravo! You accomplished everything we could have hoped for."

"Thank you," was all André managed. He was relieved when Lacroix's cell phone went off and he stepped out to take the call. Simone looked pointedly at André.

"How do you feel towards him now?"

André looked down, then to the left, as if speaking to the internal audience who'd listened to his complaints these last months. "I… hate him! He rode me like an animal the entire time."

"I know. I told him to."

André faced her again, his brow contracted. "Y-you told him…?"

She smiled a little, waiting. He returned her gaze, frustrated at not getting her point.

"Lacroix was your ideal manager," she went on, matter-of-factly. "If he hadn't existed, I'd have needed to invent him."

He began to understand, but wanted to hear it from her. "Why?"

"He is the kind of person who most irritates you, who just by being himself will push you in sometimes unpleasant ways. You had to go beyond yourself, to stop being such a plaything of your hatred. In the end you did it. You not only finished the work; you changed in the process. If I had simply told you what to do, you would have completed it — but you did much better than that."

Until now his highest praise from Simone had been her handing his work back in silence. Aglow, André tried to take the magnanimous route: "I behaved badly with him. It bothered me that he's not a thinker, or even a reader — but I was wrong. That's not his job."

"I will trust your discretion here. Lacroix's talent is for discipline and order. In the background, he could grumble while doing nothing.

Being responsible for such a project forced him to use his abilities. He is vain — like you —," she said, looking at him over her glasses, "but unlike your vanity, his is not always constructive. You want to shine, but not to take anything away from anybody else, whereas I suspect he does. That was another reason I wanted you to work under him. You will meet that kind of person again in life, in the Centre or outside it."

Martin was finishing dinner when Judith finally called. The first few minutes were elated and tense, and she spoke quickly. School was a bore. It was morning in L.A. — almost time for her hermeneutics seminar, a three hour drone-fest her advisor had recommended. She'd found a part-time job; next week she'd have her own place. *Tant mieux*, because without so much as a hiccup she and her mother had resumed their old tango of petty disagreements. Then she cleared her throat.

"I wanted to know how you're feeling about... Paris and everything."

He told her about the success at the Centre, the new apartment, the final break with Swanson. But obviously that wasn't what she meant. "When are you coming back? I miss you."

She hesitated. "I... I don't know. Look, I'm not sure where we are, really."

"What do you mean?"

"Just that... we hadn't been connecting all that well. I mean, my last night there was fantastic, but over the previous month or two, it didn't seem like you were that into it."

"Wait, I'm the one who convinced you to move in, remember? It wasn't some half-assed thing. You were on my case so much toward the end, I thought *you* weren't into it." The hurt that she'd taken so long to return his calls poked out. "I assumed you weren't happy," he went on, "since I seemed to need correcting in so many ways." If she was calling to dump him, he'd get that in, if nothing else.

"You're right," she said, in a soothing voice that brought him back from the edge. "I was unfair to you in a lot of those conversations. But it was because I cared so much, not because I didn't. I hated that Swanson was abusing your good nature. Plus, the last weeks in Paris I'd been imagining pretty much every permutation of the future, but it felt like you were just taking it all for granted. You kept talking as if we'd somehow stay together by remote control."

"Yes," he admitted. "I thought if we couldn't survive a little time apart, we didn't have enough going to begin with. But I only looked at it from my side."

"I did the same. One thing I want to say: you have changed a *lot*. We could never have had this conversation when we first met."

"Being with you changed me," he said simply.

The silence that ensued seemed full of promise now, not impending doom.

"So what do we do?" she said.

"Well, you're stuck there. I can't leave either, for now. But I want to be where you are. Or for you to be where I am. Or something."

Chapter Twenty-Nine

Though Swanson was watching a televised football game, an impartial observer would have seen a man spending more time looking out the window, where the afternoon sun daubed an amber glaze on the Manhattan skyline. That same man had today turned thirty-six. Taking his emotional pulse about it, he found only indifference; his former angst had not made even a cameo appearance. Maybe it was the distractions of a new place, a new job, a new life. Yet by now he felt he'd always lived there, inhaled that peculiarly New York smell, felt the humming energy that never turned off, whether you were in the bowels of the subway, the top floor of a skyscraper, or awake at four AM in your own bed. Hard to say exactly what was different this year. Had he slowed down, passed unaware to another stage, like the proverbial boiling frog? Nah. He charged harder now than he had in the Valley. Anyway — there was no point in angst over one's lack of angst.

The game reached halftime. After reheating last night's Chinese food, he sat at the kitchen island, one hand surfing channels, the other wolfing the still-tasty Kung Pao prawns. Then he fixed another birthday drink. On the whole, he could congratulate himself. It had only taken one short year to rebound from a situation that might have felled a lesser man. A swanky apartment in one of Manhattan's better addresses. Nocturnal adventures that left nothing to be too ashamed of. Decent bucks? Absurd bucks. If the next few years went like the last six months, he'd replace his framed prints with the real things. In one of those occasionally beautiful pirouettes of fate, he now helped finance and underwrite IPOs for the kinds of jerks who'd frozen him out of the

Valley. Last month, he'd even had the pleasure of putting the kibosh on plans to capitalize Kyle's latest startup.

Cliff trusted him, was already talking about moving him up. Assistant general manager of information technologies, maybe; or, even more lucrative, a sideways move into mortgage lending, if he wanted. And he did want. That's where the real money had flowed ever since the tech crash. Buyers wanted commercial paper, so sellers would produce it — only a fool would refuse a position in the middle. He toasted himself, a winner rattling his winner's glass to hear the posh, comforting sound of ice cubes dully bonking together in their winning whisky bath.

The phone rang. He looked at the caller identification: blocked. An irrational thought occurred to him: it could be Duncan, maybe Martin. He answered cautiously.

"Hey, big boy! Lemme up!" Ralph, his old Dendroid buddy, of all people. Swanson buzzed him in. Since moving east, he hadn't seen anyone from those days he could still call a friend. And, as he'd verified by trusted third-parties, the Ralphster had stuck up for him when many hadn't.

Even with the game on, Ralph's entrance upped the volume of the room. "I'm doing a trade show on Monday," he announced. "Had a weekend to kill and was in the neighborhood. Figured I'd stop by to say happy birthday, have a look at your new crib."

Swanson walked him through the loft-style main room, showing off the sleek chrome and glass furniture, gleaming kitchen, the futuristic entertainment system that complemented such a view of the city. On the mezzanine was the babe-magnet bedroom, with its subtle lighting and high-thread-count sheets.

"Fantastic," said Ralph. "Did you keep the Lotus?"

Swanson sighed. "One of those West Coast things I had to give up."

"Too bad." Ralph looked around again. "This place definitely compensates, though. How's your new gig?"

Swanson told him about Cliff, the team, the perks.

Ralph wore a little smile now. "By the way, I heard Kyle's funding went bye-bye — I guess that was you?"

Damn, did Ralph ever have a network. "Ah… they weren't ready to go public."

"Sure, sure," said Ralph. "I don't blame you. I'd have done the same in a heartbeat."

"I was only the instrument — the dentures of karma biting the unworthy on the butt."

"Must not have hurt to be the one leaving the teethmarks."

Swanson tried unsuccessfully to repress a grin. "Nah, just one more deal. I don't have time for any of that old shit now. It was another life." Which was almost true. Squashing Kyle like a bug had checked a box, not much more.

Knowing by long experience he'd get nothing very juicy out of Swanson, Ralph left it at that. "You in touch with any of the other Dendroid folks?"

"Can't says I am."

"Not even Cardwell?"

Swanson started a little, then shook his head. If a gossip hound like Ralph didn't know, that meant Martin had kept things to himself. He could have easily talked shit for days — to a large, willing audience. How many would have taken Swanson's side, or understood why he'd detonated things? Maybe Martin had thought it over and realized how lightly he'd gotten off? Swanson knew how to do far worse. If it had been somebody else, he might've gone for the jugular: target the guy's self-esteem, his manhood, crush any one of a dozen weak points, things that would take years to recover from. Maybe he'd played his game out a little too long, but he hadn't wanted to destroy Martin, just get out of the partnership, out of his past, in such a way that it wouldn't ever come back. It was remotely possible that Martin had realized that. The thought caused Swanson such a twinge that he turned away from Ralph and went to the kitchen area.

"Lemme fix you a drink," he called. "Rock and rye?"

"I won't say no."

Swanson handed him the tumbler and motioned him to one section of the low-slung, right-angled sofa. "What company you with now?"

Ralph slowed down for a beat. "Well, I, er, um — Helladyne."

Swanson laughed. "They as bad as we thought?"

"Mostly, but you know, any port in a storm. The whole sector has gone anorexic. You made a smart move getting out."

"Smart as a move can be when it's rammed down your throat."

"You followed the money, so props to you. Poor slobs like me, we're still pecking around the barnyard, chasing our little equity pellets. But the day-traders and granny investors are long gone." Ralph walked over to the window. "So how does it feel, pulling the hidden levers of the world economy?"

"Hey, just doing my part to keep the conga line moving."

It would've taken a long time to explain. Wall Street wasn't so different from Silicon Valley in some ways. Corporate culture–wise, he'd slid right in: high-wire negotiations, wet lunches, ugly confrontations. Basically the same huge egos and incredible stress as the Valley, just without products. Here it was all money, all the time — stripped of its context by multi-layered financial instruments, always moving, abhorring vacuums, flowing like lava into new crevices, creating nothing except more of itself. The investment risks all paperized, then sanitized by the ratings agencies for the consumption of suckers. Only far downstream, somewhere in the hinterlands, did the flotsam of people's lives and actual material stuff bob along.

"Anybody famous in the building?" asked Ralph.

"The doorman told me that a senator keeps one of his girlfriends upstairs; haven't been able to verify it, though. Tenants here don't hang much with the neighbors."

Distractible as ever, Ralph sat down again, bouncing like a kid on the firm cushions. Then leaned forward to showily wipe his finger on the table, checking for the dust he knew wouldn't be there.

"Why do I feel such an urge to make a mess?" He sat back to play air-ukelele: "Oh, give me a home where the dust bunnies roam…"

Suddenly he pivoted toward Swanson, stood up, and made a sweeping gesture that encompassed the entire apartment. In a cinematic narrator's voice, he intoned: "All this looks elegant, very elegant. Yet we, your former brethren of the distant Fog City, remain hopeful. Despite Parisian adventures and big city living quarters, we sense you have returned to your roots in… The Ramen Zone. Beneath all this, you are again One Of Us. Now the time has come for the ultimate test." He stalked purposefully over to the fridge and peered inside: an uncovered pickle on a plate, a hunk of furry-looking cheese, a few bottles of Old Peculiar.

Ralph turned, smiling broadly, spread his arms ceremoniously and walked over to hug his friend. "Welcome back!"

Chapter Thirty

The conference over, the attendees were herded outside to a broad marble terrace, where uniformed caterers served refreshments. Martin drifted to the balustrade, while André, the final speaker, was surrounded by academics and administrators nibbling *petits fours*, waiting their turn to pounce with some obscure post-lecture question. As usual, André had done the talking while Martin had demoed Félix. In the two months since news of the publication deal, they'd shown their wares to the big decision makers of the French educational system, going from run-down establishments in the *banlieus* to elegant seventh-arrondissement institutes like this one. The pre-publication buzz was growing, both for André's book and the software. One company even wanted them to create a series — the holy grail of education publishers everywhere.

André was working the crowd with gusto today. Funny. At first, he'd resisted taking time off from research to do promotion, and tried to fob the task off on Lacroix. But Simone insisted with a smile that he make a few presentations to these educators, whose mental furniture was so different from his own. Once he saw how his ideas magically improved by having to defend them in public, he was hooked. When Simone then lightly offered to let Lacroix take his place, André wouldn't hear of it.

Martin popped another hors d'oeuvre and turned away from the crowd to contemplate the garden beyond the terrace. After these dog-and-pony shows he tended to be on his own. High-level pedagogues cared nothing about software details, and he was of no social or professional use to them. Fine. He'd already schmoozed with enough customers for one lifetime — let André have his turn. His own task, straightforward now that Félix worked, had been to give demos and do troubleshooting: exactly what he'd needed. The balm of work, the obligation to arrive on time and function in front of people, kept his mind off Swanson's betrayal and whether things would work out with Judith. He couldn't stop that emotional churning, but now could see that it was just energy, as powerful in its way as happiness or enthusiasm. He'd used it, not been used by it — something he couldn't have done a year ago.

He walked down the marble steps, toward a concentric labyrinth made of low shrubs. At its heart was a fountain, filled with water lilies and a blue wedge of reflected sky. Today's presentation had been the last. Already the usual end-of-project feelings, a mixture of satisfaction and emptiness, were kicking in. Soon he'd start on his long list of improvements for Félix: pretty up the user interface, adapt the software to different languages, other subjects, add voice commands... But first, vacation, when he'd finally see Judith again. Just for two weeks, he'd decided, no matter how well things went. Of course the relationship might also crash and burn. Regardless, now was the time to see through what he'd started here, to work on himself, put more sand in his bozo. Judith's own words had convinced him, but even more so those of Simone, when he'd tipsily confessed his dilemma at the celebration.

"Just be aware that if you move away," she'd said, "you probably won't come back, however much you think you will. The work and the life that matters to you now will become a road not taken. You might discover other projects important for you. But you may also find ways to justify doing nothing. Life will be pleasant, the years will go by. Perhaps one day you'll wake up, but it will be far too late to achieve what you and only you could have done."

He'd nodded, suddenly sober. How much better she knew him than he knew himself.

"It would not be good for your relationship, either," she'd added. "To connect with her, as you put it, you first need to connect with yourself. Otherwise, she will be the girlfriend of who, exactly?"

He'd been thinking about that ever since. Did he love Judith enough to be happy if she found someone else? Or would he prefer her dependent on him? No, no — she ought to always be free, even if the idea pained him. Would it really court disaster to leave the Centre, sell his apartment, move to L.A.? Yes. Simone was right — he might easily let Judith's wishes become his, find ways to let himself off the hook. There'd always be work, Judith to keep happy, children to help raise, maybe. He'd use all that to avoid himself, satisfy the needs of the day and gradually forget about everything else. Until he had a better idea of what only he could do, he'd just end up regretting trying to be a husband or a father, however much he wanted it.

The voices from the terrace faded as he tramped toward the maze through piles of brittle leaves, inhaling the heady autumnal rot in the air. Resisting a momentary impulse to spoil all the charm and step over the low hedge, he took the obvious straight path toward the calm, sparkling fountain in the middle. When it veered off into a dead end, he tried another that led to a far corner before doubling back, putting him closer to the goal.

From L.A., he'd go north to visit family. Friends and headhunters would also be there, still trying to lure him back to Mountain View, to life among the grunts, managers, consultants, money people. And the self-styled visionaries — each hoping to be the next Jobs, most only mastering the asshole part —, convinced that humanity's next developmental step was to become just like them, with their pestilential, time-sucking app or widget at the center of any well-lived life. The problem wasn't tech itself per se, but some of its purveyors, with their warped priorities, flogging products that often fulfilled no real need: built simply because they could be built. That was not going to stop, though. Not when everyone, from entry-level factory workers to big-shot investors, marched to the same rhythm, to the pulse of hope and illusion thrumming within every cubicle and test lab, every coding all-nighter, power lunch, team-building exercise, and sales pitch in the Valley.

My former life, he thought. I always compared where I was with where I wanted to be, with where my peers were. What about where I am versus where I am? It sounded like nonsense. Yet he was so often mentally elsewhere. Even now: his legs walked, his lungs breathed, while his mind, on a completely separate track, recycled memories of Mountain View, and his emotions kept coming back to Judith. Then there were the fleeting shades of feeling and thought, the body's incessant micro-tasks. Each fragment operated in its own world with its own agenda, more or less independent of his sense of 'I', which bounced among them, pretending to be commander in chief. But after what had happened in the Luxembourg Gardens, he knew that was not all there was. He stopped in his tracks. Shit! Months had gone by without his even remembering the experience, which had mattered more than all the others. Nor had he followed up on those tantalizing remarks from Simone, the only person he'd met who seemed to understand such things. He'd let hopes and worries — his daily puppet show — sideline the really urgent question of how to live like that.

He continued toward the fountain. A black dot appeared against the sky: a tiny spider, blown by the breeze, frantically spinning its web out behind it. Where had it come from? The nearest tree or bush was many meters away. Martin watched, moved by the doomed project of this brother creature, trying to connect its origin with wherever it would land, blown around meantime by a wind whose nature and source it could not possibly comprehend. He watched it for a long moment. Then, smiling a little, turned to retrace his steps for another try at the labyrinth.

Acknowledgements

Special gratitude goes to OF, gatekeeper of the *boleto*, who accepted nothing less (or more) than the essential, paragraph by paragraph. Gwyneth Cravens was very generous with support and encouragement all through the project. Tim Crouse's analysis of the first few chapters helped me vastly improve them and the rest of the book. Tatiana Ufimtseva was tireless in giving her frank and insightful impressions. Kathy Speeth aided the book's development in both direct and indirect ways. Members of the Paris Writer's Meetup group provided feedback that was often invaluable. My family and friends, especially Natalie Winterfield and the *Trois Mousquetaires de la Librairie Gibert Joseph*, listened to my many non-progress reports and apparently believed anyway.